THE BAD BOY WANTS ME

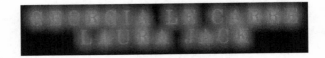

ALSO BY GEORGIA

Click on the link below to receive news of my latest releases and exclusive content.

http://bit.ly/1oe9WdE

Cover Designer: http://www.bookcoverbydesign.co.uk/
Editors: Caryl Milton, Elizabeth Burns & IS Creations
Proofreader: http:// http://nicolarheadediting.com/

THE BAD BOY WANTS ME

Published by Georgia Le Carre
Copyright © 2016 by Georgia Le Carre

ISBN: 9781910575390

You can discover more information about Georgia Le
Carre and future releases here.

https://www.facebook.com/georgia.lecarre
https://twitter.com/georgiaLeCarre
http://www.goodreads.com/GeorgiaLeCarre

Author's Note

The Bad Boy Wants Me is a fun, flirty, and humorous, standalone steamy (over 18) romance with no cliffhanger and a guaranteed HEA.

If you enjoy humour and steam this is the book for you

Happy Reading

Appreciations

I wish to extend my deepest and most profound gratitude to:

Caryl Milton
Elizabeth Burns
Nicola Rhead
Tracy Gray
Brittany Urbaniak

THE BAD BOY WANTS ME

******

This book contains mature content including graphic sex. Please do not continue reading if you are under the age of 18 or if content of this nature is offensive to you. All characters are 18+years of age and all sexual acts consensual.

Chapter One

Tori

'**I** beg your pardon,' Dr. Maurice Strong, London's top plastic surgeon, says with a perfect mix of British snobbery and scathing contempt.

Anybody else would have cringed, but not Britney. She has absolutely no problem repeating her certifiably weird request.

'I want you to make my eyes look like a cat's. You know, going upwards, like this.' She lays both her pointer fingers on the outer corners of her eyes, and pulls the skin upwards, as high as her seventeen-year-old skin will stretch.

Dr. Strong glances at me as if he suspects this whole thing is some sort of a schoolgirl prank.

I'll admit it's a feat not to laugh at the crazy scene unfolding before my eyes, but I'm damn good at keeping my expression shit-hot blank. It's more than my job's worth to express even a hint of mockery at Britney's frequent forays into lunacy. I'm paid by her father to follow her around, fetch, carry, and generally baby her.

How can I describe my job?

Well, I guess it's a bit like the ass-wipers of ancient China. No, I'm not kidding. Straight up serious. Apparently, every great emperor had a manservant whose sole duty was to carefully clean his master's ass after he'd done a number two, then carry away the precious royal droppings and dispose of them. You'd think that would have been considered the most horrible occupation a man could have, wouldn't you?

Not so.

The best part of this little nugget from the past is since the emperor was believed to be a god in human form directly from heaven, it was considered an awesome job, and eagerly fought over by many candidates. Only the luckiest guy got to smell and possibly touch a god's poop.

Unfortunately for me, other than the silent laugh factor of my job, there is no such satisfaction in mine. Getting nada from me, Dr. Strong pushes his glasses halfway down his nose (strange how plastic surgeons never have great noses) and peers frostily at Britney from the top of his gold-rimmed glasses. It's obvious that he thinks she's in need of professional help.

'You want me to operate on your eyes to make you look like a … cat?' he enunciates each word slowly, but drops the last word like a brick into the frigid air of his consulting room.

'Yes, that's right,' Britney confirms, flashing a heartbreakingly happy smile and nodding her blonde head eagerly at him.

Dr. Strong sighs, as if he has done this way too many times, or he might actually prefer the ass wipe job. He clasps his hands on his desk and looks at her grimly. 'I'm sorry, Miss Hunter, but I'm actually here to make people look better, not turn them into ridiculous freaks.'

That floors Britney. This never happens on her favorite TV program, *Botched*, where even the bizarre people asking to be turned into dolls and aliens are mollycoddled and treated with kid gloves by the two resident plastic surgeons. For a few seconds she actually looks alarmed. Her eyes widen and her mouth drops open. Then she sits forward hastily.

'No, no, no, you don't understand,' she says, sheer panic of not having what she wants turning her voice into the high, whiny drone that always hurts my ears. 'I won't look like a freak. It will be brilliant.'

'Regardless, I'm afraid I'm not the doctor for you.'

'Oh, but I want you to do it. You're the best,' she wails. He doesn't know it, but we're this close (half-an-inch between thumb and index finger) to a full-blown tantrum.

Dr. Strong takes on the expression of a man who is sitting on a toilet and has not eaten enough fiber to make it a worthwhile exercise. He sighs.

'Then take my advice and stop trying to ruin a perfectly good pair of eyes.'

'I'll pay more,' she offers suddenly.

Oh! Britney, Britney.

For the first time, a flash of anger shows on the good doctor's face. He spears her with a stink glance. 'If there is another issue you wanted to discuss then please do so, otherwise this appointment is over.'

'But ...' Britney cries petulantly. 'You did my nose and my boobs. You *have* to do my eyes.'

3

'I don't *have* to do anything.'

'Oh please,' she begs, her hands clasped under her chin.

'I will not do it, but if you insist on having cat eyes there will, no doubt, be other surgeons interested in making you happy.'

'I don't want to go to anyone else. You're the best.'

Dr. Strong shakes his head, closes the file on his desk, and looks at her with cold finality.

'This is so unfair. I want cat eyes. I'm not asking for something unreasonable ... and I'm paying. You can't just turn me away,' Britney rages.

'Miss Hunter,' Dr. Strong reprimands sternly. 'Kindly do not waste any more of my time, young lady.'

Britney jumps up. 'Come on Tori,' she orders huffily, and stalks out of the office, her nose held high in the air.

I shrug apologetically at the doctor and quickly follow her out.

She runs past the waiting room and rounds on me in the middle of an intersecting corridor. 'I have to find a way to make him operate on me,' she cries desperately. 'Can you help me to convince him?'

'Me?' I ask, startled.

'Yes. You. You're always so sensible, Tori.'

'To be honest I think your eyes are beautiful as they are.'

She looks at me the way I always imagined Cesar looked at Brutus after the knife was planted in his back.

'What?' I ask, bewildered. It's not like we're best friends or anything.

'You don't want me to be beautiful,' she screeches suddenly, and streaks off in the general direction of the toilets.

I stare after her for a few seconds before I turn around and slam into a perfectly solid wall of cologne-scented, honest to goodness, male muscles. Strong, wonderfully warm hands curl around my forearms. I look up. Okay, long tanned brown throat, unshaven jawline ...

Oh! My! God!

Amused, bright green eyes fringed by eyelashes that rightly should have belonged to a girl; straight, black, cocked eyebrows; disheveled hair, and a badass smile curved on the sexiest most deliciously full lips. The kind you just want to sink your teeth into. Oh, and just before I faint, a chin dimple just made a late entrance to the party. This is exactly the kind of man my best friend, Leah, calls 'a happening guy.' Things happen around him.

'Whoa, babe,' he drawls.

How can I describe his voice? Warmed up chocolate sauce poured slowly down my naked back. Swoon, my ass, I fucking shiver.

'Whoa, yourself,' I croak.

He bares his straight white teeth. It's one of those magic grins that begs any rational girl to suck it off his face.

'Was that my sister I just saw bolting into the toilet for a quick meltdown?'

I swallow hard. This is so not how I expected to meet Britney's famous brother. 'Could be, if you're the pop star big brother.'

Cash Hunter's green eyes look like they're on fire. 'That's me, babe. Pop star big brother.'

'Great. Er ... now might be a good time to let go of me.'

'Give me one good reason why I should?' he counters lazily.

My eyebrows fly upwards. 'My knee's reckoning on an upwards trajectory?'

Grinning, he lets go of me and raises his hands as if in surrender. 'Looks like I caught me a wildcat.'

My legs play up a little as I take a shaky step back.

He watches me. 'Where the fuck have you been all my life, Beautiful?'

I give a fake laugh. 'Are you deliberately using bad lines to save on contraceptives?'

The leather-clad, powerhouse of sexy goodness throws his head back and laughs. This early in the morning the vodka fumes that hit my nostrils are strong enough to make me dizzy.

'What's going to work on you, wildcat? My cock wants to say hello to your pussy.'

'Breath mints might help,' I retort.

'Damn girl, you sure know how to suck the juice out of a tender moment.' He rummages around in his pocket, finds a mangy mint, and pops it into his mouth. 'Now unless you don't like a long, thick cock, we're good to go.'

I look up at him with frosty eyes. 'Personally I think size is overrated. Cock doesn't have to be big to be good.'

His eyes gleam. 'Baby, we're in luck. There's a man on the other side of the corridor who can customize my dong into the right shape and size for you.'

'Hilarious,' I say unenthusiastically.

'I bet I can make you call me Daddy,'

'Thanks, but ... ugh, no.'

'Right. Change of tactics. Not that I'm giving up on getting you into my bed or anything, but want to have dinner with me tonight?'

He's too beautiful to be real.

'Cash,' squeals Britney.

Cash winks at me before he turns his attention to the figure flying at him. He catches her as she wraps her arms and legs around him like a big kid.

'How did you know where to find me?' she asks.

'Isn't this your second home?' he asks dryly.

'Not anymore. Dr. Strong won't do my eyes,' she grumbles.

'Oh yeah. Why not?'

'He's says I'll end up looking like a ridiculous freak.'

'Hmmm ... what did you want done?'

She climbs off him. 'I want cat eyes.'

Cash's gorgeous eyes widen. He nods slowly as she tells him about her disastrous appointment with Dr. Strong.

'Well, Sparkles. I think cat's eyes are a great idea.'

Jesus. Madness must run in the family.

'You do?' Britney asks brightly, her whole face shining with hope.

'Absolutely. It's a great look. It'll make you look like one of those beauties from the fifties and sixties.'

'What?' She frowns.

'Yeah, you know like Zsa Zsa Gabor.'

'Zsa Zsa Gabor. Who's that?'

'She's from dad's time,' he supplies with a wise nod. 'Oh, and like ... er ... what was the name of that comedienne who died recently?' He snaps his fingers and looks at me.

'Joan Rivers?' I suggest helpfully.

He stops snapping and points at me. 'That's the one.' With a smile he turns towards his sister who's looking at him with dismay. 'Definitely a great look,' he says approvingly.

'But they're both so ... old.'

'So what. They had style. Style never dies. Come on, let's go and see Dr. Strong together. I'll help you to convince him.' He takes her arm.

Britney holds back. 'Hang on a minute. I think Dr. Strong might have been right, after all. It's a big step and I should think about this a bit more.'

'Oh,' he says innocently. 'Are you sure?'

'Yes,' she replies lamely.

'In that case,' he turns to me, 'how about introducing me to this lovely creature?'

Britney turns to me. 'Oh, this is Tori Diamond. Dad hired her to be my PA.'

He extends a hand out. 'Hello, Tori Diamond. Cash Hunter, Britney's pop star brother. How nice to meet you.'

I step forward and put my hand into his ridiculously strong hands. Damn, these are some hands. Must be all that guitar strumming. My imagination runs away with me. *One finger inserted deep inside me, and curling to stroke me.* Oh hell! Phew! Is it hot in this corridor or what? Heat creeps up my neck. I wipe my brow as surreptitiously as I can.

He smirks. The smarmy bastard.

I clear my throat. 'Charmed, I'm sure,' I say in the poshest voice I can muster.

Chapter Two

Tori

'We really should be getting back,' I announce awkwardly, looking at Britney.

Britney turns to her brother, her voice wheedling. 'Can I go back in your car, Cash?'

'Sure, I'll take you home, but I can't stay for long.'

'Oh! Why?' she moans.

'I'm bushed, Brit. I've been up all night. I just want to get back to my apartment and crash. I'll come around tomorrow.'

'Well, you can sleep back at ours. We won't disturb you. Dad's not in, Cora never comes out of the kitchen. I'll be real quiet, and Tori here is more silent than a bloody tomb.'

He glances at me interestedly. 'A silent one, huh?'

'Say you'll stay,' she begs hopefully.

He looks down at her, his expression undecided.

'Cora's making your favorite smoked chicken pie tonight,' she says cunningly.

I know for a fact Cora is doing no such thing. It should have been a silent observation, but I hear words I never intended to say go flying out of my mouth.

'Actually she's not.'

Cash trains his starry eyes at me and I feel myself go hot. A wicked smile plays about his lips as he makes his decision. 'You know what, Britney? I think I might have to take you up on your tempting offer after all.'

Me and my big mouth.

'Yay,' Britney yells happily as she bounces up and down and jumps around like she's a frog in a rainforest celebrating a coming storm.

In a kind of hypnotic daze, I watch Cash pull a beanie from his jacket and jam it on his head. Then he takes out a pair of sunglasses and hooks them onto the bridge of his nose. I hate to be repetitive, but he is one sexy dish. Give me a man in shades any day.

Britney threads her hand through her brother's and beams at me. 'I'll see you at home?'

'Yes, yes, obviously. Of course you will,' I babble foolishly before I turn around and slam straight into a really fat man. Mortified, I make my apologies. Of course, with my luck, he would have to have a weird sense of humor. He laughs and tells me not to apologize since it's the best sex he's had all year. My face burns with embarrassment. I dart a glance back at Cash and the irritating bastard is shaking with silent laughter.

Whatever. With my head held up high I sail towards the door.

Outside the sun is shining brightly on a gleaming black on black Lamborghini parked in front of the surgery. Its macho perfection is spoiled by some heartless parking attendant sticking a yellow and black parking ticket on its windscreen. I am secretly pleased. Laugh at me, will you?

We go down the stone steps and a young woman walking past looks casually at us and then does a double-take.

'Cash Hunter?' she asks, her head pushed forward like a turtle, her eyes wide with disbelief.

'Yup, but keep it to yourself,' he says, with a magic smile.

She slaps her hands onto her cheeks. 'Oh my God. Oh my God. I can't believe this. I must be dreaming. Somebody pinch me quick. Oh, my God. I'm your greatest fan. Me and my girlfriend have even got tickets to come see you in Milan in August.' She pauses to take a breath and launches again into another gushing monologue. 'I love your latest album. I got the CD. It's really good. I think it's your best work. I play it nearly every night before I go to bed.'

'That's very nearly like going to bed with me,' he says with a naughty wink.

Oh, for God's sake. Is this guy for real?

But the fan flushes brick red. 'Do you mind very much if I take a selfie with you?' the woman gushes, flicking her hair and patting it.

'Mind? The pleasure will be all mine,' Cash drawls suggestively.

Britney unhooks her hand from his and takes a step back. She's obviously used to this scenario.

'Anna is going to be so jealous,' the woman mutters to herself as she fumbles around in her purse. She locates her phone, fishes it out, and stands there with an expectant look on her face.

Cash crooks the fingers of his right hand and she eagerly rushes up to nestle against his butter-soft jacket. I know what that garment feels like because I copped a feel earlier.

She holds her phone up at arm level and asks, 'Ready?'

Both of them grin like Cheshire cats and she snaps a few shots. The selfie excuse is over and she lowers her arm, but the silly bitch doesn't move and remains cuddled up against his gorgeous body. Smoothly, Cash steps away.

'Just one last thing. Can I please have your autograph? For my flat mate. She's also my bestie. She'll be so annoyed if I don't,' she chatters on, her face beaming.

'Why not?' Cash says, a glint in his eyes.

'Oh, thank you. Thank you. She'll be so pleased. Her name is Anna.' She roots around again in her bag, and comes up with a pen and a crumpled piece of paper.

Cash takes the pen from her and ignores the scrap of paper. 'We can do better than that,' he says with a smug grin.

Her eyes widen. 'Oh!'

'May I?' he asks.

Her head seems to waggle dangerously on her neck, but she is game. 'Of course.'

He steps forward, reaches out a hand and expertly unbuttons the top button of her blouse. Her mouth hangs open with shock, excitement,

and pleasure. Not a good look. Then he moves in and autographs the soft swell of her breast, just above her bra.

'Have fun,' Cash says, as he returns her pen. Giggling and simpering like a fool, she takes it.

Yeah, that will please your bestie for sure. Carry that home to her. I look at Britney and she rolls her eyes at me. I try not to show any expression.

'Well, it was so fantastic meeting you. I guess I should let you get on. OK, bye. See you in Milan,' she babbles, holding onto the edges of her shirt collar.

'Yeah, cool,' Cash calls moving away from her.

I see a black Bentley start inching towards us from its parked position a few cars down and I turn towards Britney. 'See you at the house then.'

She grins at me happily. 'Byeeeeee.'

Without looking at her brother or the crazed fan, I walk down the pavement and get into the Bentley.

'Hey, Victor,' I greet, closing the door after me. 'It'll just be me. Britney's going home with her brother.'

'Right, love,' he replies, and pulls out into the street.

In my peripheral vision I can see that the fan has walked off, Britney is bouncing on the passenger seat, and Cash is unconcernedly ripping the penalty ticket off his windscreen. In the light of the noon sun, their hair glows like antique gold, and their beauty makes them look like gods, or fallen angels. All that is missing are the white wings.

I sink back into my seat.

Wow! I didn't do very well back there. It hits me hard that I'm going to struggle to stay with the plan. The thought is totally depressing, but I cheer up by telling myself it's only the beginning. Yes, he won this round, but in my defense I have a few redeeming factors on my side.

a) Even I didn't quite expect him to pack such a powerful punch.

b) I was naturally blindsided by the element of surprise as I was not anticipating his arrival before the end of the month.

I remind myself not to be so hard on myself. After all, I've been crushing on him forever. For as long as I can remember, and I'm talking about the kind of all consuming crush where I even refused to look at other boys. Yup, that was me.

When it first started, my parents were all for it. Why wouldn't they be? I was twelve and Cash was sixteen. Awww ... sweet. Thinking about it now, my father actually thought it was a great development. Cash was part of a boy band called Alkaline in a faraway land called England. A quaint place still ruled by a Queen. Quite simply it meant he wouldn't need to invest in a shotgun for at least a few more years.

For years they used to buy me Cash memorabilia. I had everything and anything

with Cash's name or face plastered on it. Bedspreads, pens, pencil cases, T-shirts, life-sized posters, cushions, mugs, plates, shower-curtains, even a toilet seat with Cash's face and naked torso. My brother, Brad, bought it as a joke, but I loved it so it stayed. My room and my bathroom looked like shrines to Cash or the big publicity machine for Cash Hunter had just vomited all over my living space.

By the time I turned sixteen, my family didn't consider my crush so peachy anymore. I came home from school one day and my mother claimed she had accidentally broken my toilet seat while she was cleaning it. Wonder of wonders my father already had a replacement toilet seat handy. My mother took the opportunity to persuade me that the shower curtains were looking old and worn and no longer matched the toilet seat.

A trip to Target sorted that out.

Then the Cash sheets somehow got snarled up in the dryer and my best Cash T-shirts were dyed grey when an old, black sock got into the washing machine by mistake. The mugs started breaking and were never replaced. Brad ordered life-size posters of Nine Inch Nails since they were the other group that I liked. He insisted on hanging them up for me after taking down Cash's posters.

'They're really worn around the lips and cheeks aren't they? Want me to trash everything for you?' he asked innocently.

Even though it was like a knife through my heart to see my beloved Cash posters being taken down, I knew my family was right. My obsession was bordering on crazy. I was two mugs away from being a stalker. Still, I couldn't bear to throw my posters away. I'd been kissing them goodnight since I was twelve, so I rolled them up carefully and stored them away in the attic together with my ninety-six scrapbooks of Cash.

From that day onwards I stopped obsessively buying magazines he was featured in, and I forced myself not to go to ILoveCashHunter.com where I normally got the latest and breaking news about him. I even deleted his official website from my bookmark list.

Then when I was seventeen we heard that Alkaline was coming to Georgia. Cash Hunter was going to be performing at the Dome. My parents thought I was over him so they were quite happy for Leah and I to travel to Atlanta to see the concert.

We had to pay $30.00 for parking, wait more than an hour to check in our purses, and the Cokes were $7.00 each, but as I stood there with 70,000 other crazed fans, none of it mattered anymore. I felt more alive than I ever had. It was not like watching it on MTV or YouTube. A live concert was like nothing I could have imagined. Indescribable, really.

The very air was electric. Hundreds of roving spotlights moved over us adding so much heat to the evening that we were all bathed in sweat even before the performance started.

The massive stage suddenly lit up with winking, flashing blue lights and the music started. Nobody told me the vibrations would travel through the concrete under my feet, into my shoes, and up into my flesh and bones. It drummed into my blood and made my heart thump faster and faster. I was so excited the hair on my body stood on end.

Then the stage began to fill with smoke-like fog.

I could hardly believe I was finally going to see Cash Hunter. I thought I would stop breathing when five steel platforms began to rise out of the floor of the stage. The smoke began to clear and the crowd went crazy. My eyes found him immediately. It was unbelievable, but he was on the platform closest to us. The bright light made his hair glisten and his face glowed like an angel. He blew across the microphone.

'Are you ready to rock Atlanta?' he yelled into the microphone.

The crowd went wild.

'Let's hear that again,' he shouted, and we screamed until we were hoarse.

The exploding flash pots went off as the drums and guitars began the intro. Cash raised up both his hands as if he were a god. Tears flowed from my eyes when his voice filled the stadium. I stared at him, mesmerized.

It was my favorite song. *The Girls Who Don't Say No.*

The crowd started pulsing with the energy coming from him. The platform he was standing on grew into a kind of walkway, and to my shocked delight it was bringing him closer to us. He strutted along the expanding metal walkway in my direction and I screamed hysterically.

As he was right over me he suddenly looked directly into my eyes and sang, 'I've been waiting for you all my life.'

I froze. I felt as if he had zapped me with a cattle prod. Fine, I don't know what that feels like, but it was what I imagine it would feel like. I lost the feeling in my legs.

He moved on and sang the next line looking into the eyes of another girl, but my girlhood crush had just become love.

I was in love with Cash Hunter.

Chapter Three

Tori

https://www.youtube.com/watch?v=_tQLIyqtDxo

At that time Leah was going out with a guy from a rock band called Roll Over Beethoven. The drummer was single and she thought we might make a good team.

'Everybody knows the best way to get over someone is to go out with someone else,' she declared.

It seemed like a sensible idea. More sensible, anyway, than the fantasy love affair I was having with an unattainable pop idol. His name was Colton and he was sexy in a moody, grungy sort of way. The exact opposite of Cash. He dressed only in black, and I think he probably colored his hair jet black too, but he was a sweet guy underneath it all, and he made me laugh.

It was easy to drink one beer too many, and let him take my V card in the back of his truck. We became an item. The sex was good, but it wasn't the mind, body, and soul thing I was looking for, which was a real shame because he fell hard for me.

Then, one night I went to one of his gigs and I found him by the toilets with his trousers around his ankles and his dick inside another woman. I didn't love him, but I was still shocked and hurt.

He looked at me with bitter eyes and said, 'Now we've both cheated on each other.'

Then he turned away from me and carried on humping her. I fled the scene knowing I'd hurt him, but I told myself I would never do that to another human being again. The next time I start a relationship will be when I am well and truly over Cash Hunter.

My thoughts are interrupted by Victor stopping the car outside the house. Cash and Britney have not yet arrived, so I run up to my room and pace the floor. A million thoughts rush around in my head.

The big plan came to me when my aunt mentioned that a good friend of hers who worked in a recruitment agency in London had told her about an interesting job that had just come in. Cash Hunter's father was looking for a young woman, 19 - 25 who was independent, tolerant, and possessed a strong sense of duty to act as a companion/PA to his daughter. No actual PA experience was needed.

That sounded like a description of me. I was all those things!

The plan was simple. Apply for the job as Britney's PA, see Cash Hunter up close, and realize that he was just a manufactured, media created, playboy prick, and naturally and effortlessly fall out of love.

But at that time it seemed a very long shot since my aunt's friend had already warned her there were hundreds of applicants. Imagine my astonishment when I was called for an interview and my shock when I actually got the job. I was convinced it was fate. It had to be. Me, chosen out of hundreds of applicants. I was meant to be here.

So here I am. Close enough to see Cash for what he really is.

Why then am I pacing the room like some caged animal?

I hear the distinct thunder of his Lambo, followed by voices on the street below. I run to the window to stand behind the curtains and watch them. Britney skips up the steps. He says something to her and she laughs.

I think I'm pacing because in spite of everything I'd told myself in the car ... Cash Hunter is even more potent in the flesh than I gave him credit for, and it's already pretty obvious that there's no falling out of love with someone like him.

I freeze when I hear their voices come up the stairs. They stop at the top.

Then I hear Britney call out, 'Sweet dreams.'

Quick light footsteps come towards my room.

'Come in,' I call when she knocks.

Britney puts her head around the door. She looks happy. 'Just wanted to let you know that Cash is sleeping in the guest bedroom and Dad just came home so we're off to buy me a birthday present, but we won't be long because I know exactly what I want.'

I force a smile. 'Great.'

'By the way I've already told Cora we're having chicken pie for dinner.'

'That's good,' I say, stretching out my smile until my cheeks hurt.

After she goes I look at the time. It's just after one. I had brunch so I'll skip lunch and save myself for one of Cora's lovely teatime treats. Unless I am mistaken, I believe she is making scones today. I open a magazine I picked up at the newsstand yesterday evening and go right to the horoscope page at the back of it. Hmmm ... Aries.

Acting impulsively is not the best idea this week. Resist temptation. Don't eat that last cookie in the packet. Instead, take stock, get your ducks in a row, and get ready for the best adventure of your life. Life is about to surprise you.

I read it again. Got it. Don't act impulsively.

I flick the pages disinterestedly. Imagine my surprise when I turn a page and see a large picture of a shit-faced Cash in leather pants and silver shirt. A disheveled blonde is snuggled up to him. They are in a nightclub or restaurant.

The title of the piece is:

Is Cash Hunter the most eligible man in the world?

On closer inspection I note from their reflection in the mirror behind them that his right hand is full of blondie's butt. Inappropriate and quite frankly tasteless butt grab, but the blonde seems to dig it. She is looking up at him with an awed, stupid expression on her face. I let my eyes move over to his free hand. A sigh escapes my mouth. I've always loved his hands. They are big, strong and manly. *Mooning over his hand, God, you're lame.* I leave the picture and start scrutinizing the next one.

That turns out to be a to-die-for picture of him at a sunny beach. All his lovely, hard muscles are on display and he is with a different blonde this time. This one is curvier and seems more self-assured. She has a pair of sunglasses pushed up on her head, one hand is resting on her tanned hip, and the other is placed possessively on his chest.

He's always had a thing for blondes.

A stray thought pops into my head. *I'm blonde.*

I turn the page quickly and there is a full-page, black and white photo of him in a tux at some kind of award ceremony or music bash. This time I recognize the woman he is with. Octavia Harding, his manager. Except for her fake breasts, that actually look like two halves of a tennis ball shoved underneath her skin, she is two lean nuggets away from being an anorexic.

I don't like her. I never have.

From the first moment I laid eyes on her I felt that there was something cold and malicious about her. A couple of times I have seen videos of her standing next to the band members, an arrogant smile stretching her crimson mouth; she actually makes my skin crawl.

I could easily have sat there gazing at his picture a bit longer, but I close the magazine with a snap and drop it into the wastepaper basket. Seeing the magazine in the bin makes me feel mildly victorious. I'll conquer my silly crush if it is the last thing I do. I decide to have a bath. Britney will be at least an hour, and being in the bath always relaxes me. Allows me to think and clear my head.

I run the bath, pour in a whole load of fragrant bath cubes, put my hair into a messy topknot, and lower myself into the scented water. Mmmm ... this was definitely one of my better ideas. I lean my head back against the folded towel and close my eyes.

Let's think this thru.

I shouldn't be so harsh on myself. First off, I've been in love with this guy for years. Obviously the first encounter is going to be either traumatic, disastrous, or both. It was both. So what? The worst is over. From now on I'm prepared. I've read the side effects warning label: This asshole is likely to break your heart.

The good thing is I now know just how hot he is and how strong he comes on and things will

be different. If I just stay calm and unaffected, bit by bit he will reveal his true self and I'll discover that he ain't all that. Once I see that my memories of him are all flawed and he is far from perfect, I will realize that he is a hero only in my mind.

At that point I will either be put off, or better still, so totally sickened that I will wonder why I ever wasted so many years pining for him. On that happy day I will put in my notice and go on to my aunt's house in Surrey and wait for Leah to join me for our victory backpacking tour of Europe.

Sitting here in this fragrant steam, I see clearly that I over reacted. There is nothing to worry about. Everything is under control. I'm in charge of my body and my decisions. And in a way it is good, because he has shown his hand. He tries it on with every female he meets. Slut. Manwhore. Womanizer. Prick.

So, now that I have redefined the parameters, I can relax. I wave my arms a little to circulate the hot water and exhale slowly.

'Mmmm.'

I start to chill.

My mind wanders lazily away. I don't check it. Whatcha gonna do? I'm in the bath. It goes to ... Cash ... no, not Cash, of course not Cash, just a man who looks like him. He is in bed. Between white silk sheets, his tan intense, some kind of lop-sided smile on his face. He pats the space next to him.

And I, I'm in a slinky black nightie, my hair's freshly washed and bouncing like a shampoo advert as I walk up to him with a sexy, totally sophisticated smile. As I reach the bed, he is so eager for me he jumps me and throws me on the bed. Before I can say, 'You called?' he has his face between my thighs and starts feasting his heart out.

My fingers move to the hard nub between my legs. Swirl. Swirl. In the silky water. Ohhhh. Oh, Cash. Yes, Cash. Yes. Just like that. Oh, God, yes—

Suddenly everything in my head disappears with a jolt. My bathroom door slams open, and my eyes open wide. Oh Good Lord!

Cash freaking Hunter has dropped out of my fantasy and into my reality.

Chapter Four

Tori

'What the hell are you doing in here?' I screech, ducking down so violently water slops over the edges of the tub onto the floor. From my position where only my neck and head are visible above the soapsuds, I stare open-mouthed with a mixture of disbelief and reluctant admiration at him.

Oh my! So much gloriousness is on show. Obliques, traps, pecs, biceps, six pack. Actually, the whole works ... everything is irritatingly tight, cut, evenly tanned and finished off in a gorgeous tattoo wrap of Maori art.

The life-size posters never did him justice. He was a boy then. This is a man's body. And that V, that's a V to beat all Vs. He's wearing faded blue denim jeans with the top button unbuttoned, and wait, what? My eyes bulge like a freaking TSA inspector's when he finds a restricted item in some poor guy's baggage. Oh, my, God. His dick is massive.

And totally hard.

My senses reel out of control and I feel hot all over. I could be coming down with a fever.

'This used to be my bathroom,' he says conversationally, as he steps into the bathroom and closes the door.

His hair is endearingly sleep-mussed, and his lips are slightly swollen and red, the way children's are when they first wake up, so it's damn hard to remain infuriated and forbidding, especially when my insides are buzzing with wicked thoughts, but a lot is riding on this. My plan will crumble if I don't put a stop to this right now. I need to get him out of my bathroom right this minute.

'It's not your bathroom anymore. If memory serves, the guest bedroom has an en-suite. So: kindly GET OUT.'

'I didn't come in here to take a piss, wildcat,' he says, his eyes all hot and crazy.

Holy cow. 'What?'

'I've discovered I have a thing for ballsy girls. I've actually woken up with a raging hard-on.'

Is he freaking kidding? 'You're batshit crazy.'

He looks genuinely surprised. 'Batshit crazy because I want to see my cock disappear into your sweet lips?'

'How dare you?'

He gives me a smug, self-satisfied look. 'How dare I? I just saw you stare at my cock like it was a lollipop you wanted to suck.'

I can feel color exploding up my neck and cheeks. I did make that a bit obvious. Fine, it was not a bit obvious, it was a get-in-my-mouth-right-now stare.

'Any woman would have stared at an erect cock being shamelessly displayed less than five feet away from her,' I counter as scornfully as possible in my circumstances.

He shakes his head slowly. 'An uninterested woman would have looked away.'

'You seem to be laboring under the mistaken impression that I'm interested in you. News flash: I'm not.'

He shrugs. 'Why not?'

'You're not my type,' I lie boldly.

'Everyone wants a taste of celebrity cock,' he states confidently.

See. There is merit to my plan and a method to my madness, after all. These are exactly the kinds of things that will eventually get me out of my crush. Rude, crude, pompous jerk. Like I'm lucky to be getting a chance at having his cock. A few more statements like this I can go home with my mancrush obliterated for good. To my joy I find myself gloriously angry with him.

'I know you think you're hotter than shit and irresistible to the entire female population, but some women don't care for guys whose hobbies include throwing clothes-optional parties, fucking girls who don't wear panties in toilet cubicles at concerts, and banging whatever crawls into their beds.'

'For a girl who's not interested you know a lot about me.'

'It's public knowledge. Cash don't show up unless pussy is involved,' I defend.

He grins. 'You can strike off sex in toilet cubicles with chicks who don't wear panties from your list. It lost its charm after a while.'

'Whatever. Will you please get out?'

Instead of leaving he walks over and sits on the edge of the tub. 'Give me one good reason I should.'

'Karma is a bitch and you'll have to pay the price of being an asshole?'

He laughs. 'Don't worry. This has a happy ending.'

'Are you kidding me? One-night stands are not considered happy endings.' I scoff.

'What makes you think I'll only need you for one night?'

I sigh elaborately. 'Look. I work for your father and, shock horror, screwing his son's brains out is not in the small print of my employment contract.'

'We'll just have to tear that contract and have a new one drawn up.'

'This is all a big joke to you, isn't it?'

'No,' he says, waggling his pointer finger between us. 'Don't you think we've got a lot of sexual vibes going on here?'

'No we don't. First off you hit me with the worst pick up lines in the history of shitty lines, then you barge in here uninvited and tell me you've got a hard on. It's downright insulting. You've got a hard-on. Go fuck yourself.'

If anything the expression in his eyes heats up. His eyes glint with interest. 'I would if I didn't suffer from Masturbator's wrist.'

My mouth drops open. Did he really say what I think he said? 'What?'

'It's from indulging in my other ... er ... hobby. Ya know, like tennis elbow, gamekeeper's thumb, writer's cramp. It's a repetitive strain injury ...' he trails off, his voice full of barely suppressed laughter.

The thing is. He is funny and I am starting to really like our snarky back and forth. And that is a bad thing. A very bad thing. I definitely do not want to like anything about him. I squeeze my lips together in a bitter line.

'Careful, you were about to crack a smile there.'

'You know what? I've had enough of this bullshit. I know you're my employer's son and everything, but if you don't get out right now I'm going to scream, and I can scream loud enough to wake the dead.'

He crosses his arms over his chest and grins. 'Go ahead and scream. Dad and Britney are still out, and Cora is well used to hearing women screaming in my bedroom.'

'What do you actually want, Hunter?' I demand sternly.

'One kiss.'

'What? No.'

'Come on. What've you got to lose? If you don't like it, we'll call it a day.'

'No. Absolutely not,' I say very, very firmly. I have a plan. I have it all figured out, and this is certainly not part of the plan. Who knows where one kiss could lead. Even the idea is already giving me goosebumps.

'You chicken shit, Diamond?' he taunts.

'No,' I deny, jutting my head and bobbing it the way kids do when they are trying to annoy you. 'I'm not chicken shit. Has it *ever* occurred to you that maybe I just don't want to kiss you?'

'No.'

I gasp at the arrogance. Unbelievable. 'Well, I don't.'

'Prove it.'

I throw my hands up in exasperation. The action pops my breasts out of the water and his eyes immediately dip down to them. I slide back down and his eyes take the slow route back up to my face.

'Nice tits,' he says, his eyes doing a slow burn.

Suddenly he stands and takes a stride towards me. A totally Alpha move. I panic. Oh my god. I can't let him kiss me. I just can't.

I hold both my hands out, palms outstretched, as if I am in a horror movie and warding off Dracula or some other evil. 'Let's talk this out,' I say urgently.

'Let's not,' he says, and before I can do anything he is already bending over me. His hand claws into my hair, making my topknot loosen and my hair tumble all over his hand. He fists the hair at the back of my head and tugs downwards, pulling at my neck.

'Tori,' he whispers, and then his lips touch my exposed throat. His mouth sears my skin. My gut constricts and my sex starts to throb and crave something. Something called Cash. My hands come up to grip his shoulders and my back arches and pushes my chest out of the water.

Then his lips touch mine and, to my shock, I moan into his mouth. At any other time I would have cringed. I sound like an animal, but at that moment I don't care. I open my mouth, our tongues touch and ... Oh Lord, everything goes white. The whole world drops away. I fall into a huge vat of warm chocolate or toffee and I get sucked deeper and deeper into the thick sweet liquid. I feel myself melt. I could have stayed in that moment forever. The kiss going on and on ...

But he snatches his mouth away from mine.

'Wha—'

'You can thank me later,' he mutters, his voice so thick it is almost harsh. With dazed eyes I watch him stride to the door, open it, and walk out without looking back. For a few seconds I stare at the closed door blankly. What the hell just happened? Then I hear Britney's laugh come from the top of the stairs. Cash says something indistinct and their voices move away.

Oh, sweet Jesus, I was so involved I did not hear them come in. I could have been killed by an axe murderer and I would not have known.

Yup. That's me all over.

No sense of self-preservation.

Chapter Five

Tori

'Tori, can I come in?' Britney calls from outside my bedroom door.

For heaven's sake. The last thing I need is to see anyone. What if she notices that I have been kissing her brother? Then I take the long view. I'm in the bath. Of course I'll be flushed.

'Come in. I'm in the bath, Britney,' I call out.

She comes in and sits at the very place her brother had occupied. I definitely did not need to have worried about her noticing anything. She's in a world of her own. Her eyes are shining.

'Will you come with me to a pool party tomorrow, Tori?'

I sigh inwardly. A party full of spoilt teenagers is not my idea of a fun evening. 'Of course,' I say politely.

'Guess who will be there?'

'You got me.'

She excitedly clasps her hands in front of her chest. 'Taylor Swift.'

Britney is a massive Taylor Swift fan.

'Great,' I say, injecting some enthusiasm into my voice. 'Where is it being held?'

'At Cash's house.'

'Oh! Oh I see.' I pause to cough. 'Look, since it's at your brother's house maybe Victor can take you there and back. You don't need me to come and cramp your style.'

She stares at me astonished. 'You don't want to come?'

'Well, I thought I could stay home and read. You know, have some time to myself.'

Her eyes fill with tears. It never fails to amaze me no matter how many times I see it, how Britney can go from super happy to the pits of depression in a New York minute.

'Oh, no,' she cries dramatically. 'You have to come. You know Dad won't let me go if you don't come. Please. This might be the only chance I ever have of seeing Taylor.'

Tears are running down her cheeks unchecked. Britney truly is the queen of exaggeration, but it looks like I'm stuck. I paste a smile on my face. 'Of course, I'll come.'

She leaps to her feet and, running up to me, slaps her hands on either side of my cheeks, and plants a noisy smacker right on my kisser. Oh, for heaven's sake. First the brother then the sister.

'I really do love you, Tori,' she says with a laugh. Then she goes to the door and, hanging on to the edge, she begins to twerk and sing a made-up song.

Oh, yeah. I'm happy. So happy.
Tori said, yes. She said yes.
Oh yeah. I'm happy. So Happy.
Tori said, yes. She said yes.

She looks funny doing it and I laugh. I kinda like Britney when she is like this. She's cute and adorable. When she stops twerking, she twirls around the small space like a ballerina and says dreamily, 'I can't believe I'm going to meet Taylor tomorrow.' Then she stops suddenly and looks horrified.

'Oh my God! I've just realized. I've got nothing to wear. We'll have to go shopping tomorrow.'

'You've got karate at two o'clock,' I remind. 'We can go in the morning if you want.'

She pulls a face. 'Do I have to go? Can't I just skip this once?'

'Look, Britney. You know your dad really wants you to be able to defend yourself. It's only an hour.'

'But I won't be in the mood, and I'll be tired after all that shopping. And I want to go to the hairdresser. I need to get my roots done,' she whines.

'OK. This is what we'll do. I'll call Mr. Wong and see if he can fit you in sometime in the morning, then we'll spend the rest of the day shopping.'

'All right,' she agrees reluctantly.

'Good. I'll try to make it for nine, OK?'

'OK.' She brightens. 'We'll have to get you something super-sexy too. You never know there might be a hot guy there for you.'

'I won't bother. I've got loads of stuff I can wear.'

She puts her hands on her hips. 'No you don't. You only have jeans and T-shirts.'

'I thought it was a pool party.'

'Pool party dress-code is: come in something that looks amazing when it's wet.'

'Right.'

'OK, I've got to go. Cash is taking me out for ice-cream.'

'Have fun,' I say.

'Wanna come with us?'

'No,' I say immediately.

Her eyes widen in surprise at the abruptness of my reply.

I smile to soften the rudeness of my refusal. 'I would have loved to have come, but I can't because I promised to call my friend in the States and she'll be waiting for my call.'

Fortunately she accepts my explanation at face value. 'OK. See you later then,' she sings.

'See ya.'

She skips out, then pops her head around the door again. 'You will make that appointment for me at the hairdresser, won't you?'

'Of course.'

'Oh, and can you make sure it's not Eileen that does my hair. She drives me mad talking about Cash all the time.'

'Oh? Yeah, I'll make sure you get someone else.'

'Thank you,' she sings and is gone from my room. My brain starts ticking again. In a funny sort of way I feel numb and detached from the weird situation I have gotten myself into.

The bad boy kissed me. And I kissed him back.

The water is cold. I really should get out.

Chapter Six

Tori

I dry myself and look at my reflection in the mirror. Tori Diamond. Blonde with a really guilty look in her cornflower blue eyes. OK, so the big plan is basically in tatters. Leah will have a fit when she hears where the plan has gone.

I look at my watch. It's too early to call her. She will still be sleeping. She's an author and she works at night and sleeps until noon.

I put the hairbrush down and wander over to my bedside table. Picking my cell phone up I call Mr. Wong and yeah, no problems. He'll take Britney at 9.00am. Then I call the hairdresser.

'Er ... is Eileen around tomorrow afternoon?'

'No, it's her day off tomorrow,' the receptionist says, after checking their roster.

'Shame. Never mind, can I book an appointment for Britney tomorrow afternoon? Anything available about threeish?'

'She's booked with Pauline at three,' she says crisply.

'Wonderful.'

'The nail technician will be around tomorrow. Do you want to book her at the same time?'

'Why not?"

'Manicure & pedicure?'

'Excellent. See you tomorrow,' I say and ring off.

I throw my phone on the bed and take Monstrosity out of my bedside table. Monstrosity is my diary. I call it that because there is a long fanged monster made with furry blue material on the cover. I sit cross-legged on the bed, unlock him, and flip the pages to today's date.

Dear Monstrosity,

I think it's safe to assume I f**ked up.

Out of sheer spite the enemy kissed me and I, well, I kind of kissed him back.

In my defense:

1. *There is no logic to a crush.*
2. *I was in a weakened state.*
3. *I was caught woefully unprepared, and*
4. *The enemy is, while clearly rude, crude, vulgar, unrefined, whorish, cocky and just low, also very experienced. On a side note I suspect he may be sugarcoating his lips on the sly. Seriously, no man should taste that sweet. Either that, or it could be some dark magic.*

It's true he won this round, but I will take heart from the fact that one battle does not

make a war. All is not lost. If I get desperate I might even invest in body armor for the lower half of my body. By hook or by crook I will try to release myself from this torment. As a last resort I will even considering initiating Plan B.

It is now four in the afternoon and to console myself I'm going down to the kitchen to eat some scones. I deserve it.

I will start over tomorrow.

Wish me luck.

I lock my diary, put it back into the bedside drawer and go out of my room.

The Hunter residence is a five-storey, London town house decorated in a limited color palate of white and grey, black, and an occasional splash of bright color to add glamour to the contemporary feel. I take the stairs with its black runner carpet, my hand sliding down the smooth intricately patterned wrought iron banister.

I walk past Crittal style windows that serve to section off the living room where there are fabulous sixteenth-century antiques brought in from Milan, canary yellow sofas and a seventies chandelier by Seguso.

The kitchen is behind a door with a black and white mural. I push it and enter a large rectangular space done up in walnut and cream. Simple, clean, and smelling like a food lover's paradise.

Cora, a tiny woman with sandy hair and warm hazel eyes, is sitting at the island watching

TV. I glance at the screen and notice it is not one of the usual shows she watches. Cora is a fierce romantic. Occasionally it will be *Cake Boss*, but more often than not, she will be watching *Say Yes To The Dress, I Found The Gown,* or something that features a happy bride in it.

'Whatcha watching?' I ask as I take the seat next to her.

'*The Real Housewives Of Beverly Hills*,' she says without taking her eyes off the screen.

'How come?'

'I missed last Sunday night's show so I'm watching the repeat.'

'Is it any good?'

'There's only ten minutes left. Watch it with me. See this bitch talking now. She's the one I hate the most. Everyone else thinks that Lisa Vanderpump is the bitch, but this is the real bitch. She's always causing trouble.'

I smile at how involved and mad Cora is. The camera pans to a beautiful, flawlessly made up blonde.

'This one here is Erika,' Cora explains. 'She's the richest of them all. The rest of the housewives are all secretly jealous of her. They don't own private planes, but both Erica and her husband each own one.'

The next shot cuts to what seems to be an enormous argument.

'They've got all this money and they're always fighting about stupid things,' Cora says disgustedly. 'Sometimes I just want to shake them and knock their silly heads together.'

I hide a smile at her passion. While the shit is still flying around the screen, the show is over and Cora shakes her head with exasperation and gets up. She goes to the oven and peers through the glass door. Nodding with satisfaction, she opens the door and pulls out a tray of hot scones. Cora has asbestos hands so she peels the scones from the parchment with her bare hands and arranges them on a cooling rack.

From the fridge she fetches the container of clotted cream and puts it on the island table together with a jar of homemade strawberry jam. I have to say, Cora makes the best jam in the world, every spoonful will have at least one chunk of strawberry in it.

I start laying the island surface with two plates, a couple of knives and two spoons. I tear off four pieces of kitchen paper and lay them besides the plates.

Britney, who has been to Mrs. Ottilia Flutie's finishing school where she has learnt how to eat oranges with a knife and fork, says that there is a very clear etiquette involved in eating a scone. As a matter of fact, there are only two approved ways to eat scones properly.

First you have to cut it horizontally. That then is the last time you can use the knife on the scone. The scone must then be eaten open faced. The jam and the cream added bite by bite, or one half scone at a time. Basically, don't ever turn it into a damn sandwich.

I spread enough jam and cream on my warm scone to leave long teeth marks and do the one-half-scone-at-a-time thing, and Cora employs the bite-by-bite method. The scones are so good we do not even speak. Mrs. Ottilia Flutie would have a heart attack if she saw me pick up every last crumb with my fingers and suck it off.

'What are you making tomorrow?' I ask as I clear the table.

'Apple pie,' Cora says, wiping her mouth with a napkin.

I put the dirty plates and utensils into the dishwasher. 'With custard?'

'You can have yours with custard if you like, I'll be having mine with rum and raisin ice cream. Scrummy combination.'

I think about it for an instant. It does actually sound good. 'I think I'll join you.'

'You won't regret it.'

'Same time tomorrow?'

'All right, love.'

As I leave, Cora increases the volume on the TV. I trudge upstairs, open my laptop, and see that Leah is already awake. I Skype her and she answers holding a bowl of cereal in her hand.

'Hmmm ... let me guess? You met the singing sensation.'

'Yeah,' I say with a small laugh. She knows me so well.

'And,' she prompts.

'And he kissed me.'

'On the cheek? On the forehead? On the hand?'

'On the lips.'

'Oh sweet Jesus. You fell at the first hurdle.'

'Well, I didn't fall exactly. It was just a kiss. I was taken by surprise. It won't happen again.'

'Just a kiss? Then why is your face red?'

'It's hot here.'

She shakes her head disapprovingly. 'You know what I think?'

'What?'

'I think you should skip all preliminaries and move on to plan B. Get it over with, draw a line in the fucking sand, and then let's go on our holiday.'

'No way. I'm not throwing in the towel yet.'

'You've already thrown in the towel.'

'Look. I have more self-control than you think. I just ... need a bit of time to adjust. This is not easy for me.'

'I've got news for you, Tori. It's not going to get any easier.'

'I'm *not* moving on to Plan B,' I say stubbornly. 'Well, not yet, anyway. I don't think I need to.'

She puts down her bowl of cereal and sighs. 'Before I do some straight talking, you know that I love you, right?'

'Right,' I say slowly. A lecture is coming my way.

'Stop being delusional. You're wasting your time trying to resist him. The more you resist temptation the stronger and more potent it becomes. The longer you keep spending time with the guy the more entrenched your feelings will become.'

Of course, she is right.

'The man is well and truly unavailable to you, long term anyway, but if you play hard to get you will only make him chase you which will make you fall even harder. You need to say yes, sleep with the guy once or twice, and put an end to your girlish crush once and for all. I mean, a guy who looks that good has probably got a small dick.'

'He doesn't,' my mouth blurts out before my brain can get into gear.

'What?' she explodes, her eyes popping open.

'Um ... he has a big dick.'

'And you know this because?'

'He had an erection and I saw it through his jeans,' I confess.

'Oh Lord. Just get your condoms ready, OK?'

'You should have more faith in me.'

'I do. There is merit to my strategy. Good looking and a big dick means he's definitely a lousy lover. You'll be wanting to be rid of him sooner than you think.'

Not if his kiss is anything to go by. Fortunately I'm not dumb enough to voice this particular thought.

'So when are you seeing him next?' she asks, picking up her bowl again and spooning another mouthful of cereal into her mouth.

'Tomorrow. He's throwing a pool party. Britney is all excited about it because Taylor Swift is coming.'

'Hmmm. Do you think you can swing an autograph for my sister?'

That evening Cash doesn't turn up for chicken pie. I eat my dinner without tasting it, and wonder if Leah might have been totally wrong. There will be no need for condoms at all because Cash has already lost interest in me.

Chapter Seven

Cash

Hunter by name and hunter by nature.

Goddamn. She's something else. My head's reeling and the blood is pounding so hard in my dick I feel like pulling over to the side of the road and fucking taking care of it myself, but I don't need to see grainy pictures of me jacking off in my car on the evening news. Been there. Done that. And I definitely don't need Octavia breathing hot air down my neck *again* about imaging, branding, target audience, or urban cool.

Nope.

Still? Tori fucking Diamond, eh?

My little sister's PA. Who'd have thought she'd be the hottest thing to cross my path in a long, long time? She's so hot she's bouncing with it. And that attitude of hers. Talk about a badass mouth. I can already see it full of my dick.

And my, my, what a sweet picture that is.

I was a walking zombie this morning. I'd been up all night partying hard and all I wanted to do was go back and crash in my own bed. Yeah, I know, it's called a hedonistic lifestyle.

But as Fate would have it, I'm driving down the road when I spot the Bentley with Victor cooling his heels in the driver's seat. On Harley street? There's only one scenario: Britney was up to no good again. Believe me, I fucking cuss the air blue, but I stop and go in, and there she is like a long, cool drink on a hot day. Blonde hair down to her waist and the ass on that bird. It's one of the reasons I still believe in miracles.

Oh, yeaaaaah.

If a jaw ever dropped ... but damn if she didn't look at me as if I was a bit of chewing gum stuck to the bottom of her shoes. It made me want to rip the clothes off her back and give it to her right there.

You see, when every woman you meet can't wait to choke on your dick and lays it all out on a silver platter for you, you start to yearn for the woman who throws you a bit of shade. You miss the buzz of a chase. You wish someone would resist you. Everyone wants a piece of Cash. She doesn't. That makes her fucking precious.

I just had to break off a little piece of that Kit Kat.

I chased her all the way to my father's house and right into my old bathroom. So she's naked and in the bath and giving me all the sass, but I catch her staring at my dick like a starving animal looking at a fuckin' feast.

I don't know. Maybe she never saw a dick so big, but fucking hell I could have roasted a pig in the bonfire in her eyes.

You gotta respect a contradiction like that!

I mean, one minute she's slaying you with her tongue and giving you spicy ass attitude, next moment she's looking at your junk like it should be registered on the endangered species list. It's a challenge and an invitation, but in my case it's a red rag to a bull.

Tori Diamond just put hunt back into Hunter and poured a little bit more awesome sauce on to my already fantastically awesome life.

I glance at the speedometer. 102 MPH.

There are no speed cameras on this stretch of the road so I lean on the accelerator and revel in the rush of watching my metal baby eat up tarmac at incredible speed. Music is blasting from the stereo and adrenaline is coursing in my veins. The high is unbelievable. This is my life. Money, pussy, and speed.

What else is there, anyway?

Chapter Eight

Tori

A cousin of mine who once won a minor beauty pageant used to say real beauty requires hard work and discipline. I didn't truly know what she meant until I go shopping with Britney.

We spend *hours* looking for the right dress. She tries on what seems like a hundred different outfits in at least thirty shops. She twirls in front of me in dresses that are, quite frankly stunning, and decides that they make her grasshopper long legs look stumpy and fat or her augmented and perfect 32C chest look flat and blah.

She almost bursts into tears because the color of one of them, she believes, makes her glowing teenage skin look washed out. Another classically simple dress gets the ultimate insult.

'I'd rather wear one of Kanye West's plain white T-shirts that he has the cheek to sell at $150.00.'

I flash a placating smile, find a broken sweet in my jean's pocket, slip it into my mouth, and crush it to death between my teeth. Then, just as I am about to tear my hair out with sheer boredom, we go into Couture Couture and Britney finds a mini-dress in Clementine. Even I have to admit this dress is special. It is super-sexy, trendy, and perfect for her body shape. Good, I think we can take a break for a couple of hours before her appointment at the hairdresser, but life is never that easy.

'Now,' Britney says, moving again towards the dress rail, 'we have to find something for you. I think I saw something that might be perfect just now.'

There is absolutely no way I'm buying anything at Couture Couture. Even the tiny dress Britney is swanning around the shop in carries a £695.00 price tag. That's more than three weeks' worth of wages to me, and there is no way in hell I'm about to go traipsing around the shops all over again.

'I have a little black dress. I think I'll wear that,' I say trailing behind her.

Britney stops in her tracks, balances her weight on one hip, and looks me up and down. She reminds me of one of the divas in that Real Housewife reality show that Cora likes to watch.

'What little black dress?' she asks.

'You haven't seen it. I didn't bother to unpack it.'

She folds her arms across her chest. 'I *have* seen it. Isn't it made out of T-shirt material?'

'Well, yes, but I can dress it up.'

'Absolutely not,' she says imperviously, and turning away from me resumes rifling through the dress racks.

'Look, even if I do decide to buy something, I definitely can't afford to get anything from here.'

'Hmmm ...' she says, ignoring me and moving quickly through the rack.

'Britney,' I call, my voice louder and more impatient.

'You're not paying for this dress. I am,' she says without turning around.

I puff air out of my cheeks. 'It's really nice of you and everything, but you will not be paying for it, will you? Your Dad will be, and I don't think he'll appreciate being forced into buying me such an expensive dress.'

She turns to look at me in surprise. 'Dad's not going to mind me buying you a dress. It's not like it's every day that Cash comes home and throws a party.'

I shake my head.

'If you don't believe me I can call him right now and ask,' she challenges.

'That won't be necessary. It's not that I don't believe you. I'd just feel uncomfortable accepting such an expensive dress from my employer.'

'Think of it as a uniform. You have to come to the party with me and you need an outfit that won't show me up.'

'OK, let's compromise. Maybe we can stop by Topshop or Miss Selfridge and I'll find something suitable there.'

She wrinkles her nose in disgust. 'Tori, you don't understand, do you? Everybody there will be dressed to kill. You might as well come naked instead of a little number from Topshop.'

I stare blankly at her. My mother calls it my owl look.

'It's just a dress,' she says persuasively.

'Fine.'

'Good,' she says with satisfaction, and turns back to the rack. Less than a minute later she yanks something out from the rail. 'How about this?' she cries triumphantly.

I stare at it in amazement.

'It'll be gorgeous when it's wet,' she says, walking towards me.

Wow! I don't know about it being gorgeous when it's wet, but it's awesome dry. I mean, I would never even have considered a zebra print, semi transparent, maxi dress with a plunging neckline and long sleeves, but now that she has pulled it out and is waving it temptingly in front of me, I have to admit she knows her fashion. I take it from her and look at the price tag. An eye-watering £799.00. On sale. Supposedly reduced from £1,399.00.

'Have you seen the price?' I whisper, horrified.

'If you don't hurry up, we'll miss my hair appointment,' she prompts, one eyebrow raised expectantly.

I take the dress from her and bustle into the dressing room. I wriggle out of my clothes and pull the dress over my head. I zip it up and I can quite honestly say I have never worn anything so revealing, sexy, or glamorous before. I feel slinky and sheer, and in a funny sort of way like my grandmother's favorite movie character, Suzie Wong.

'Come out then,' Britney calls.

I step out. 'How do I look?'

She gives me the critical once over, grins and says, 'I think I officially hate you.'

'You don't think it's too ... er ... sexy?'

She comes closer to me. 'It'll be tremendously sexy when it gets wet, but that's the whole point,' she explains, tilting her head slightly as she adjusts the material around my hips.

I swivel my head to look at the back of the dress. Actually, it's already tremendously sexy. 'Are you sure your dad won't mind?'

'I have a credit limit. Sparks only start flying when I go over it.'

I smile at her awkwardly. 'Well, thank you for the dress. It's very generous of you.'

She looks down at her bare feet, and for a confusing moment she looks young and vulnerable. 'It's only a dress. You do a lot for me.'

'Thank you,' I say softly.

She raises her eyes to mine and smiles shyly. 'You're welcome, Tori. I really like you.'

For a fraction of an instant I can't bring myself to reciprocate. Then I realize that she's just a kid. A lonely, rich kid. Telling her I like her won't be a lie. Sometimes, like now or when she was hanging on to my bathroom door and twerking, I do like her, a lot.

'Me too,' I say.

Her smile widens into a massive grin of pure joy. It is infectious and I start grinning back at her too.

'Are you planning to put your hair up or let it down?' she asks suddenly.

'What do you think?' I ask, bowing to her obvious expertise when it comes to clothes, fashion, and pool parties in the homes of celebrities.

'Without any doubt, down.'

'You don't think that would be too ... obvious?'

'God, no. It's an asset. I wish my hair was as beautiful as yours. Actually, I wish my everything was as beautiful as yours.'

I frown. 'I think you're way cuter than you give yourself credit for.'

'No,' she says gloomily. 'Cash got mum's lovely coloring and looks and I got dad's.'

'I think you're beautiful, Britney,' I say sincerely.

She shrugs. 'You're hardly going to tell me I'm ugly even if you think so, are you?'

Astonished, I stare at her. 'Why on earth would you imagine that I think you're ugly?'

She shrugs again.

'I don't think you're ugly at all. In fact, the opposite. You're beautiful. People are always telling you that.'

'Sure they are. Everybody wants to be Cash's sister's friend.' Her voice is husky, almost tearful.

'That's not true,' I deny immediately, but we both know that there is no real conviction in my tone.

She smiles suddenly, a forced stretch of her lips. 'Never mind. Let's settle the bill and go get us some killer shoes.'

We pop into Russell & Bromley and Britney gets a pair of mile high platform sparkly shoes and I buy silver stilettos. My shoes come to £120.00 and I insist on paying for them. They are more expensive than what I would normally splash out on a pair of shoes, but what the hell? We only live once!

After buying our bikinis, black for me, and white for Britney, we head off to the hairdressers. While I wait for Britney, the girl from Thailand who does nails comes and asks me if I want to have my nails done. My nails are actually pretty rough looking.

'I make pretty,' she says, nodding her head vigorously.

How can anybody resist such an invitation?

'Oh, go on then,' I say. A little part of me has started to get excited about this pool party and seeing Cash again.

'Manicure and pedicure?' she asks, sensing an easy prey.

'OK,' I agree, and she shows me her color swatches.

To be honest she does make both my hands and feet look very pretty. Feeling generous I leave a good tip.

'Thank you,' she says with a small nod. She immediately roots around in her basket and carefully presses a small crystal onto my thumbnail and finishes it with a layer of clear varnish.

'Hmmm ... your carriage awaits, Cinderella.'

Chapter Nine

Tori

'She most popular girl in bar. She got sex
appeal.'
- The World of Suzie Wong

The cool air smells of roasting meat and
pulses, with techno music and the sounds of a
seriously good party in progress. As soon as the
car noses through the gaggle of paparazzi
gathered outside the gates, the guard waves us
through and we turn into Cash Hunter's drive.
The house, a massive, modern, glass and steel
monster structure, is lit up like a mother ship.

Britney and I get out of the car and walk up
to the team of bouncers standing around the
front doors. We go through the tall doors and,
I'm not kidding, step into every manslut's wet
dream.

The living room has —wait for it—an
Olympic-size swimming pool. OK, Olympic size
might be a bit of an exaggeration, but you get the
picture. It is infested with nearly naked, nubile,
squealing bodies. As my dazed eyes watch more
super-excited, shrieking, gloriously perfect,
scantily clad girls land in the water with a splash.

Oh, you should also know that the living room boasts a dance floor (that's right, a slightly raised square platform that flashes), two well stocked bars (on either side of the pool), and a giant movie screen with images of whales swimming underwater in slow motion. The whales, I'll admit, is a cool and surreal idea.

Honestly, the whole thing looks like an MTV music video.

Right in the middle of all this fun and laughter is Cash Hunter. Lying on a giant purple inflatable bed between two giggling babes. One of them is pouring champagne straight from the bottle onto his chest. Talk about living a cliché.

Still, awesome, fantastic, wonderful.

This is exactly the kind of stuff I was hoping to run into. Right this minute, the lead singer of ALKALINE doesn't seem all that attractive. In fact, he looks like a shallow, selfish, vain, egocentric, show-off, media created, hateful, sexual deviant of a jerk. Who in their right mind would ever want a party god like this?

Beside me Britney screams, 'Cash.'

His head swivels in our direction and our eyes meet. Suddenly the blood in my veins starts fizzing like soda water. Oh God. Apparently, I'm not in my right mind. Because I want him so bad it hurts my stomach, and until he decides to break the eye-fuck I find myself totally, completely, and absolutely unable to look away. I just stand there frozen and stare idiotically at him.

Until his eyes flicker and he turns his gaze to Britney. A smile breaks out on his face.

Rolling the girl next to him into the water, he slips into it himself and swims strongly towards us. Placing his palms on the tiles at the edge of the pool, he hauls himself out easily. His eyes are luminous with water reflections.

From his crouched position, he uncoils, full of sexual energy. Water sluices off his body in fast flowing rivulets and I actually feel my eyes widen. Holy crap. What a rush! He lifts his powerful arms and slicks his hair back, and my eyes just follow like some starving, stray dog.

It's just not fair. Why should *anybody* look like that? I shake my head to clear the weird hypnotic effect he is having on me. It's not like I want anything to happen between us.

Britney takes a step forward and pecks delicately at his wet cheek.

'Great party,' she says stepping back.

'There's not much to your dress,' he notes darkly.

'We're here to have fun,' Britney giggles.

His eyes narrow disapprovingly. 'Watch it, Brit. I don't want to have to bash anybody's head in.'

'Oh for God's sake don't be such a spoil sport, Cash. I never get to go out and have fun,' she groans.

He scowls at her. 'I mean it. I'm not your BFF. I'm your older brother.'

"What time is Taylor Swift coming?' she asks, craftily changing the subject.

'Not until later.'

She clasps her hands together. 'I'm so excited. I can't believe I'm going to meet her.'

He smiles indulgently. 'She said she's bringing something special for you.'

Britney's eyes become dinner platters. 'What?'

He lifts one wet, muscular, tanned, taut shoulder. Phew. This man could start a new category of porn – shoulder porn. 'It's a surprise,' he tells her.

'But do you know what it is though?' she wheedles.

'Nope. You'll just have to wait.'

'All right,' she agrees easily. 'Where's Prince anyway?'

'Locked in my bedroom,' he says.

'Can I go see him?'

'Yeah, but don't let him out.'

'Oh why not?' she complains.

He raises his eyebrows meaningfully. 'Because he'll do what he did the last time you let him out.'

'I thought it was a great laugh,' she says with a little naughty giggle.

'Seriously? You want a repeat?'

'So he jumped into the pool. He's friendly. It's hardly his fault that everybody else was silly enough to behave as if a man-eating crocodile had got into the pool with them,' she defends.

'Britney,' Cash says patiently, 'after he emptied the pool he ran outside and shook himself all over the buffet table and slobbered on the barbequed meat so no one had anything to eat.'

'Your friends don't eat anyway,' she retorts.

Way to go, Britney. This is the version of her that I could really start to like.

'Prince doesn't get out, or you're never coming to my parties again,' he says. His voice is flatter than the flattest thing you can think of.

'Fine,' Britney agrees sulkily. 'I won't let him out.' She turns toward me. 'Do you want to come and meet Prince, Tori?'

I do very much want to meet Prince. I know that he is an enormous, pale tan beast of a Kangal. Two years ago it was all over the news how he had been found in a drug dealer's backyard, snarling, his bones showing, and his ears chopped off so that he would look fiercer. He was already in the police dog pound waiting to be put down since Kangals are classified in some countries as one of the dangerous dog breeds, but Cash had seen his picture in the newspapers and fallen in love with him. I suppose he must have called in a whole lot of favors because he got the dog.

Kangals are intimidating monsters, capable of warding off wolves, bears and jackals, but the only photos I have seen of his dog are those where he is standing on his hind legs and resting his great big front paws on Cash's shoulders while he licks his master's face like some great big puppy.

I'm about to agree to go see him when Cash speaks up.

'No, you go on ahead. Let Tori stay here and say hello to me.'

'All right,' she agrees and moves away.

I take a deep breath and look up at Cash.

He lets his smoldering eyes slowly travel down my body. I think I manage to keep a version of a too-cool-for-school expression going on my face, or maybe not, since my skin gets so hot my eyebrows feel like they are on fire.

Baring icy white teeth, he drawls, 'You look ravishing, but ... Zebra prints? That's false advertising surely.'

I frown. 'What are you trying to imply now?'

'I'm not trying to imply anything. Just sayin' it might have been more truthful to go with wildcat prints, but I guess we both know you're not very honest.'

'And what the hell is *that* supposed to mean?' I demand, getting more and more annoyed.

'You want some of this,' he flicks his hand down his annoyingly hunky body, 'but you pretend not to.'

'God, you sure have an extraordinarily big head, don't you?' I mutter, irritated that he is 101% right in his assessment of the situation.

His eyes gleam. 'That's me. Big head, big mouth, big cock ...'

I roll my eyes so hard it hurts my head. 'Oh, here we go again.'

'Why are you so mad at me? I'm just trying to be helpful. You know, reading out the label so there are no surprises later.' He drops his head, looks down at his feet so his wet eyelashes are almost sweeping his cheeks, then looks at me through the spiky curtain.

God, damn him, even though I know it's all callous manipulation and technique, it still stirs my heart. It's so freaking difficult to keep pretending and saying no, when all I want to do is fall into his fantastic arms and let him sweep me off to his lovely bed. I desperately need to put some distance between us.

'You're not that cute, and I will *never* fall for that tired, old stunt,' I say, pulling together my scattered wits.

'Never?' he asks.

'Never,' I say firmly.

'You could crush a guy saying things like that,' he murmurs.

'It doesn't seem to be doing you any harm,' I retort.

'I'm worried about the drip, drip effect,' he says softly, his eyes twinkling with mischief. 'Over time even very hard things can be worn down.'

I ignore the sexual innuendo. 'Don't worry, I don't think I'll be around long enough for you to notice such an effect.'

'I don't know. After a mind-blowing climax with a side of wow, you might want to stay around. Maybe even stalk me.'

If only he knew. I was already stalking him. 'Men like you badly need to slip on a banana skin and fall flat on your butt.'

'I'd love to see you eat a banana. I bet you kill it,' he says huskily.

I open my mouth to reply and nothing comes out. God help me. I have a vision of myself running kisses along his jaw.

Without warning he moves in for the kill, his mouth inches from mine, his arm brushing mine, the clean male smell of him making my senses reel. Horrified, I lean back.

'By the way,' he whispers seriously. 'That's not pussy you're smelling. I just ate a tuna fish sandwich.'

There's no fishy smell. Gross bastard. He knows I want him and he's just keeping me in the sexual prey zone. An image of his head between my legs slips into my mind and something inside me lurches. I should shove him away, or say something cutting.

'I hate to break it to you, but you're a very shallow person,' I croak.

His breath is hot against my cheek. 'For a very shallow person I can go very deep.'

'You're unbelievable,' I breathe shakily. It's clear I should push him away and I do want to. Really, I do.

'I'm hoping you'll be keeping to that storyline later,' he says with a chuckle.

'You're so full of shit there can't be much room left to house your brain.'

'I'm a simple man. I keep my brain in my dick.'

'Cash,' a hard voice raps.

Shocked by the sudden intrusion, I stumble away from him, and snap my head towards the voice. Octavia Harding. In real life she looks like she lives on low fat, no sugar, gluten free toasted wheat crackers with lettuce and half a slice of tomato, and sucked out whatever little bum fat she had and injected it into her lips. She is everything I am not. The contempt in her eyes is calculated to try and make me feel worse than a used condom. Completely ignoring me after that first dismissive glance, she fixes her attention on Cash. She flashes an insincere smile.

'I need to speak to you privately.' Her voice is professional with a tinge of sexy.

Cash takes his own sweet time answering her. 'Relax, Octavia. It's a fucking party.'

'EMI has sent three executives out. I'll relax once you've met them.'

Not taking his eyes off me he says, 'Say hello to Tori Diamond first.'

Something dismissive and resentful flashes in her eyes. 'I'm not paid to say hello to every bimbo you fuck, Cash.'

My back prickles. Wow! First time for me. I've never come face-to-face with a twenty-four carat bitch before.

'Don't mind her, Tori, she's been digging into her stash of bitch crisps again,' he mocks, before turning back towards her, his eyes hard. 'Tori is Britney's new PA. You could be seeing a lot of her, so it might be a good idea to play nice.'

Octavia's lips stretch into a malignant smile. 'Hello.'

'Hey,' I say, unsmiling.

Her eyes narrow. 'Are you an American?'

'Yes.'

Her eyes glitter. 'Hmmm. Do you have a permit to work in this country? They don't usually hand out work visas for lowly PA jobs.'

Don't sock her. Don't sock her. I take a deep calming breath and open my mouth.

'Tori is allowed to work here. Her mother's English, so she holds a British passport as well as an American one,' Britney explains cheerfully, having come back from seeing Prince.

'Hello, Britney. You look wonderful,' Octavia says, her voice one degree warmer.

'Thanks, so do you,' Britney says unenthusiastically.

'I'm afraid I'm going to have to steal your brother away. He has very important people waiting for him.'

'They can wait. Nobody asked them to come,' Cash says coolly.

'I did,' Octavia says. She appears to take stock and realizes she is going about this the wrong way. She softens her tone. 'Come on, Cash. It will only take a minute. Gavin and Joseph are already there. You can party after you finish with them. How about that, hmmm?'

'Go ahead, Cash,' Britney says. 'Tori and I will go help ourselves to the fruit punch. I'm dying of thirst.'

He turns his eyes away from Octavia and looks down sternly at his sister. 'Go easy, you.'

'Stop worrying. I'm not a bloody child. I'll be eighteen soon, and anyway, Dad said I could have a couple of drinks.'

'Right.' He turns to me, his expression warming up. 'Don't lose your head until I get back.'

I flush to the roots of my hair. He's like a safety pin to the bubble I have spent so long blowing.

Chapter Ten

Cash

'**G**ot the hots for your little sister's PA, have you?' Octavia says as we walk through the party.

'Since when have you cared who I had the hots for?'

'Excuse me. You're talking to me, Octavia, the mug who is constantly getting you out of trouble.'

That pisses me off. I hate it when she treats me like I'm still sixteen. 'Bullshit,' I snarl.

'Oh yeah? Two DUIs?' she reminds sweetly.

One of these days Octavia will go too far. 'I was fucking seventeen.'

'I broke the law for you.'

'And still holding it over my head like the sword of Damocles. You did what you did and got handsomely paid for it.'

'And the pregnancy?'

'Oh, for fuck's sake. It wasn't even mine,' I grit.

'What about the girl I had to pay off?'

Is she kidding me? 'That was Gavin,' I say in a bored voice.

She laughs. 'True. He hasn't got the sense God gave a goose so he goes around laying his eggs in every woman he meets.'

I don't say anything. No point. In her eyes I'm still whacking off in socks.

'That doesn't change the fact that I don't trust that girl. I've been in this business a long time and I know when something's not right, and there's something very wrong about her. She might have designs on you.'

'Designs? I'm the one doing all the chasing here.'

She shakes her head as if I have just said the stupidest thing on earth. 'I can't believe how gullible men are. Of course she wants you. It's just a technique. Playing hard to get.'

'In that case, well done to her. Her technique is definitely working. I can't wait to get into her pants.' I'm actually sick and tired of people treating me as if I'm only good enough to jump around on a stage and sing the words they ask me to.

'I'd be careful if I were you,' she warns

I bite back the nasty retort. One day. One day, she'll hang herself on her own rope. 'Just chill, will ya?'

'Just remember you're worth millions. Don't get caught in a gold digger's claws. You could ruin your entire future with one stupid move. We talked about this before. Stay single. Play the field. Lots of girls. Often. That way your fans think they have a chance with you. They can keep warm with the fantasy that they'll be the one who ties you down.'

I stop walking and look at her. Sometimes I think it is Octavia who has her claws in my flesh.

The older I get the more irritated I am by her constant meddling in my affairs.

'I'm just doing my job,' she says.

'Thanks a bunch, but I think I have this one covered,' I say. When we get to the studio, I hold open the door and she sails in, her grotesque lips stretched into a smile. I walk in after her and catch Gavin's eyes. He looks bored out of his skull. He raises his eyebrows at me and I shrug. Joseph is staring into a glass of whiskey as if he's just found the meaning of life at the bottom of it. The other band members have had a lucky escape. Robbie and Steve are already in Milan getting ready for our upcoming concert.

At the other end of the room, Octavia is saying, 'So glad you could make it, Tony.'

She is in her element.

Tori

The punch is too sweet so I settle for a bottle of beer. Carrying our drinks, Britney and I walk into the grounds towards the pit where the meat is being cooked.

Britney tells me that the meat and the men preparing it have been flown in from Argentina. This method of slow cooking in the ground to allow the fats to infuse through the meat while using lots of coarse barbeque salt is called Asado. It makes the meat so tender you can eat it with a spoon.

As we get closer, the smell of sizzling meat makes my stomach rumble. The men are

71

wizened and burnt brown, their faces greasy. They joke and laugh in Spanish as they unload large chunks of short ribs, rib-eye steaks, blood sausages, and sweetbreads on metal racks. Another man expertly cuts them into more manageable sizes and arranges them into large trays.

I fill my plate up with steak, grilled provolone cheese, garlic bread and salad. Britney has a bit of salad and a tiny portion of ribs. We take a seat on one of the chairs laid out on the lawn and start to eat. The meat melts in my mouth and the cheese is delicious, but I find I can't eat a lot. I keep thinking of Cash, wondering where he is and what he is doing. As soon as Britney finishes pecking at her food we go back to join the party.

Britney sees someone she knows and goes to say hello. I stand by the bar, drinking my beer and looking around me. Secretly I am searching for Cash. You're dreaming. He might change. He might change. He won't change. He'll just freaking break your heart. A dull ache starts somewhere in the region of my chest.

'Looking for me?' his voice asks from behind me.

'No,' I lie, my eyes flicking from his delectable dimple all the way down to his totally suckable toes. The man is a powerhouse of raw sex and testosterone. It puts my nerves on edge. I feel amped and nervous.

'You're just saying that to get a rise out of me,' he parries.

'If I wanted to get a rise out of you I'd just take my bra off.' Hot, lion's teeth! I can't believe I just said that. What the hell was I thinking of? I feel the burn rush up my neck and face.

His eyes gleam wickedly. 'Finally, an idea we can both enjoy.'

'Please, I'm trying to enjoy my drink here.' I raise the cold bottle to my lips and take a sip.

His eyes drop to my mouth. 'You're gonna suck my cock like that bottle?'

'Ugh,' I cry, pretending to be exasperated. Any more of this and I'm going to crumble. I glare at him. 'I swear I've never met a man more happy to be classed under young, dumb and full of cum.'

He chuckles. 'That's the best you can do? I'm more offended by the interest rate my bank pays out.'

In spite of myself a small reluctant smile tugs at my mouth. I know it looks like I've got the self-restraint of a puppy, but it's very, very, very hard to even pretend to stay mad with a guy who looks like he ate a whole fridge full of gorgeous.

He cocks his head. 'Come on, you know you want me,' he says persuasively.

I actually feel breathless. I really should walk away, but I just can't. He's like a magnet. The more I try to push him away, the more he pulls me towards him. 'You should quit while you're ahead,' I advise.

He crosses his arms. 'Ahead? How do you figure that? You've still got your dress on.'

My stomach twists with sexual tension. Leah is right. This is a game I can never win. 'Back off. You've got zero chance of getting my dress off.'

'Is that a challenge or an invitation?'

'Neither. It's a statement of fact.'

'Let's test it, shall we?' he says, and in a flash he plucks my beer from my hand, puts it on the bar top, and picks me up in his strong arms. For a few precious seconds I am too embarrassed and humiliated to do anything. Then I realize where we are heading and it's too late.

'Don't you dare,' I shout.

Seconds later I'm flying through the air, a scream tearing through my throat. Next moment I hit the water with a great splash, and sink like a sack of potatoes. Vaguely I hear clapping and cheering. I emerge spluttering. Treading water, I look around. He is standing at the edge, a smirk on his face. I am so furious I can't even think straight. Bastard. I turn and swim to the opposite side of the pool. As I reach the edge a hand reaches down, grabs my hand, and hauls me out of the water.

Cash

What the fuck? I watch Gavin's hands linger around her wet body and a ball of fire rushes up my spine and explodes inside my skull. My blood boils as I see his arm go around her. Fucking shitbag is trying to move in on my territory! Look at him with the stupid spit curl that he spent an hour getting into shape.

Yeah, sure, we've shared girls before. But Tori? Not even if hell freezes over. I'll rip his throat out before I let him lay a finger on her.

She is mine.

Striding around the pool, my brain slowly melting in my skull, I see her put her hand on the smarmy bastard's chest. Fucking fool has a tattoo on it in Moulin Rouge font that reads I'm The Greatest. Yeah, sure, Gavin. Next time just send out a fucking Twitter message. Idiot. You know what I'm sayin'?

As I come up to them I hear a snippet of their conversation. Puke fest.

'I ain't gonna lie I don't wake up looking this good. There's about twelve products that have gone into this look,' he says proudly.

'Twelve?' She sounds dazed.

'Straight up,' the fool boasts.

Chapter Eleven

Tori

'**Y**ou're pissing on my patch, Gav,' Cash growls.

Gavin looks dumbfounded.

'Hit the pedal, man,' he says, his eyes shooting sparks of fury.

'Right, man. Right,' Gavin mumbles, takes a step backwards and throws a bizarre little laugh while simultaneously looking around to see if anybody else has witnessed his humiliation. Noting that his pride is still intact, he grabs a passing girl and whispers something in her ear. She giggles and nods. He drags her away in the direction of the gardens.

'You're pissing on my patch? What are you, a dog?' I fume incredulously.

He shrugs the macho territorial posturing like it's a coat or something, and the flash, brash bad boy comes back into town. 'It's a guy thing. You wouldn't understand.'

'You're such a dick.'

'No,' he corrects, his eyebrows raise innocently, sensuality shimmering in the green wells of his eyes. 'I have a dick. A big one.'

'Oh my God, I'm stuck in a time loop,' I say sarcastically.

He grins, all sex, lust and trouble. 'Lean in, sugar drop. This is a secret. What happens next between us has never happened to you before.'

'I'm wet and pissed and not in the mood for cheap innuendos, or the whole asshole act.'

His eyes twinkle. 'You were doing so well with the first part of your sentence, but I get your point.' His eyes linger on my body, now that the dress is wet there is not a curve or line that is not completely exposed. I suppress the desire to wrap my hands around my body. He takes my hand. 'Come on, let's get you out of that dress and you dried off.'

I let him lead me away from the crowd towards a corridor on the ground floor. He opens the door and we are at the threshold of a scrupulously clean, minimally furnished room dominated by a massive round bed. Of course it has a mirror over it.

Suddenly I find myself grabbed and propelled forward until a wall is against my back. My eyes open wide.

'Scared?' he taunts, his breath tickling my skin.

I raise my hand and swing it at him. The crack reverberates in the empty room. I hit him so hard there is a white handprint on his cheek and my hand is throbbing furiously.

He laughs, a deep growling sound. 'I've always liked a girl with a temper.'

'This is sexual harassment,' I hiss.

'So show me you don't want me. Say no.' He pushes his body closer to me so his hot, thick erection presses into my stomach. I gasp, liquid fire rushing through my body. 'Go on, I'm waiting,' he challenges.

I stare up into his eyes as the scent of his wet body, his cologne, his excitement, swirls into me. I feel as if I am twelve again, and just as hopelessly in love with him as I was back then. Not one tiny iota of the love has gone away after all these years. In fact, it has grown up, and become infused with lust. My heart is hammering wildly in my chest and my breath is coming hard and fast. I want to say no. I must say no. I will say no. The answer is no, obviously.

My palms press against his chest to shove him away and encounter the stone-like slabs of his pecs. I swear I try to fight the thick heat rising between us, but it is in my veins, my skin, his half-hooded eyes, oozing out of his pores. It's everywhere.

At that instant I realize something. You can't outrun lust. It was moronic of me to even think I could. Pure lust is like a spell. It dazes and compels you to do what you know you shouldn't. It is impossible to resist.

In fact, I don't want to resist any more. I want anything and everything he's offering. I want that mind-blowing climax with the side of wow. Why shouldn't I have it? Maybe Leah was right all along. Just sleep with him and get it over with. My grandfather once told me the only things he regretted are the things he did not do.

He fixes me with his mesmeric stare and I stop thinking.

I let my body take charge. My hands reach out and grab fistfuls of hair as I pull his head down and feast greedily on his mouth. It's like matter and antimatter touching. We explode. There is no other way to describe the violent hunger. I've never felt more alive.

Every nerve, every cell in my body screams out for him to take me. The passion is as uncontrollable as a forest blaze. All I want to do is tear his clothes off and impale myself on him. I've never felt this way before. Lost to everything except Cash. My sensitized body throbs and feels strangely out of control.

I spread my palms over the broad, strong chest. My fingers look very pale. Moving my head, I bite his nipple. He draws in his breath sharply, but he doesn't stop me.

'Oh yes, Wildcat. Oh yes,' he encourages instead.

He unzips my dress, peels it away and groans at the sight of my bikini-clad body. He reaches behind me, pulls the string of my top and my breasts spring loose. They feel swollen and heavy. His eyes blaze possessively at the sight of my body nude, but for a tiny triangle of black material.

Expertly, he rolls a hard nipple back and forth between his smooth fingers. My body arches into him and he growls low—the sound is erotic—and sucks my lower lip. Hard. I shiver helplessly.

'God! You're so beautiful,' he murmurs as he gets down on his haunches. He bites at the string of my bikini and rips it off my body roughly. I feel his strong large hands lift one of my legs and put it over his shoulder. I begin to move my hips, desperate and seeking.

He grasps the outer lips of my sex and pulls them apart so the secret, pink inner tissue is exposed, and stares at the glistening flesh. I squirm impatiently. My whole body is hot with desire and excitement.

His expression is enigmatic as he gazes at the show between my legs. I never thought it would be, but it is an incredible turn-on. I feel dirty, slutty, and shameless ... and absolutely fucking vibrant.

'This is what I wanted, wildcat. To see your legs wide open and desperate for me. Keep them spread open.' His breath fans my fully opened sex, inflaming me. His fingers touch the wet whorls of flesh, and tendrils of excitement snake through my body. He drags his fingers through the soft, sensitive layers. My head tilts back involuntarily, my eyes half close.

'Go on,' I urge.

'What do you want, Tori?'

'Suck me,' I say hoarsely.

He moves his mouth toward my sex, and for one second I look down and take a mental picture of him, breathtakingly handsome, his curling eyelashes long against his cheeks, and then the shock of his mouth attaching itself and greedily licking the wet core between my legs drives all thought from my mind.

It feels so damn good I writhe, whimper, and push my aching center down hard against his mouth. His tongue moves between the folds, tasting, eating, sucking, and then I feel his finger thrust into me and I suck in a startled breath. Juices flow over his finger as he moves it in and out of me, maddening me. The heat and the hunger increases, and my thighs starts to shake with the approaching orgasm.

'Tori,' a voice echoes from somewhere.

I freeze. Sweet heaven! Tori. Not now.

'Fuck, don't you dare stop. You're coming,' he orders harshly.

'She'll come in,' I whisper in a panicked voice.

'I locked the door,' he says, and goes back to devouring my pussy while his fingers pump me hard.

'Tori, where are you?' Britney calls again, and this time she tries the door handle.

I try not to scream, but suddenly all hell breaks loose. It's the kind of orgasm that takes over your body. You have no control of your responses. My nails dig into his shoulder, my mouth opens, and a scream flies out. Super quick Cash lifts his hand and clamps it over my mouth so the sound is muffled. A groan rumbles in his chest. Cash leaves me immediately. I am still leaning against the wall, panting hard when Cash comes back with a bathrobe.

'Wear this, quickly,' he says, and sliding open the window he climbs out and disappears into the night.

'Tori, are you in there?' Britney calls and rattles the door handle.

I take a deep breath. 'I'm coming,' I choke out.

Chapter Twelve

Tori

I hurriedly pull my arms through the sleeves of the bathrobe, pull the edges together, and tie a knot at the front as I run to the door. I know my face must be flushed and strange, but there is nothing else I can do but face Britney. Taking a deep breath, I unlock the door and Britney almost falls into the room.

She looks at me accusingly. 'What are you doing in here?'

'I … I … er … got wet. Your brother said I could dry off in here.'

That sounded so lame I cringe inwardly, but she is too distraught to notice. She sniffs loudly and comes further into the room. 'Where's Cash now?' she asks tearfully.

I stare at her anxiously. 'I don't know. He must be back at the party. Are you OK?'

'Yeah. I think I had too much to drink.'

How could that be? She had two glasses of fruit punch.

'I want to go home,' she says.

'What?'

'I want to go back home.'

'Now?' I ask in disbelief.

'Yes,' she almost sobs.

I open my hands out in confusion. Ever since she knew about this party she has not stopped talking about meeting Taylor Swift, and now she wants to go back without meeting her. 'But what about Taylor? She's got a gift for you and all.'

Huge drops of tears roll down her face. I stare at them in amazement.

'It doesn't matter,' she sobs.

'Britney, what is the matter?'

'I just want to go home, OK?' she wails.

I hold my hands up. 'OK, OK. Just wait here. I'll go find Victor and tell him to bring the car around.'

'No, I'm coming with you,' she says quickly.

'Come on then,' I say.

She comes close to me and takes my hand. Hers feels small, hot and damp. I touch her forehead with the back of my hand. She seems to be running a fever. I frown. How strange. She was fine when we arrived. I lead her through the party-goers.

We walk quickly, but I can't help my eyes from scanning the crowd looking for Cash. Unexpectedly my eyes meet Octavia's. She is watching me with a strange expression. She knows. She knows about me and Cash. I let my eyes slide away quickly and pull Britney towards the front door.

A hand curls around my wrist. I look up into Cash's eyes. They are bright. He has changed into a dry T-shirt and black jeans and is looking sexy as hell. I feel myself go hot with the memory of what we did only minutes ago.

'Britney is not feeling very well,' I tell him. His eyes move from my face to hers. His brow knits.

'What's wrong, Sparkles?' he asks.

'Nothing. I think I just drank too much.'

'How much?'

She shrugs sulkily. 'I can't remember now.'

His eyes narrow and his voice sounds concerned. 'It's OK. Tori will get you home safely and I'll call you tomorrow.'

'Can you tell Taylor that I desperately wanted to meet her, but I wasn't feeling very well so I had to go home?' she asks in a small voice.

'Of course I will,' Cash soothes, but his eyes are watchful and disturbed.

For an instant I'm aware of undercurrents. I look again at Britney and suddenly I see it. She's not a spoilt rich girl. She is somehow terribly damaged. I'm not really her PA. I'm kind of guarding her.

'Is Victor bringing the car around?'

'No, he's parked at the side so we're just going to walk there.'

'Come on, I'll walk you both to the car,' he says and gets on the other side of her. Together we walk towards the car in silence. Each of us lost in our own thoughts.

Victor is sitting in a group with the other chauffeurs eating a piece of roasted meat using his fingers. When he sees us he drops the meat onto a big plate full of bones, and wiping his hands on a napkin, rises from his seat. He walks towards the car and holds open the back door. Britney looks up at her brother.

'Bye,' she says unhappily.

'You'll be fine in the morning,' he says.

'See you around,' he says to me.

'Yeah,' I say awkwardly.

We get into the car and Victor pulls away. I look at Britney and she is lying back with her eyes closed. I assume she doesn't want to talk so I turn away and stare at the dark countryside.

'There's something wrong with me,' Britney says suddenly, her voice sounding very childlike.

I face her. In the light from the streetlamps her eyes look big and frightened.

'Is your head spinning?' I ask.

She nods.

'There's nothing wrong with you, Brit. You've just had too much to drink. When we get home, we'll get a big glass of water and two aspirins into you and I promise you, you'll wake up completely fine again.'

'It's not the alcohol,' she says softly. 'There's something missing in me.'

'What?'

'I'm not like other people. I don't feel like I'm whole. I feel empty all the time and nothing I do will fill it.'

I stare at her, speechless. What do I say to that?

'Have you ever lost something really important?' she asks me sadly.

'Uh ... no, not really.'

'That's what it feels like. As if I have lost something really important.'

'I ... I'm sorry.'

She lets out a thin wail that makes the hair at the back of my neck rise and I cover my mouth with my hand.

'Help me, Tori,' she whines.

For a second I stay frozen with my hand clasped over my mouth, and then something inside me gives, and all the petty resentment I have ever felt about her dissipates into nothing.

'Come here,' I say and hold open my hands. Like a small hurt child, she scrambles into my arms. I hold her thin body and rock it slowly, as if I am her mother.

'Shhh ... Shh ... Shh,' I croon again and again as she sobs her heart out.

With some shock I realize that I have misjudged her badly. I thought she was an appearance obsessed, shallow rich kid who spent all her days on selfish pursuits. But in fact she is suffering some deep pain and there is nothing I can say to her to make it better. Her suffering seems so profound.

I pull tissues out of the box at the back of the headrest and pass them to her. Her sobs finally subside just as we get into London. She straightens and moves away from me. When I look at her puffy, reddened face I don't feel as if there are only two years separating us. Suddenly she seems to be years younger than me. She blows her nose noisily and sniffs.

'We're nearly home,' I tell her.

She looks outside the window, nods tiredly, and falls into a morose silence. The car comes to a stop and I open the car door and get out. The air is cool. Victor opens Britney's door and, to my surprise, he scoops her up in his arms and proceeds to carry her to the door. I shut the car door and run ahead to put the key in the front door and throw it open for him. He takes her all the way up the stairs and to her bedroom. I follow behind anxiously. He lays her in her bed and turns to me.

'You can take over now?'

'Yes,' I say quickly.

'Right I'll be off. Goodnight.'

'Goodnight,' I say, and he goes out and closes the door.

I look at Britney and she has curled up into a ball on her bed. I walk over and sit beside her.

'Shall I help you get into bed?' I ask softly.

She makes a strangled noise but it is so low I have to get on my haunches to try and catch her words. 'Do you want me to get you a couple of aspirins?'

'No,' she chokes.

'I'll just go and get a glass of water, OK?'

She reaches out a hand and grasps a chunk of my bathrobe. 'Don't go,' she whispers.

'OK, I won't,' I say reassuringly.

She looks up at me, absurdly grateful for that small concession.

'Do you want to come on the bed?' Her voice small and pleading, her face is full of childlike trust. How on earth is this girl going to survive in the big wide world?

'All right.' I take off her shoes and put them on the floor. Then I pull the duvet over her and lie on top of it beside her.

'I'm here,' I say. She snuggles up to me. Her body is hot. For a while I lie on my back, frozen and stiff, staring at the ceiling and not knowing what to do next, but then it feels right to offer her comfort. So I turn towards her, and lying on my side, gently stroke her hair.

'Go to sleep, Britney,' I say softly.

Eventually her breathing becomes even and deep. Very gently I prise her claw like grip on my bathrobe and slowly edge out of her bed. I stand over her and experience shame and guilt.

Lord, what a judgmental bitch I've been.

I never gave the poor girl a chance. I took one look at her designer clothes and things and her obsession with her physical appearance, and just judged. It never even crossed my mind that it might be a symptom of a deeper suffering.

My attitude this entire time has been condescending, tolerating her with the kind of politeness that barely concealed my impatience, but all this time she has looked at me as if I'm someone she can trust and call a friend. Her complete innocence touches me and I suddenly feel strong sense of protectiveness. She becomes the little sister I never had and always wanted when I was a little girl.

Looking down at her softly breathing figure I vow to find a way to help her. There must be something I can do. I tell myself that before I leave this house I will get to the bottom of her pain.

Bending down I whisper in her ear, 'Sleep little Brit.'

She mumbles in her sleep.

Tiptoeing out, I close the door softly and go to my room. I enter my bathroom and switch on the light. In the harsh light I examine myself in the mirror and suddenly I feel quite detached from everything that has happened. As if it all happened to someone else. As if Cash eating me out and the time with Britney in the car didn't happen to me. I cover my eyes with my hands.

'Wow! What a night it's been.'

I think of myself pressed up against the wall, one leg thrown over Cash's shoulder while he ate me like a starving man and how the whole world had fallen away then. Even now thinking about it makes my sex throb. I look up at myself in the mirror again. At my pink cheeks, my wild eyes, and feel a shaft of fear. This is not at all going according to plan.

'Maybe it'll be all right,' I try to reassure myself. 'Maybe this is the way it is meant to be.'

Avoiding my eyes I remove my make-up, brush my teeth, and use the toilet. My hair has died into a rat's nest, so I brush the tangles out and braid it into one long plait down my back. Back in my room I slip on a pair of panties, pull a super-large T-shirt over my head, and sit on my bed. I open my drawer and take out Monstrosity and begin to write in it.

Dear Monstrosity,

Despite my best efforts, sadly, I have lost another battle. A big one. It is now one in the morning so I won't go into the disgraceful and humiliating details of my defeat at his hands right now, but in the interest of truthfulness, three painful observations must be made:

1. *It was an easy victory for the unscrupulous one, and ...*
2. *The enemy being mad, devoid of reason, and cruel will almost certainly rub my nose in it and mock me at every chance he gets.*
3. *I am too weak to resist the enemy and it is clear now that the war will be lost. It may even be tomorrow!*

On a brighter note, I think I found a friend in an unexpected place. I will tell you all about her tomorrow.

Goodnight, dear Monstrosity.

I lock my diary, put it back into my drawer, switch off my bedside lamp, and lie on the top of the duvet. The room is full of moonlight. It's a hot night and I'm glad for the cool breezes that blow in through the open windows. The night must have exhausted me far more than I realized, because I fall asleep very quickly.

Chapter Thirteen

Tori

I am jerked awake suddenly.

A hard body is pressing against me. Seized by an unthinking panic, my immediate reaction is to kick and scream as loud as I can. I only have time to open my mouth before a large hand clamps down over it. In the silvery glow of the moon my fearful eyes collide with Cash's beautiful ones. They seem bizarrely bright and as translucent as emeralds.

He places his index finger against his lips. 'Shhh ...' he says, and as he sees realization come into my eyes he takes his hand away from my mouth.

'You scared the shit out of me. What the hell are you doing here?' I whisper fiercely.

'Finishing what I started,' he replies coolly.

'So you just decided to jump me in my bed like some freaking prowler?'

'Sorry,' he says sounding not the least bit sorry. 'But my cock couldn't rest for thinking he missed out on all the action earlier.'

His shoulders are naked, the skin gleaming like burnished gold. My heart is still pounding like a drum, but the fear and panic have disappeared like a puff of hot breath on a cold night. As the exact nature of the situation hits my sleepy brain, my body tightens with excitement. Oh. My. God. *He came for me. He came for me.* Cash is in my bedroom. On my bed. I can hardly believe it. My most amazing most secret girlish fantasy has come true.

I gaze into his gorgeous eyes and all the logical, rational objections of why I shouldn't fall away. I know I'm just another girl who is willing to get fucked by him, and maybe I will regret it. Maybe I will get hurt, maybe he will break my heart or scar me forever. Or maybe ...

You know what?

Cancel all that bullshit internal dialogue.

I'm here. He's here. He wants me. I want him. Call it plan B. Call it whatever you want. Who cares? I've waited this long. So what if he's all the terrible things he is? Let me have my one night with him so I can put this endless longing and craving behind me, and carry on my merry way. I deserve this.

'What the hell is he waiting for then?'

With wide eyes I watch him lift himself away from my body. Completely naked and his dick as hard as a rock and already sheathed, he kneels astride my thighs like some kind of avenging angel. The strong muscles of his thighs look bunched and powerful, and the golden hairs shine silver in the moonlight. It sends a thrill through my body just to look at him.

With one hand he pulls my upper body off the bed, and with his other he yanks my T-shirt smoothly over my head.

'Your tits are fucking perfect,' he growls, feasting his eyes hungrily on them.

He grabs my wrists roughly and holds them above my head.

For a few seconds more he stares down at the picture I make, my body stretched out, and my hands held high above my head. Then he swoops down and takes a nipple in his mouth.

I draw in a harsh breath.

He licks it gently, and when I moan he flicks his tongue back and forth over the hard tip. I arch into his mouth and he soaks it with saliva. Oh Jesus. He has no idea how many years I have waited to feel that. My breathing becomes heavy and erratic and my body starts to burn with need as he continues sucking. I move my head from side to side. I want to moan. I want to groan. I need to make some kind of sound, but I clench my teeth to keep myself silent.

Watching me through half-hooded lids, he bites down on my nipple.

My eyes fly open and an involuntary shocked gasp is torn from my throat.

With his gaze fixed on me he continues sucking until the needle sharp pain mingles with pleasure and takes on a different hue. It begins to ache and throb for more. I know I can't stay silent for long.

I look at him with pleading eyes. 'I'm going to make a sound and someone will hear.' My voice is hoarse, unrecognizable.

'I've got it covered, Wildcat,' he says, and lifting his thighs away from my body he drags my panties down my legs. Balling them in his fist

he stuffs them into my mouth. I cannot imagine what I must look like, my hands held together at the wrist high above my head and my mouth filled with my own panties, but something primal and possessive glitters in his eyes as he looks down at me.

'Hold your position. I want to see your body submit' he orders, as he lets go of my wrists.

Like a wild animal he licks my stuffed mouth, my face, my neck, my nipples, my belly button until my body feels as if it is on fire. Finally, he opens my thighs and lets his finger brush along my heated crack.

'You're dripping, Wildcat,' he says, and swipes his tongue along the slick gash.

My hips writhe upward and my hands claw at the sheets while he expertly and mind-blowingly does what no one else has ever done to me: rolls my clit in his fingers. Then he places both his palms under the cheeks of my ass and lifts me up. He places his thumbs in the creases between my thighs and my body. Holding me as if I am half-a-coconut he worms his tongue into me.

The sensation is insane, but he follows it with something that supersedes everything else. He locks his hot wet mouth on my clit and sucks it real hard, making me throw my head back in pure ecstasy as my whole body begins to heave.

I wriggle and grind my sex into his face as he tightens his hold and inserts two fingers into me. I start purring like a frigging cat. The sucking just goes on and on while his fingers pump into me until my back arches, my teeth clench together, and my pussy gushes uncontrollably into his mouth. It fascinates and shocks me when I collapse back on the bed to realize that my hands are still obediently held over my head.

'It's time to feed pussy,' he growls, and before I can even form any kind of coherent thought, he lays his hands on either side of me and drives his hips forward, impaling me completely.

I scream at the speed with which he drives his long, incredibly thick cock into me. Once buried deep inside me he goes completely still. Our eyes catch. Mine are widened and shocked and his are excited and glazed.

'You're so fucking tight,' he snarls.

As my sex adjusts and tightens around the invading shaft, I revel in the sensation of being stuffed so full of Cash. It is like nothing I have known before. It is far, far better than any of my girlish dreams or even my most forbidden fantasies.

I am panting so harshly my body is heaving.

'Relax,' he orders, his big hands caressing and sending beautiful heat into my skin.

'Go on. Don't stop,' I say, but it comes out as muffled, meaningless sounds.

'Wrap your legs around me,' he commands.

I obey, my hips lifting off the mattress.

With his eyes locked on mine he tears into me so hard it makes me cry out. He withdraws and when he is about halfway out he slams back in. I groan. He finds a steady pace. Pounding me so powerfully, the flesh of my entire body jiggles. It feels as if the whole bed is jumping and bouncing. Mewls of pleasure are escaping my mouth as I thrust my clit onto his hardness. Incredibly my entire body starts tightening once again as if I am about to climax! I dig my heel into his ass and cry out his name as my body shakes and spasms with release.

'Go on, Wildcat. Cum all over my hard dick,' he snarls, his eyes fevered as he pushes faster and faster into me.

The sensations exploding inside are intense and uncontrollable as his pelvis slaps my clit relentlessly. I feel my eyes roll back and my senses slip away. Gasping with pleasure I cling to him with my legs as my world breaks apart. The contractions go on and on until I lose muscle co-ordination.

My body convulses and vaguely I sense that I am being held, arched, and open, even as he continues ramming into me. Even after my orgasm has subsided, he keeps my exhausted body in the same position so I can feel the full thrust of his hardness against me. Then it's his turn: he tips his head back and, with a low guttural roar, rams into me one last time and lets go.

My mind is still spinning from the intensity of my climax and my pussy is trembling when he lowers my hips to the bed. I do something I have never done. I moan in protest and claw at his hips to keep him locked onto my body so his cock doesn't slip out. Resting on his elbows he pulls the saliva soaked knickers from my mouth.

'I thought I was pretty impressive,' he murmurs into my ear.

OMG! Cash's cock is still inside me. 'Really? I've seen more action at basket-weaving classes.'

He laughs quietly. The sound low and washing over me like waves. 'Damn girl, you're hard to please. You came so hard it felt like someone detonated a bomb in your pussy.'

'I need a bath,' I say, and start rolling away from him.

He grasps my shoulder, rolls me onto my back, and smirks cheekily. 'Don't bother. I'm the type of dirty that doesn't wash off, Wildcat.'

I stare up into his eyes. 'I can't believe I had sex with you.'

'If it's any consolation you didn't stand a fucking chance. From the moment I saw you, I knew I wasn't stopping until you were mine.'

A warm thrill tingles through my spine and my heart thuds loudly against my ribs and I can't think of a single comeback, so I just roll my eyes and pretend like I don't care.

He springs off the bed, takes the condom off, and starts pulling his jeans on. I watch him with disbelief. That's it. He's leaving just like that. All kinds of crazy thoughts and scenarios run through my head at the speed of light.

In that instant I decide that yes, he's had my body, but I'll never let him see how crazy mad I am about him. He'll never know that his casual rejection hurts like the stab of a knife. He wants to go, fine, I'll just say, bye, and turn over as if he means as little to me as I do to him.

At least in this way I will leave his father's house with my pride intact. He will never know I stalked him for years or that my appearance in this house is not a random act of fate.

But as I make my plans he turns to me, holds his hand out, and says, 'Come on.'

Chapter Fourteen

Tori

https://www.youtube.com/watch?v=u9Dg-g7t2l4

I get up on my elbows. 'Where to?'

'Up to the roof.'

I cock my head to one side. 'Is this British humor at its best, or are you talking in code?'

He shakes his head in mock wonder. 'Unless my cock is inside you, you find it hard to simply obey instructions, don't you?'

'Watch it, lover boy. You're straying into dangerous territory there,' I warn.

'I like living dangerously,' he says, shrugging into his shirt and doing up a couple of buttons.

'Are you serious about going up to the roof?' I ask.

'Of course.'

'Why do you want us to go up there?'

'The better to push you off when you give me sass,' he says with a deep growl.

'Ha, fucking ha.'

'Have you never been up there?' he asks curiously.

'Of course, I haven't. I'm like other human beings. I tend to spend my time under roofs and not on them.'

'Come on,' he urges putting on his shoes. 'You'll like it. It's good up there. I'll show you my ultra, super-secret hiding spot when I was a boy.'

For a few seconds I look at him half-undecided, then I jump out of bed, and slip my T-shirt back over my head.

'I never thought I'd ever say this, but you need to wear some pants, girl.'

I grin at him. 'There's hope for you yet,' I say, and pull on a pair of jeans.

'Ready?' he asks.

I nod.

He opens the door and we pad noiselessly along the corridor to the narrow steps that lead up to the attic. The stairs creak and I freeze. Cash winks at me.

'Relax, you need to swing a bat into my father's head to wake him up.'

I giggle softly at the thought of mild mannered Mr. Hunter sleeping one floor below us.

In the attic there is a desk, a couple of cupboards and black bin bags of old toys that Britney hasn't the heart to part with. Quietly, Cash pushes the desk so it is under the sash window. He opens the window and, placing his hands on either side of the frame, hauls himself up and scrambles onto the roof. I climb on the desk and Cash offers his hand. I hesitate. The roof looks pretty steep from the ground and we are three floors up.

'Are you sure this is safe?'

'Don't worry we won't be having sex up here. At least not this time around.'

'Will you give it a rest for just a few minutes,' I grumble.

'It's you. You bring out the horny beast in me. Every time I see you all I want to do is fuck you senseless.'

'What if the tiles break?' I ask worriedly.

'It's perfectly safe. Watch,' he says and jumps about, making a horrible rattling noise.

'Whoa, are you crazy?' I whisper urgently.

'Good quality tiles can last at least a hundred years. These tiles are only fifteen years old.' He stomps his feet in a tight circle. 'See.'

'OK, OK,' I concede quickly. 'Just ... please ... don't do that anymore.'

Flushing all over with a strange excitement, I put my hand into his. I'm not sure whether it's because I could easily end up an unrecognizable splat on a London sidewalk, or because I'm with Cash finding out something about him which is not on ILoveCash.com.

Effortlessly, he hauls me up and suddenly I am on the roof and so close to his body I feel the heat coming off it. The night is colder than I thought.

'I gotcha,' he whispers, his breath hot and damp against my cheek.

I grip his hand nervously as he leads me a couple of steps up towards the chimney. The edges almost make for a seat and we sit side by side, our bodies touching. The tiles are rough and cold under my butt. From the corner of my

eyes I can see just how far away the ground is. From up here the pavement looks very hard.

I turn my head and he holds out a flat silver box with the cover open. Inside are hand-rolled cigarettes. 'It's good weed,' he says.

'I don't smoke.'

I watch him extract a joint and, cupping his hands around it, light it with a cigarette lighter. He draws deeply making the tip burn orangey red. Then he throws his head back and exhales the smoke. I watch the pleasure it gives him. He takes another draw and turns his head to look at me. Embarrassed to be caught watching him so intently, I let my eyes slide away to the night sky, full of stars and a nearly full moon.

'It's beautiful here,' I say softly.

'Yeah, I used to come up here all the time when I was a kid.'

I turn to look at him. He is staring at a far away dot in the horizon. He looks nothing like the playboy celebrity.

'Yeah?'

'Uh huh. My balls dropped early so I used to come here with my smokes and a dirty magazine to lie here, look up at the stars and dream of becoming rich and famous.'

'And now you're rich and famous.'

An odd expression crosses his face. 'Yeah. Now I'm rich and famous.'

'What's wrong?'

He shakes his head. 'The grass is always greener on the other side. Maybe it's not what I thought it was going to be.'

'What did you think it was going to be?'

'I thought it would be more satisfying.'

I nibble at my bottom lip. 'How can it not be satisfying? You are leading the life that most men would kill for.'

For a moment he is silent as he flicks ash from the end of his cigarette and takes another lungful of warm smoke. 'I'm not making the kind of music I want to make.'

I stare at him and he stares back. 'Tell me truthfully do you like my music, Tori?'

I shrug. 'I guess nobody can have everything.'

His face shutters. 'I guess not.'

I hold my hand out, my fingers pinched, and he slips his cigarette between my fingers. I take a drag. Wow! It's been a long time since I smoked this stuff. He's right. It's good. I exhale and close my eyes.

'What kind of music do you want to make?' I say, and inhale again. Already I feel less uptight. More relaxed. I think I really like this guy.

He takes his phone out of his pocket and scrolling through it finds the music he wants me to listen to.

'Lie back and close your eyes.' I return the joint to him and lie back. He puts his phone close to my ear.

'Who is this?' I ask.

'Disturbed singing The Sound of Silence.'

'OK,' I say. I close my eyes and this deep, deep, hauntingly beautiful voice pours like oil from a jar into my ear. Smooth. Smooth. It is so poignant I feel tears start to gather at the backs of my eyes. In my mind Cash is singing it. As the song progresses, the man's voice becomes richer and richer and the words resonate and ring in my ear. Under that patch of Cash's night sky, I became witness to someone else's darkness. Finally, the man's voice becomes rousing and powerful, a screaming crescendo like the kind of thing you would hear at a heavy metal concert.

When it is over I turn my head and look at Cash with new eyes. I thought I'd see the real him and he would not live up to my fantasy, but he is even greater than what I believed him to be.

'Why don't you make music like this then?' I ask softly.

'My record company doesn't want it.'

'Why?'

'The fans don't want it,' he says with a shrug of his broad shoulders.

'How do you know your fans don't want it?'

He sighs. 'Your fans never want something different from you. They just want more and more of the same. Every artist in the current climate, no matter how successful, has found that out. When they produce the kind of music that they think is special, their critics are quick to accuse them of indulging themselves and their fans simply don't buy their records.'

'But if you don't love what you are doing ...'

He flicks away the cigarette butt and laughs, a short bitter laugh. 'Well, Wildcat, we all have to do things we don't want to. I'm sure all those people working in chicken processing factories or collecting the refuse or finding things to recycle from rubbish dumps would rather they weren't doing those jobs, so I can't complain too much about singing teeny-bopper stuff.'

'They don't have a choice. They'd probably go hungry, or be homeless if they don't. You have enough money behind you to be brave.'

He stands up and looks down at me, an odd expression on his face. 'Brave? You want to see bravery?'

I feel fear clutch at my stomach. He has just smoked a joint. We're a crazy distance from the ground. He's going to do something stupid. We're both going to die. 'Don't be an idiot,' I say sternly.

Fixing his eyes on me, he lifts his hands out to shoulder level on either side of him and he starts walking backwards on the narrow ridge with a kind of elegant dance move.

'Stop it. This is stupid,' I shout, my voice full of panic.

'Why? You wanted me to be brave and this is what bravery means when you go against billion-dollar record companies,' he says as he carries on walking backwards.

'OK, I got it. OK. I got it. Now stop. Please. You're scaring me.'

'Look, handstand,' he says, and suddenly he is on the palms of his hands.

With my heart in my mouth I stand shakily. 'I'm going back in, you stupid freak. Go ahead and break your neck. As if I give a shit,' I cry, my voice trembling with emotion.

He rights himself and stares at me. For a few moments we are both standing on the roof staring at each other. Then he hunkers down on his haunches.

'Don't give me them eyes, baby.'

'Yeah, well,' I breathe, embarrassed by my own outburst. 'Can we just go back into the house now?'

'I'm sorry I scared you,' he says softly.

I wrap my arms around myself and nod. 'Apology accepted.'

'Remember when Prince was so furious with his record company he went around with the word slave written on his face. He was not kidding.'

I lower myself back down into a sitting position. 'But you could create something original. Something special,' I say earnestly.

He shakes his head. 'The record companies don't want creativity or something special from their artists. In fact, they do everything in their power to turn us into homogenized, processed 'stars'. Fucking puppets, that's what we are. They give us the tune, they give us the words, they even give us our dance steps. We sing their words and move to their commands and even before our sell-by date comes around the machine will have already picked and begun grooming our replacements.'

'That's exactly why you need to follow your heart. You should reach for the stars. I believe you can touch them because you have a truly unique talent.'

I lean back against the chimney and he walks up to me. 'Your concern is touching though,' he says softly. 'Thank you.'

I open my mouth to deny that I care, but I can't. Not when his eyes are so naked and sincere. For a few seconds neither of us moves. Then the mask drops back over his face and he is Cash Hunter the star, the celebrity, the irrepressible skirt-chasing bad boy again. He puts his finger under my chin and smiles cheekily.

'Ready for another round of basket weaving?' He smiles wickedly.

'No,' I whisper, but my eyes look at his lips hungrily.

'Fuck,' he says, dragging his thumb along my lower lip. 'You're driving me mad, Wildcat. I can't even think when you look at me like that. All I want to do is bury my cock inside you.' He drags his thumb along my lower lip.

I stare at the smoldering pits of green fire as they come closer and closer. Sparks fly between us. His mouth is warm and tastes of smoke. I thought I would hate it, but it is sexy. Everything about him is infuriatingly sexy. Our lips part reluctantly. I stare at him. The silky strands of shoulder-length brown hair dusted with gold lift in the breeze and fall about his strong neck. I reach out a hand and curl a silky lock around my finger.

'What shampoo do you use?' I whisper in a hypnotic daze.

He grins. 'Something called Ten Voss. Why? Is it turning you on?'

'Screw you, Hunter.'

'Excellent suggestion,' he growls and, putting his spread palm on the small of my back, pulls me close to his body. I know that I will never forget this moment for as long as I live. When I went up on the roof and shared something real with Cash Hunter.

He helps me down the roof and through the window.

I watch him close and secure it. Then we walk down the corridor, silent as mice. At my bedroom door I turn to face him. I see the look in his eyes.

'Cash ...'

'Uh ... huh?'

'What happened between us earlier was a kind of temporary insanity. I ... we really shouldn't do it anymore. It's ... er ... not right. I ... well ... work for your dad,' I stutter.

'You're right, we shouldn't do it again,' he murmurs as he reaches behind me, opens the door and pushes me in.

Chapter Fifteen

Tori

He kicks the door closed with his heel and our mouths crash together, our tongues twine, and our hands pull and rip each other's clothes off in a wild frenzy.

Then we are naked. His fingers are like fire on my skin. Everywhere he touches burns. I press my naked body into his hardness and rub myself restlessly against him. He propels me backwards until the backs of my legs hit the bed.

Locked in a kiss I vaguely hear the sound of a condom packet tearing. Our mouths make a sucking sound as he pulls away. He takes a pillow and throws it on the bed.

'There's no one to save you now,' he says thickly, and turns me over. My face lands in the pillow.

'Lift your ass higher and show me your pussy,' he orders.

I obey, spreading my legs wider to give him a better view.

'Look at that. Hot, wet and ready.'

Splaying my legs wide open, he gets between them and finger fucks me. A fiery stream of pleasure rushes through my veins as juice gushes out of me and soaks his hand and the bed. My orgasm is immediate and shockingly explosive. I bite the pillow to keep my scream muffled. Possessively, he grips my ass and keeps his thumb jammed inside my pussy while the waves of contractions race from my core to the tips of my fingers and toes. I hear his voice come from far away.

Gripping my butt cheeks he pushes into me. Thick, hot and incredibly hard. It seems to take forever to journey into me. Finally, he is in and I squeeze and milk his cock with my pussy. My muscles dance around his cock making shudders race through him and his dick pulse inside me.

'Goddamn you,' he says in a low lusty voice, and starts to ferociously pound my pussy.

'Oh yeeees,' I hiss

With the sinews of his shoulders straining and his neck and chest red, fucking me hard, he shoots hot cum into me.

'That was so amazing,' I pant, gazing up at him.

Pulling out of me, he crouches between my legs and, to my shock, I feel his hot, velvety tongue lapping at my wet folds, his tongue slicing through. His mouth suckling.

'Oh God! Again?' I squeak.

'I'm gonna make your sweet, achy pussy come so hard, you're won't be able to breathe,' he says, and spreads my slit with four fingers of his magic hands. Opening me right to my sphincter he gets engulfed in my heat, my scent, my flesh. Until I go rigid and climax again. When the aftershocks subside, he pulls up to me.

'Nice basket,' I whisper hoarsely.

He chuckles. 'I was working with a grade A, premium pussy. I could spend all day weaving.'

I turn my head to look at him. 'Do you realize that your thumb is still inside me?'

He grins. 'Yup. Pussies are where I'm at.'

'Would you mind terribly taking it out?' I ask in a mock English accent.

That makes him laugh. 'Only if I'm going to replace it with my cock.'

'Holy crap. What are you? A sex addict or something? Have you *not* had enough?'

'Are you kidding? I've barely started.'

'Oh, yeah?' I look down and his cock is already an exclamation mark.

I roll on to my side and crouch next to his body. 'Do you ever think of anything else but getting laid?' I ask, wrapping my hands around the base of his cock.

'Sometimes I think of making baskets,' he says with a devilish grin.

'I want to taste you,' I whisper.

'I'm not going to argue with that.'

Bending my head, I slowly lick the entire length of his shaft before enveloping the head with my mouth.

He groans. 'I love to see my cock disappear into your pretty face.'

I look up at him and slowly, very slowly, start swallowing his cock. Inch by inch I let it enter my throat.

'Oh fuck. That feels amazing,' he moans.

He holds my head with both hands and starts to fuck my mouth. Pre-cum drips down my throat and flows out from the sides of my mouth.

'I'm gonna cum,' he warns.

I grab his hips and suck ever harder. The muscles in his buttocks tense as he starts to lose control, and his rocking becomes faster and more frantic. With his hands gripping my head he fills my mouth with his seed. I look into his eyes and swallow. Then swallow again when he spurts more hot cream into me.

'Whoa. That was amazing,' he says, pulling me up to his mouth. We kiss. It is so gentle, my breath stops. The kiss ends and I realize I am now on my back, my hands clasped around his neck. I stare into his gorgeous, gorgeous eyes.

'What about Tori? Tell me about her,' he asks.

I don't want to talk about myself. I don't want to spoil the moment with lies. 'I'm actually tired. I think I should go to sleep.'

His expression becomes guarded. 'Sure, babe, but I'll be asking that question again.'

I watch him get ready. He comes to the bed and looks down at me. 'Can we keep this a secret?' I ask softly.

He touches my hair. 'I never met a girl who wanted to be my dirty secret,' he teases gently.

'I'd rather Britney didn't find out right now.'

His eyes narrow. 'Why?'

I nibble at my lower lip. 'I can't properly explain it so that it would make sense to you, but we have just found a kind of bond tonight and I think she will feel that I cannot be trusted with all her secrets if she knew we were having sex. Does that make any sense?'

He nods. 'Sure. My sister is a complicated girl, but how long are you planning on keeping it a secret?'

'Just until she feels safe. Maybe a few days.'

Chapter Sixteen

Tori

The alarm was set for eight o'clock. I wake up groggy and unrefreshed, and almost immediately smell Cash on my sheets. Wow! It was not a dream. For a few more minutes I hug my pillow and replay last night. Creeping around in the dark, sharing a joint on the roof, coming back to my bed. Heat fills my face as I think about how bold I was. How amazing it was. Could this really be my little life?

After a while, I drag myself out of bed and get into the shower. Dressing in my usual uniform of T-shirt and jeans, I go one floor up and knock on Britney's door.

'Go away,' a sleepy voice scolds.

I open the door and enter her room.

She sits up and, when she sees me, smiles at me. 'Sorry, I thought you were Jacinda. She's always trying to clean my room when I am trying to sleep.'

I walk up to the bed. 'It's only me. I wanted to make sure you were all right. How do you feel this morning?'

'Super,' she says a bit too brightly, and pats her bed. 'Sit down. I want to talk to you.'

I sit at the edge of her bed.

115

'You won't tell Dad about what happened last night, will you?'

'Of course not,' I say.

A look of relief passes over her face. 'Oh good. Thank you. After all, nothing bad, not really bad, happened so no need to worry him.'

'If you ever want to talk about anything, I'm here, OK?'

She looks down at the pattern of pink roses embroidered on her duvet, her expression undecided, before she looks up with a determined smile on her face. 'OK. Thank you.'

'Good. Want to have breakfast together?'

She beams. 'Yes, I definitely do.'

'Go on then.'

'Give me five minutes,' she says and leaps energetically out of bed. I walk to the window and stand looking out at the garden. It is not a beautiful garden. No one in this house cares for it. Someone comes to cut the grass and trim the hedges, and the tall wall of rhododendron bushes at the bottom of the garden flower and die unnoticed.

Britney is out in less time than it takes me to squeeze toothpaste onto a brush. We walk down the stairs together while she chatters on about one of her bitchy friends. To be honest I have to agree with her. I met the girl once and I didn't like her one bit.

The breakfast room is full of sunlight from the lantern roof. Cora has already laid out all the breakfast stuff. We drop our slices of bread into the toaster and while we are waiting for it to pop we fill our cups with coffee.

We sit opposite each other at the long table. I butter my toast and cover it liberally with blueberry jam while Britney thinly spreads her slice with butter and an even tinier amount of Marmite. I can smell it from where I am sitting. Ugh. How is that even food?

'Dad's taking me to lunch at Groucho Club. Do you want to come with?'

I hold my toast suspended in front of my mouth. 'Have you forgotten, Brit? I go back to my aunt's every second Saturday. I'll be back Sunday evening.'

'Oh,' she says, her little face crumpling. 'What time are you going?'

'Right after breakfast. My aunt is taking me to an antique fair.'

'Oh,' she says as if being dragged around an antique fair is something she has wanted to do all her life.

I smile. 'Britney Hunter? You hate antiques!'

She bites into her slice of toast. 'Yeah, I know, but I hate being here on my own more.'

'You don't have to be here on your own. Why don't you ask Natalie to come over?'

'Natalie is in France.'

'Right, how about Victoria?'

'Nah. Don't worry about me. I'll probably just paint all afternoon.'

I take a sip of coffee. 'How come you've never shown me your work?'

She worries her lower lip. 'I've never shown it to anyone.'

I stare at her. 'Why not?'

She shrugs. 'But I'll show you.' She pauses. 'If you have the time.'

'Of course I've got time,' I say immediately.

'Only if you want to.'

I look her in the eye. 'I want to, Brit.'

'OK,' she says and a simple, childlike joy fills her little face.

We finish our breakfast and go up the stairs. We pass the room that leads to the attic where Cash and I had been in last night, and go towards the last room. It bears a skull and cross bones sign on it. When I was first shown around the house this was the one room I had not gone inside. She stops in front of it and turns towards me.

'I feel really nervous.'

'If it helps I still draw stick figures.'

She giggles. 'OK. I trust you. You always tell the truth.'

I feel my ears becoming red. She turns and puts a key into the lock and turns the handle. It is quite a big airy room with a bare wooden floor. There is a mannequin parked at one corner, a tall easel in the middle of the room, and a massive, deep-red velvet armchair by the window. On the floor next to the chair are empty packets of crisps, discarded chocolate wrappings, and a couple of detective novels. Along the walls there are many canvasses lined up with their backs showing to the room.

'This is my secret room,' she says in a small voice.

I turn to look at her. 'I love it.'

She grins. 'So do I.'

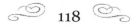

'Come on then. Show me your art.'

I follow her to the canvasses lined up against the wall and one by one she shows them to me. I say nothing. Just look at each one carefully. They are beautiful, but very strange, and leave me with a sense of unease. Most of them are images of unfinished humans or humans with holes cut out of their bodies and children curled up inside the empty spaces. Other figures are white and featureless standing against a dark background. They have a string, like an umbilical cord coming out of them.

'Well?' she asks, when I have looked at the last painting.

'I think they are strangely beautiful. I don't mean that they are chocolate box pretty, but they have a lot of passion and they are different.'

'Really?'

'Absolutely. I don't know much about art, but these are good. I've never seen anything like this before. They are completely original.'

'Thank you,' she whispers.

'Who are these figures? I ask pointing to the featureless people.

'Me,' she says simply.

I look at her curiously. 'What do you mean?'

'It's how I feel sometimes. Unfinished. The most important parts of me missing.'

'Oh, Brit,' I whisper softly, my heart breaking for her. Her art is the outward manifestation of her instinctive knowledge that something is missing or lost inside her.

She shakes her head. 'I don't want you to pity me.'

'Come here, you silly Billy.'

She takes a step towards me and I stroke her hair. Strange how much affection I have for her now that I have seen the real her.

'I don't pity you,' I tell her. 'You have everything. You're beautiful, you're talented, you have a family that loves you dearly, you've got friends, you've got a trust fund, even if you never work a single day in your life you will never starve or be homeless. Why on earth would I pity you?'

She stares at me as if she can't believe I mean what I say.

'In fact, I wish I had half of what you have,' I tell her honestly.

'No you don't.'

'Actually I do. Do you know that you are luckier than anyone else I know? Everything falls into your lap. Designer clothes and shoes, music classes, expensive holidays. You just have to open your mouth and ask for it and it's yours. It's not like that for me. I've had to take summer jobs to get the things I want. When I go back I'll have to take out a student loan just to complete my studies. A debt that I will spend a great deal of my working life paying back.'

She doesn't say anything, but I can see she is thinking about what I said.

'When I was young my dad told me a story and it kind of changed the way I thought about things. You want to hear it?'

'Yes, please,' she says quickly.

'It was about this set of twins. One of them was an eternal optimist. No matter how bad the situation he would find a reason to be happy, and the other was the eternal pessimist. He would do the opposite and find something to be sad about no matter how good the situation was.

'So one day their father decided to see if he could change their attitudes. On the boys' birthday he filled the pessimist's room with every imaginable toy. He practically bought his son a toy store. Then he filled the optimist's room with donkey dung. Just a big stinking pile of dung right in the middle of the poor kid's room. When the boys came home from school the father said, 'Boys your birthday presents are in your rooms.'

'The pessimist ran into his room and began to berate his father for buying so many toys. He complained and cried about how he would never have enough time to play with all of them. In the other room the optimist began skipping around the dung heap, laughing. 'Woo hoo,' he sang happily. 'There's a pony around. There's a pony around.'

Britney laughs. 'I'd like to be the pony boy in your story. He's cute.'

'You could be,' I tell her softly.

'Thanks for the story. It's a good one.'

'You're welcome.' I look at my watch. 'I have to go. My aunt will be waiting for me. Let's talk again when I get back on Sunday, OK?'

'OK,' she says slowly.

I start to walk to the door.

'Tori,' she calls. 'I'm sorry you have to take out a student loan just to finish your studies.'

I smile at her. 'It's OK. Most people have to, Brit. Just be grateful for everything you have.'

'My brother likes you, you know.'

'What? Why?' Whoa, that had come out like high pitched squeaks. I clear my throat. 'Er ... what makes you say that?'

'Everybody knows you only get pushed into the water by a girl who's jealous of you, or a guy who has the hots for you.'

'Oh.'

'Do you like my brother?'

'Um ... I never really thought about it.'

'Really? Most girls can't stop thinking about him.'

'Well, he must be very bored of it all then.' I look at my watch. 'I should get going.'

'Have a nice time with your aunt.'

'I will. You have a lovely lunch with your dad.'

'Bye.'

'Bye.'

Chapter Seventeen

Tori

I take the tube to Waterloo and get on the train to Virginia Water station. The train is almost empty and I sit in a carriage with one other person and stare out of the window unseeing. My mind churning with thoughts. Sometimes I catch my reflection smiling like some lovesick fool. I wonder what he must be doing. Probably still in bed. I think of his lips going down my stomach, kisses fluttering like butterflies.

When the train gets to Staines I call my aunt, and by the time I exit Virginia Water Station she is already waiting at the car park. I fling my knapsack into the boot of the car and get into the passenger seat.

'You all right?' she asks, smiling at me and turning the key in the ignition.

I smile back. 'Yeah. Did you have to wait long?'

'No, I just got here.'

'So where is this antiques fair then?'

'At the Runnymede Hotel. It's only ten minutes away. Hopefully we'll find something special for your mom's birthday.'

'I hope so too,' I say, and suddenly miss my mom. I take my mobile out and send her a message.

I love you, mom. <3x

Her reply is instantaneous.

Me too. Love you with all my heart, my darling. Call us tomorrow. We're at grandad's. Send your aunt my love. <3 <3 <3

'Mom sends her love. She's at grandad's,' I tell my aunt.

She smiles. 'I'll call her tomorrow.'

Her phone rings and she fits her ear piece and says, 'Hello.'

With a sigh I turn to look out of the window.

Virginia Water is a stockbroker belt and fittingly we are flanked on either side of the tree-lined road by massive mansions. My aunt often says that her family is the poorest in Virginia Water. My uncle bought his property for an unthinkable sum of £220,000 twenty years ago before it became the real estate heaven for the city boys. Now her home is worth more than £2.2 million. 'One day I'll sell my house and be a millionaire,' she always jokes.

Less than ten minutes after we hit the A30, we turn into Runnymede Hotel. I trail after my aunt from table to table looking at brick-a-brac that I would have cheerfully thrown out, but it is apparently still considered of value.

A chipped porcelain cup that a woman wanted £5.00 for, a dusty doll with a scratched face going for £20.00, yellowing tablecloths, a purple feather boa, but none of it puts my aunt off. She is determined that she will find a gem in that junk, and she is right. We, well she, finally finds a surprisingly pretty Victorian Cameo brooch pin with pearls that I know mom will love. My aunt bargains and gets £7.00 taken off the price. I hand over £30.00 and the vendor wraps it up and puts it into a bag for me.

Afterwards we have lunch at the hotel, then we head over to her house. My niece, Tabitha, who is eight years old comes running from the garden next door. She is wearing her swimsuit and her hair is in pigtails.

'Come for a swim, Aunt Tori,' she begs.

'I'm too tired. I didn't sleep well last night and now that I have had a big lunch I think I'll take a nap for a couple of hours, but look what I got you.'

'What?' she asks excitedly.

She runs off after I give her a packet of gummy bears. I throw myself on the couch and almost immediately fall asleep.

I wake up to the sound of my aunt's panicked voice calling me.

'There's a big black Lamborghini stopping outside the house.'

I blink sleepily.

'Heaven's above, a man who looks very much like Cash Hunter is coming out of it.'

I sit bolt upright. 'What?'

My aunt turns away from the window and looks at me, her eyes shining with inquisitiveness. 'Looks like he is coming up our driveway, Tori.'

I stare at my aunt with horrified eyes.

'Would you like to freshen up first, or are you OK with him seeing you with drool on your face?' she asks calmly.

With a yelp I jump up and dash up the stairs.

At the top of the stairs I hear my aunt say graciously, 'Do come in. She's upstairs. I'll give her a quick shout.'

She then pretends to call up the stairs. 'Tori, you have a visitor.'

I rush to the bathroom and my aunt is right. I look a right mess. With shaking fingers, I hurriedly repair my hair, splash some cold water on my face and slick on a lick of lip gloss and spray some perfume from a glass bottle. Too late I realize that it is air freshener. Shit. I try to wash it off my skin as best as I can before I go downstairs.

'Hello,' I greet, with a little awkward wave of my right hand. Cash looks like a living god in my aunt's sitting room.

He lets his eyes wander hotly down my body. Damn him. I feel my cheeks begin to flush and my heart rate soar.

My aunt smiles at me. 'I'm just about to make some tea. Would both of you like some?'

'That's really kind, Mrs. Carter, but I was hoping to take Tori out on a picnic.'

My aunt's eyebrows shoot up into her hairline. 'Oh. Yes, of course. What a splendid idea. Yes, yes, you must take advantage of this fine weather. That's if Tori is happy with the idea, of course.'

I feel both eyes turn towards me.

'What have you got in your picnic basket?' I ask.

He grins. 'I have no idea. I ordered the deluxe picnic basket from my local delicatessen.'

'That'll do,' I say with a grin.

'What time will you be bringing Tori back?'

I laser my aunt with an I'm not twelve look.

'Just kidding,' she says with a laugh.

Both Cash and I pretend to laugh with her.

'Right, we should be off,' Cash says.

'I'll call you later,' I tell my aunt.

'Please do,' she says with emphasis, as she walks us to the front door. She remains at the doorway and watches as we walk down the drive. There is at least half-a-foot between us.

I smile up at him. 'So how did you find me?'

'Do you remember answering a little question called next-of-kin on your employee form?'

I nod. 'I thought that information was personal and confidential.'

'I slipped into that category last night when I was eating you out. Now might be a good idea to wave at your aunt, Buttercream.'

'Don't call me that,' I say as I turn around to wave jauntily at my aunt.

My aunt waves back.

When I turn around Cash too is waving at my aunt.

He opens the car door and I slip into the black interior. Inside it is all sleek lines and so super masculine, I feel a bit like Naomi Watts when she was carried in King Kong's oversized, leathery palm.

'Fancy,' I say.

'It's always nice when a girl is impressed by your ... equipment,' he says with a predatory grin.

'Do you know I sometimes fantasize about slapping you?'

He laughs and guns the engine. The roar is incredibly Alpha. I get why these kinds of cars are standard issue for successful men the world over. It's a good ole my-roar-is-louder-than-yours chest beating competition.

Chapter Eighteen

Tori

'**W**here's your security?' I shout over the noise of the engine.

'Let's just say they're still somewhere on the M25 driving in a standard issue Range Rover SUV and hoping I get to where I'm going to in one piece so they don't have to look for a new employer tomorrow,' he says flashing me a wide grin.

'Why would you do something so selfish and juvenile?'

'You wouldn't understand, but sometimes I feel like I'm living in a bubble. I can't go anywhere like a normal person. When I am in the States I can't even fucking walk to my car, I have to run surrounded by beefcakes in suits. Today I wanted to just be any guy to take a girl on a date.'

'Where are we going?' I ask.

'Pennyhill Park,' he says.

'Very posh,' I say.

Minutes later we turn into an impressive set of black and gold gates. The grounds are beautiful with mature trees and hundreds of rabbits running around. The winding road takes us to a stupendous mansion house. Cash cuts the engine.

'Wow! This is amazing,' I exclaim.

'Isn't it just?' he says as he hits a button. The door slides upwards and I get out and look around me in awe.

'I thought we were having a picnic.'

'We are. In our hotel room.'

He holds out his car keys to a liveried valet and tells him about the picnic basket that needs to be brought in. Then he holds his arm out to me. With a small smile I take it. I feel as if I am in a dream. How is it possible that this is happening to me? A small voice jeers. 'Better enjoy it, Buttercream. It's all based on a pack of lies and it's going to come crashing down on your head very soon.'

'What?' Cash asks as we stand in the grand stone portico.

'I didn't say anything,' I say.

'Yes, you did. You said no.'

'Oh. I didn't mean to. Just overwhelmed by the beauty of this place, I guess,' I lie quickly.

As we walk into the grand reception with its massive stone fireplace, I have the first inkling of what life is like for celebrities. The wide smiles, the excessive politeness, the starry eyes, the cannot do too much for you attitude. We are shown to the Heywood Suite, which is lavishly furnished in opulent fabrics.

'This is the only suite with its own private terrace,' the bellboy tells us as he opens the door to the terrace. I step out and the view over the grounds takes my breath away. I stand outside admiring the lush greenery while Cash tips the bellboy and closes the door. He comes back out to stand behind me.

'Do you like it?'

I turn around to face him. He has taken off his leather jacket and the magnetism of the man hits me like a brick wall.

'What's not to like? It's unquestionably beautiful.'

'Apparently it is very popular with honeymooners and people celebrating special occasions like us,' he says.

'Is this a special occasion?'

'Is there any reason why it shouldn't be?' he asks softly, advancing on me. I know I keep saying it, but he really is very hunky. 'Unless you've got some deep dark secret you're hiding from me?' he finishes.

I feel the color draining from my face. 'Why would you say a thing like that?' I ask. My voice is high pitched and panicked.

'I don't know. You tell me,' he says quietly.

I take a nervous backward step. 'What do you mean?'

'Like a boyfriend maybe?'

The relief that pours into my body is indescribable. Oh, thank god. I'm not going to be horribly exposed miles away from anywhere, after all. Elated, I bat the air with my right hand as if I am swatting away a fly, or he has just expressed the most insane idea I've ever heard. 'Me? Boyfriend? I mean, Pffff.'

He looks at me curiously and I realize that it is possible my reaction might have been a bit over the top.

I take a deep breath. 'What I meant to convey is that it's not special because we're just foolin' around. Right?'

'Yeah, we're just foolin',' he says as he scoops me up and throws me over his shoulder like a sack of potatoes. He carries me off to the bedroom and throws me still squealing and protesting onto an enormous bed.

'Sex in the afternoon in a hotel room? It's a bit decadent even for you, isn't it?' I laugh.

He grabs my right foot, pulls my black sandal off, and throws it behind him. 'It's backbreaking work, but someone has to do it,' he says, grabbing my other foot.

I unbutton my jeans. 'Don't put your back out on my account,' I say as I wriggle out of them.

'My cock would never forgive me if I didn't step up to the job,' he replies, grabbing the hems of my jeans and tugging them clear off my legs before he chucks them somewhere behind him.

I grasp the edges of my top and, lifting slightly off the bed, I pull it over my head. 'You talk as if your cock has a mind of its own.'

'Rule number one. All cocks have a mind of their own. Any man tells you otherwise, he's a lying, son-of-bitch fuckboy,' he says, popping my bra open, and flinging it south.

I hook my fingers into the waistband of my panties. 'What's a fuckboy?'

'Fuckboy: typically, a man who refers to his conquests as his body count, expects sex after buying you a cheap meal, messages you, or worse turns up at your place during booty call hours—'

'Excuse me,' I interrupt, completely nude. 'Didn't you turn up in my bed during booty call hours?'

He kicks off his shoes, his eyes twinkling. 'That doesn't count. I dug my seduction trap well before twelve when official booty call hours begins.'

'I'm sure hell will freeze over before anyone mistakes you for a fuckboy,' I say sarcastically.

As a response he pulls his black T-shirt over his head and it's like a magic trick. Just like that he is a whole lot hotter. Molten hot. Suddenly I don't want to talk anymore and he's won the discussion. Shocking how just the sight of this man can have my whole body in an uproar like this. Until I met him, I can count on my hands the amount of times I've had sex. Now I can't get enough.

I feel lust spreading in my veins like an electric current. Arousal courses through my body. Between my legs I start leaking. I stare at the tattoos, the muscles, the utter deliciousness of Cash Hunter as he takes his belt off and yanks his jeans down his muscular thighs. His boxer shorts are terribly tented.

I crawl to the edge of the bed. Extending one hand out I hook one finger into his boxers. Holding his eyes, I slowly pull at the material. He comes with a wolfish growl. When he is close enough I sit on my haunches and drag the black and white striped material down his muscular thighs. When it reaches his knees it becomes slack and falls of its own accord to pool around his feet.

He is buck naked.

I cup his heavy sack, as soft as the finest kidskin with one hand. His testicles are two perfect ovals. With my other hand, I grasp the base of his erect cock. It is only inches away from my mouth and it looks monstrously big and angry. Green/blue veins dance over the pale sienna surface. He stares down at me with an intense, sensual look in those beautiful green eyes. I move my head forward and wrap my lips around the satiny soft skin.

He groans and shoves his hands into my hair and pulls me against him, forcing my jaw open, forcing me to take his thick cock head deeper.

'Oh god, yes,' he encourages.

I start sucking him wildly, furiously bobbing my head back and forth, taking more and more of his hardness in my mouth with each trip down his shaft. I nearly gag, but I keep going, determined to swallow all of him, until he suddenly pulls me off his cock. In an instant he grabs me and throws me shocked on the bed.

I watch him roll a rubber on to his tool with wide eyes.

The weight of his body settles on me, pushing apart my thighs. Immediately I spread my legs wide and push my hips up in an open invitation as I lock my legs around his hips.

'Yes,' he growls as the hot head of his cock finds my pussy and enters. I feel every inch of his cock as it slowly slides into my tight, slick opening. My muscles clench around the thick intrusion. He lowers his body on top of me. The sensation of his body hair rubbing against my breasts and stomach as he moves over me sets my skin on fire.

The deliciously male smell of him makes me feel light-headed as he jams deeper and deeper into me until he is balls deep. Slow thrusts, fast strokes, sliding deep, stopping shallow, he goes on and on, rocking my body until I feel my teeth sink viciously into his shoulder.

He slams hard into me. 'You gonna fucking come? Yeah?' he snarls.

I keep the death grip on his body as the glow inside me becomes a raging inferno. While my arched body jerks and convulses, his rhythm suddenly falters and he cranes his neck and cries, 'Tori.'

He rolls off my limp body and lays at my side, staring at the ceiling. Our breathing evens out slowly.

'I keep getting whiffs of the smell of apple,' he says lazily.

Shit. I shift slightly. 'Er ... I think I saw an apple tree outside the balcony.'

He turns his head and fixes me with his emerald eyes. 'It's coming from you, isn't it?'

'I may have accidentally sprayed some apple scented room freshener on my wrists, but I washed it off, so it can't really be me.'

He takes my wrist and smells the inside deeply. 'I think you've just ruined all apples for me.' He stares at me. 'I'm going to get a hard on every time I see one.'

I look at the bruise my bite has given him and swallow hard. What is it about this man? He just has to look at me and I'm gone. It's unfinished business swirling between us all over again. I think he might have been about to bend his head and kiss me, when I fart. A surprisingly loud one. I feel my eyes widen and see his do the same. We stare at each other for a few seconds. Did I have broccoli at lunch? Thank god, no.

Then my mouth opens and I ask, 'Was that you?'

His eyes widen even more. 'No. I thought that was you.'

I shake my head slowly, my face is rapidly becoming redder and redder and his eyes are becoming more and more sparkly.

'That is some cold-blooded shit to deny,' he says.

I shrug. 'So what you gonna do about it?'

'There's only one thing to do,' he says mock seriously.

'What?' I ask reluctantly.

'I'll have to identify it by smell,' he says, and lifts one corner of the duvet and smells the air coming out.

I take a quick surreptitious sniff too and there is no smell coming out. Everyone knows noisy farts don't smell. 'Well?' I ask.

'Inconclusive. I'm going to have to smell the source of the smell.'

'No, you're not,' I blurt out and start wriggling away. He catches me by my upper arms and half lies on me, trapping me completely.

'You have a choice. I smell your butt or I make you confess.'

I giggle. 'Make me confess.'

I thought judging by the smoldering look in his eyes he was going to kiss me or do something sexy to me. It never crosses my mind that his idea of making me confess is to tickle me. He is very good at it. He tickles me until I am curled up into a ball and laughing so hard my stomach hurts, and I am gasping for breath.

'It was me. It was me,' I gasp finally, unable to take another second more.

He stops tickling me and kisses the tip of one breast. 'See how much better life is when you tell the truth.'

I become cold inside. Oh God! If only he knew. Everything about me is a lie. I touch the hard plane of his cheekbone. 'I didn't mean to lie. I was just messing with you.'

He looks at me curiously. 'I know that.'

I smile. 'Just wanted you to know.'

He rubs his chin. 'Are we talking about the same thing here?'

'Yeah. Did you say you brought a picnic basket?'

He vaults off the bed and I watch his long tanned back and tight butt as he pads completely naked out of the room. I close my eyes. It's OK. It's OK. It's just a fling. He'll lose interest soon and no one will be the wiser.

I sit up.

Chapter Nineteen

Cash

https://www.youtube.com/watch?v=YXSpXO4N-tI
- Down in The DM,
The Art of The Hustle

By the time I come back with the basket she has pulled a large bath towel around her body and tucked one end between her breasts. It looks hot as fuck. I stand at the doorway and stare at her. Tendrils of gold hair fall in twists around her face and neck. The girl is too damn cute for my liking.

'What?' she asks, her mouth red and swollen from sucking my cock so long and hard. Just thinking about her lips wrapped around my dick makes me go hard again.

Fuck. This is going to be a problem.

I've never wanted a woman so completely, even after banging her this many times. I got rules, man. Normally by now my cock and I would already be finding a way out. Saying our goodbyes in the most diplomatic way possible, which we have discovered doesn't actually exist. Goodbye has the unfortunate tendency of making eminently rational girls turn in the blink of an eye into raving psychos. My experience: the sooner you make your exit the better it goes down.

I walk up to the bed, put the basket on it, walk around the side, then up to her. I start unbraiding her hair. Don't be nobody you ain't. That's my motto, but fuck me if this shit doesn't feel real. I fluff her mermaid hair out.

'That's better,' I say softly.

She stares at me with big eyes.

The mood in the room changes.

'Are you an angel?' I ask. Fuck, look at me being cheesy.

'No, but thank you for the awkwardness you have created,' she says, biting her bottom lip.

'Did you think about me last night after I left?' I ask.

'No,' the barefaced liar says.

'I did. I fantasized about what you would look like with your ankles by your ears'.

She flushes bright red.

'You've gone an interesting shade of red,' I mock.

She covers her heated cheeks with her palms. 'What do you expect? It's a graphic image.'

'What the hell? You've just sucked my dick and I've just fucked you senseless.'

She drops her eyes. 'It's different when it's done in the heat of the moment.'

I part the towel.

'Cash,' she protests, but not too hard.

'Open your legs. I wanna peek.'

Slowly her thighs open to reveal her blonde thatch and underneath, wet folds of pretty pink flesh. Ain't nothing sweeter than a fully swollen pussy after a good pounding. My cock twitches. In my world you get addicted to drink, drugs and pussies. Notice I said pussies. Always plural. Why settle for one when you can have them all? But she's blindsided me, big time. I can't keep away. One look at her pussy and I want to fuck her again and again and fucking again.

'Slide your finger in,' I tell her.

'Stop being such a pervert,' she says and closes her legs with a snap.

'Go on, be wild for me. Play with yourself.'

She opens her legs slowly. Thick honey is oozing out of her. She places her palm on the gold triangle of hair and slowly moves her finger around and around her slick clit. She is so aroused it is protruding like a little white pearl from its hood of flesh. Her sex is actually throbbing.

I reach out and push my finger into her opening.

She gasps.

I push it in and out of her.

Her breathing becomes faster and I shove two fingers into her and hers start circling her clit faster. I watch her laying there pleasuring herself and it is a glorious sight. I stick a third finger inside her, pump her hard until her whole body arches back.

At that point I can bear it no more and I push her back on the bed and plunge hard and deep into her. Her moan is a beautiful sound, and I feel the blood surging and pulsating in my veins as I ram my entire length into her. I don't stop until we both explode.

'Fuck, we didn't use any protection,' she says, startling me.

I frown. What the fuck was I thinking of? I can't believe I did that. I've never gone bareback with anybody.

'Are you on any kind of protection?' I ask urgently, lifting my sweat drenched body upwards.

'Yeah,' she says. 'I've got one of those five year things under my skin.'

I breathe a sigh of relief. Hell, I'm losing it with this girl.

Chapter Twenty

Tori

'Is this meant to be for two?' I ask pulling more and more packets of food out of the picnic basket. 'The delicatessen sure packed a lot of food.'

'You eat what you can and I'll finish the rest. After that session I need the sustenance,' Cash says, looking extremely smug.

Attached to the lid of the basket there are plates, cutlery and glasses. I take them down and put them on the bed. Cash goes and gets the champagne that has been sitting in ice and fills our glasses.

We clink glasses and drink.

'To the good life,' Cash says.

'To the good life,' I echo.

I open a transparent box of antipasto and nibble on a bit of cold meat while he takes a chunk out of a pork pie.

'Good stuff,' he says with relish.

'Yeah, very tasty,' I agree, swallowing a bit of potato salad.

He picks up a Muffeletta sandwich. It is made from the sturdy heel of a loaf of Italian bread and piled with cured meats, tangy olives and salad. 'Do you like Italian food?' he asks before stuffing his mouth with food.

'Love it,' I say.

'Same here,' he says. 'So where in the States are you from?'

'Georgia.'

'Oh yeah?' He wipes his hands on his napkin. 'I had a tour stop a few years back in Atlanta.'

I clear my throat and try to look at him with an interested expression. The truth is I never took into consideration how difficult lying to him would be. Not admitting that I was in Atlanta for his concert feels horribly, horribly wrong, but to admit it means everything will fall apart.

'How was it?'

'Yeah, it was good,' he says with a languorous look in his eyes.' I distinctively remember that Georgia girls were gorgeous.'

Shocking, but I never had an inkling as to what a jealous person I am. I feel like slapping him across his smug face. I take a sip of champagne and smile tightly. 'I'm glad you had fun.'

His eyes light up. 'Are you jealous?'

'Probably as jealous as you are of the guy I was with at that time,' I say coolly.

He tears off a bit of bread and dips it into the olive and fig tapenade. 'Now you're just being a cloud over my sunshine,' he grumbles.

I smile inwardly. 'Want some potato salad?'

'Yeah, pass it over,' he says and chews thoughtfully. 'So who was this guy then?'

'No one you know.'

'I know that. Were you in love with him or something?'

'Yeah, I was in love with him. Look can we not talk about him anymore?'

I pick up a packet of biscuits from the basket. 'What on earth is a garam marsala biscuit?'

'They have Indian spices in them,' he says.

I make a face. 'A biscuit with Indian spices?'

'Try it.' he suggests.

I open the packet and take a small bite of a biscuit. 'This is not bad,' I say.

'Let me have a taste,' he says, and catches my hand. I watch him bring my hand to his lips. He bites into the biscuit while staring in my eyes. 'Tell me more about Tori,' he says softly.

'There's not really that much to tell. I come from a family of four, my parents and my brother and me. My father analyses numbers and data on computer spreadsheets, but none of us have figured out exactly what he does. My mom is a housewife. She's funny and sweet and I miss her, and my brother is in college. I'll be joining him this fall.'

'What were you like as a child? I bet you had some mouth on you.'

'Actually no. I was a very quiet and insular child. My mother said I refused to speak to anybody unless they gave me sweets first, and even then I was a bitch about it'

He laughs.

'And you?' I ask.

146

'I was a messed up kid. I can't explain it, but thoughts came really fast into my head. So damn quick it was like a tap left open on full. Water continuously rushing down a sink hole. It was like being bombarded. I couldn't process them so I acted out.'

He shrugs and picks up one of the plastic dishes of prawn cocktail.

'ADHD wasn't an available condition then, so the doctors thought it might have been a mild form of autism. They wanted to put me on medication to calm me down, but my dad refused point blank. I was seven years old. He thought it was a passing phase.'

He takes a sip of champagne.

'It was hard for me, but it was hell for all those around me since I was constantly lashing out. I think my father might have been about to cave in when we were passing a music shop one day and there was a shiny red electric guitar in the window. I was seven years old but knew straight away that I wanted to play it. He took me in and the salesman let me put the strap over my head and hooked it up to the amp. It totally dwarfed me.'

He shakes his head with the memory.

'I couldn't believe it. The moment the first notes hit my brain the unceasing river of thoughts stopped. I wouldn't leave the shop without the guitar. It became my salvation. I didn't want to take classes. I played it just to stop thinking. I'd lock myself in my room and play for hours. As the years passed, my brain calmed down, or fucking rewired itself, who knows, but by the time I was eleven I guess I was a pretty normal kid.'

'Oh my god. That is amazing,' I say.

He nods. 'It was pretty amazing.'

'So how did you end up as the lead singer of Alkaline?'

'When I was fifteen I saw an advert in a newspaper. The ad was calling for young street smart, extrovert, ambitious boys who could also sing and dance. I applied and the rest is as they say history, but enough about me.' He raises an enquiring eyebrow. 'How does a girl from Georgia end up working as my sister's PA?'

I take a deep breath. I don't need to lie. The only thing I will omit to mention will be my reason for wanting to work with his sister.

'My best friend Leah and I had decided to take a year's break before we went to college. We wanted to backpack around Europe and Asia. It made sense for us to start our journey from England since my aunt was here. The plan was for me to come over first and spend a couple of weeks with my aunt and niece, but then my aunt told me about a PA job to a young girl that did not require any PA skills. It was more of a companion thing. It seemed like the perfect thing.'

I shrug and smile. 'So I applied. Your dad interviewed me, and to my shock he offered me the job while I was still at the interview. He said he picked me over hundreds of other applicants because I was exactly the kind of smart go-getter he was looking for to broaden his daughter's horizons. Apparently I was the only applicant from America and he was hoping some of my independence and bravery would rub off on his daughter. After listening to your guitar story I think he is expecting me to have the same effect on your sister that your guitar had on you, and he's going to be very disappointed.'

Cash smiles. 'How's the job working out?'

'Well, to start with your sister didn't endear herself to me. I thought she was waaaaaay too spoilt, selfish, and ridiculously obsessed with her appearance, but the job paid well. It was live-in which meant I didn't have to look for digs or worry about living expenses, and so I thought I'd stick it out.' I pause and take a deep breath. 'However, I've had a change of heart since then. Britney's grown on me.'

He smiles. 'Yeah, my sister is like a fucking creeper. Before you know it she has entwined herself around your heart.'

I frown. 'How come your dad let her have plastic surgery when she was fifteen?'

'She saved her pocket money and did her boobs secretly. She had arranged a fake ID and everything. One day dad is sitting in his office and gets a call from the hospital to come and pick up his daughter. She had already been operated on. My dad was livid.'

'Wow,' I say in wonder. 'My dad would have killed me.'

'Yup, and he let her do her nose, because she was so determined to do it she wouldn't come out of her room for weeks. He made her promise that if he did let her do her nose she would wait until she was eighteen before she thought about any other reconstructive surgeries. Once she gave her word he took her to the best doctor in London.'

'And now her eighteenth birthday is coming up and she's making enquiries about cat's eyes.'

'Exactly.'

'Can I ask you something about Britney?'

'Shoot.'

'Did something bad ever happen to her when she was young?'

He stares at me hard. 'No. Why?'

'You know she paints right?'

'Yeah, but she won't show anyone.'

'Well, she showed me.'

'What?' He looks at me astonished.

I nod. 'She did, and here's the weird thing. She draws unfinished people and people with holes in them or strings coming out of their belly buttons, and she says that she always feels as though some important part of her is missing or lost. Can you think why she would feel that way?'

Cash stares at me.

'What?' I ask.

'Shit,' he breathes.

'What is it?' I ask again.

'It can't be. It's too incredible,' he says almost to himself.

'Tell me what it is?' I demand impatiently.

'My mum died shortly after she gave birth to Britney and it was a very traumatic time for all of us, so my father made the decision not to tell Britney that she had a twin who died that day.'

I gasp in shock, my hands rushing to cover my mouth. 'Oh, my god. I know that twins are supposed to have an invisible bond, but is it really possible that at some level she is missing her twin?'

He shrugs. 'It sounds totally out there, but there really is no other explanation for the paintings you describe. Britney has had the best of everything my father could provide.'

'Will you tell her?' I whisper.

'I'll tell my dad. He'll know what to do.'

Suddenly tears fill my eyes when I think of Britney. How misunderstood she was. 'Poor Britney,' I whisper.

'Hey, why are you crying?' he asks, shocked.

'Damn onions,' I sniff.

'What onions?' he asks, as he scrambles over to my side of the bed, making some of the food tip onto the duvet.

'You're destroying the bed,' I mumble, embarrassed that I cried in front of him.

He pushes me onto my back. 'Your tough guy attitude is just an act, isn't it? Inside you're as soft as a marshmallow.'

'No, I'm not,' I deny.

'Don't,' he says softly. 'You're beautiful when you cry for someone else.'

Chapter Twenty-one

Tori

After I put the food away we go for a walk in the lovely grounds with their flowering bushes and tall majestic trees. There are rabbits everywhere and I put the salad and cut carrots that I found in the picnic basket on the ground, and watch delighted as the tame creatures come up to us and eat them right in front of us. They are so cute that I make a video of them on my phone to show my niece.

When every last bit of food is gone and nose twitchers have scampered away, I suddenly spot a strawberry plant with a single, bright red strawberry nestled in the bushes.

'Look at that,' I cry. 'It looks like a jewel.'

'I'm going to get it for you,' Cash says.

'No, just leave it. You don't know what's hiding in the bushes,' I warn.

'I'm bigger than whatever's hiding in there,' he says, as he walks towards the plant. He stands in the middle of the bushes next to the strawberry plant and takes a bow.

'And now to win the coveted prize for my lady,' he says, and bending down plucks the strawberry with great flourish.

I shake my head and laugh. He brings it back to me and places it on my lips.

'Your eyes are such an unusual green,' I say, looking into the swirling green depths.

He shrugs carelessly. 'When I was a baby they were like yours, bright blue. Then one day when I was about five they became green.'

Looking into those green depths, I open my mouth and take a bite.

'Oh yeah, babyyyyy,' he says in a deep sexy voice, as my tongue comes out to lick at the juice squirting down my lips.

Then his face changes, he blinks.

'What?'

'Oh fuck,' he curses, and sitting on the grass starts ripping his shoes off and tossing them away. Then he stands up and starts unbuttoning and unzipping his jeans before yanking them urgently down his legs. He kicks the pants off and I see them.

Ants. Angry red ants. All over his legs.

Cursing, he begins slapping at them and frantically brushing them off his legs and I feel laughter bubbling up inside me. I can't help it. I laugh so much I have to drop to the ground and hold my stomach. He collapses beside me.

'I risk life and limb to get you a strawberry and you laugh at me,' he says with mock petulance.

'Excuse me, Mr. Act First Think Later, but I did warn you. Remember? I'm bigger than whatever's hiding in the bushes? Though you were right about that bit.'

'Funny girl. You can at least kiss me better,' he says.

'Let's go back and get some ice on it,' I suggest.

He laughs. 'It doesn't hurt that much. I was just trying it on.'

I punch his shoulder.

'Awww,' he screams.

I shake my head. 'You're such a drama queen.'

'And you're sour as balls.'

I look at him. 'I'm sorry you got bitten by ants,' I say, and spoil it by giggling.

He raises his eyebrows. 'Doesn't look like it.'

'I tell you what. Let's get your mind off your ... er ... injuries.'

'I know exactly what'll get my mind off the damn bites,' he cuts in.

'No, not that,' I say quickly. 'I'll ask you a question and you answer me, but really fast without thinking about it.'

'How is that going to help?'

'It'll be fun. Then you can turn around and ask me whatever you like, OK?'

He rubs his hands. 'Cool.'

'Right. First question. Name your favorite actor.'

'Matthew McCononaughey.'

'Favorite actress?

'Angelina Jolie.'

I nod. 'Name the actress that you fancy the most.'

'She's like god knows how old now, but Cameron Diaz.'

'For real?'

'Oh yeah, for real. And can I have one more?'

I grin. 'Go on.'

He grins. 'Jennifer Lawrence. Now she ...'

'A celebrity you *wouldn't* want to do?' I interrupt quickly.

'Kim Kardashian.'

I look at him curiously. 'Why?'

'Have you seen her sex tape? Man that's one lazy woman.'

I laugh. 'Seriously?'

'Seriously, someone showed it to me.'

'Right, favorite color?'

'Lucky blue.'

'Favorite food?'

'Macaroni and cheese.'

'Favorite musical artist?'

'Aww, babe. That's like asking me to choose between my ribs. They're all necessary.'

I smile. 'Give me a few.'

'Led Zeppelin, Prince, Chuck Berry, Pink Floyd, Bob Dylan, Tupac, Michael Jackson, The Beatles, Oasis, Coldplay, Green Day, The Killers, Maroon Five. The list goes on.'

'Are you secretly gay?'

His eyes widen. 'Come here, you little ...'

I giggle. 'Favorite word?'

'Sex.'

I shake my head. 'Do you have to be so predictable?'

He opens his palms out. 'What'd you want from me? I'm a man.'

'Biggest regret in life?'

'Pass.'

'Biggest mistake in life?'

'Pass.'

We stare in each other's eyes and I realize he has a huge regret that he doesn't want to talk about.

'Favorite TV show?' I ask.

'Fresh Prince of Bel Air. Is it my turn yet?'

I grin at him. 'Yes, it's your turn.'

'Your smile is killing me.'

I feel myself blush at the intensity in his eyes. 'That's not a question. You're supposed to be asking questions.'

'Can I have your number?'

'No.'

He laughs. 'Favorite movie?'

'How To Lose A Guy In Ten Days.'

He nods sagely. 'Ah ... Now it all makes sense.'

'You're supposed to fire the questions really quickly,' I remind.

'Favorite animal?'

'Hummingbird.'

His eyebrows rise. 'Favorite color?'

'Green.'

'Favorite person?'

'My mom.'

'Favorite singer?'

'You.'

He freezes. 'I thought you didn't like my songs,' he says slowly.

'I love your voice, I just don't dig your music,' I reply quietly.

He stares at me. 'I'm done playing. Let's go back to our room.'

My heart flutters as he takes my hand. Then we are running back to our room. We arrive breathless, laughing.

I love this man. God, I love him so much.

I was so tired after we had sex I nodded off. One moment I'm lying in Cash's arms and the next I'm gone. When I wake up again it is dark and I am alone in the bed. I remember we went into the vast bathroom and bathed in the stunning glass roll top bath. Our bodies slipped and slid over each other.

How I had giggled.

I wrap myself up in the bedsheet and go outside. I find Cash on the terrace. He is sitting on the floor wearing his jeans. The picnic basket is open and there is food all around him.

He turns his head to look at me, his lips greasy, a chicken drumstick grasped between his fingers.

'You sick freak! Eating chicken after dark like a caveman,' I say softly.

'Want to see what else I do after dark like a caveman?' he asks.

I smile. 'What time is it?'

'Nearly nine. Are you hungry? There's still loads of food here, or they have an award winning restaurant downstairs. We could eat something.'

'Nah, I really should get back.'

'You sure you don't want to stay the night?' He sounds disappointed.

'Yeah.'

He stands and comes towards me. 'Why not?'

'I don't think my aunt would like it. It's setting a bad example for my niece. Kids nowadays are so sharp. They pick everything up. Besides, it's a big thing for Tabitha and me to make pancakes for breakfast on Sunday morning. It's like a tradition ... ' I trail off because he is watching me, his perfect teeth gleaming in the dark.

'I know why my father chose you now,' he says, smiling big.

Chapter Twenty-two

Cash

'**A**re you two coming in?' Tori's aunt asks after yanking open the door so suddenly that Tori almost falls into the house.

Automatically I reach out and grab Tori's arm while she finds her footing again.

'Oh, I'm sorry, dear. Were you leaning against the door?' her clueless aunt asks.

I try to keep a straight face as Tori mumbles something indistinct and her aunt turns towards me. 'Would you like to come in for a drink?'

'Actually, I've got to hit the road.'

'It'll only take a minute.'

I look at Tori and she shrugs with an expression that says, your funeral.

I turn on the charm. 'All right, but I do have to leave soon.'

I step through the hallway, and what do you know, there are about ten people in the living room. All of them are staring at me and smiling. Aww fuck. I glance at Tori and she grins. For the next ten minutes I sign autographs. Even before the ink on the last one is dry, I stand, say my goodbyes, and turn towards Tori.

'Maybe Tori can see me out.'

'Of course,' she says, her voice sweeter than sugar.

We go out of the front door and I turn to her.

'Thanks for the warning,' I tell her.

'I'm sure you'd do the same for me,' she says.

'Damn right,' I say and grab her by the forearms.

'Don't you dare,' she warns.

I bend my head and kiss her on the lips. I make it long and passionate. Behind the windows there are many open mouths. Many questions that need answers. Poor Tori.

'You're going straight to hell, you know?' she spits.

'Been headed that way for some time now,' I say, tipping my head at her. 'Sleep well, Wildcat,' I say with a wink.

She slams the door before I get to my car. It just makes me smile wider. I have a quick glance around the area. No paparazzi hiding in the bushes or among the dustbins. All is well today.

From the car I call my dad and tell him I've got to talk to him. He asks me to go over so I drive to his house. After Britney goes to bed we go to his study to share a cognac. Then I tell him what Tori had told me about Britney's art. To my astonishment my father breaks down in tears. I never realized that even after all these years my mother's death still hurts him so much.

'I can talk to Brit about it,' I offer.

 160

'No. No. That's my job, son. That's my job,' he says sadly.

By the time I leave it is nearly one in the morning. On my way to the car Gavin calls. There is a party. Do I want to go?

I want to fuck, Tori. 'Nah, man. I'm bushed. Have fun.'

'What, you kidding me? Francine is here,' he says.

I think about Francine. Long dark hair, fantastic tits, sucks cock like a top notch pro and likes it up the ass.

'Enjoy her,' I say and end the call.

My cock is not hard for Francine. It's straining in my jeans for Tori. She's the only fuck I want. The only party I want to go to. For a second I stop in wonder. I don't sound like myself at all. Not one little bit.

I get into my car and roar through the streets of London. In my mind Tori is on her knees. She opens her goddamn beautiful mouth and asks, 'Do you mind if I give you a blowjob? I'm dying for a taste of your cock.' I see her eyes open wide and staring up at mine. Her mouth and tongue hungry for me. I knock her hand off my dick and take control. Thrusting into her wicked sexy mouth.

Making her take it all in. Fucking her, and fucking her, and fucking her until I explode inside her. Then I hold her face to my cock and let her drain me. Every last wild, dumb drop of cum.

'Now make me yours,' she says and opens her legs to show me her sweet pink pussy. Fucking gorgeous.

Fuck, it's like I lick my lips and taste her pussy.

I get to my apartment, close the door, and go straight to my sound-proofed room. I close the door and start playing my music. The rest of the world dissolves. It is like I have taken a really good hit. I'm good and chilled. I stop thinking of the sweet, wild taste of Tori Diamond.

I plug in my guitar. It's been a long time since I played it. In here the music I make is real. It won't be the crap I'm forced to sing for the rest of the world. In here I won't let the music down.

Chapter Twenty-three

Tori

By the time I return to the Hunter's residence on Sunday evening, Britney has already been told about her twin brother. She comes to my room and I see straight away that there is something different about her. A new inner-confidence.

Now she knows that there is nothing wrong with her. She truly did suffer a loss, and even though she was not told about it, her body knew and suffered. All these years she was mourning for her twin and did not know. Now that she understands it perhaps she can start to heal. For a second she stands there looking at me, then she rushes into the room and throws her thin arms around my neck. I hug her back tightly. It's a funny ole life. I never dreamed I would come to love Britney like this, and yet I have. I realize now that even if I leave England tonight, never to come back, at least I have done some good to her.

'Thank you,' she says simply and pulls away from me.

I shake my head. 'I did nothing.'

'Dad's right. You're special,' she says.

I flush with pleasure. I like Britney's dad. He's a nice man. He reminds me of an absent-minded, kindly professor. 'You know when I told you that twin story. I hadn't heard about your twin then.'

'I know that. Anyway that's a cute story. It taught me something,' she says with a happy smile.

'Good. How do you feel now?' I ask.

'I feel as if I finally figured out a 10,000-piece jigsaw puzzle that I've been working on for seventeen years. I don't feel happy or victorious, but I do feel vindicated. I don't ever have to think that I am weird, or there's something wrong with me anymore. I'm just like everybody else, only I lost my other half.'

'Yeah?' I say, smiling at her.

'Yeah, and you know what else, I feel stronger and more sure about the future.'

'Oh, Britney. I'm so happy for you.'

She lowers her voice. 'I guess while I'm here we might as well discuss the surprise birthday party that Dad is throwing for me this Saturday.'

'Huh? You know about that?'

'Duh! Of course. Dad's got a mark on his calendar saying, 'Britney's surprise birthday party.''

I laugh. That is exactly the kind of thing I would have expected from Britney's dad.

'Don't you think you should tell me about it so I can make some of the important decisions, and it doesn't turn out to be a complete disaster?'

I laugh. 'No flies on you,' I say.

It is nearly midnight and I'm already in bed when Cash texts me.

Meet me?

As soon as I see the message my heart starts pounding.

Where r u?

His answer is instantaneous.

Around the corner.

My hands are shaking with excitement as I type.

C u soon.

I don't know where he was when he texted me, but I have only enough time to leap out of

bed and get dressed before the door opens and he is standing there, scruff on his face and some kind of dangerous in his eyes. Bad ass sexy, he is.

'Hey,' I whisper.

He doesn't speak, just walks up to me and molds his body to mine. 'God, I missed your body,' he whispers hoarsely. Our eyes lock, his eat me up. He bends his head and inhales the smell of my hair.

Thank God I washed it this evening.

'Come on,' he says. 'I'm taking you to a party.'

'What?' I blurt out. 'I'm not dressed for a party.'

'We'll dress at my place,' he says.

'What do you mean?'

He lays his fingers on my lips. 'Shhh ... just trust me.'

Suddenly, the night seems to hold the most exciting adventure.

'OK,' I whisper, and we tip-toe out of his father's house.

Outside the front door, he stops to light a cigarette and puts it between his lips.

'No security again?' I say.

'Nope, but they'll be around later.' He lights up, inhales deeply and we walk down the street to where his car is parked. He flicks away the cigarette and we get in.

It is a strange feeling driving through the mostly empty streets of London, the top down, the wind in my hair. I turn to look at Cash and I cannot help the sensation that my heart will break with all the love I feel for him. He turns towards me and smiles crookedly.

His apartment is in Park Lane, on the top floor of an old building. We take the lift and Cash puts his key in the door. His apartment is like his house. All glass and modern. The living room is a vast empty area. The walls are lined with couches. Perfect for a party. There is a large modern painting on one wall.

'Where's the party?' I ask.

'In easily the most unique club in London. It's called The Box.' He adds, 'No mobile phones or cameras allowed so everything that happens in The Box stays in The Box.'

He opens a door to a room where there is a bed with a whole load of shoe boxes on it, and a clothes rail on wheels.

'Go on. Find something there to wear. The dress code is glam/posh.'

'How did you know my size?'

'You left your dress behind at my house. I gave it to my PA, Alison. What you see there is her best effort.'

I stare at him. He went to a lot of trouble 'Thank you,' I murmur.

'I'll be next door getting my gear on.'

He shuts the door and I rifle through the clothes. O la la! Each one is quite simply to-die-for stunning. I have never owned anything so expensive or so fine in all my life. It's really hard to choose, but eventually I settle for a gorgeous black and gold dress.

The label says Orchidees Noires and it is very Great Gatsbyish. The bodice is made entirely of burnished gold flowers, with shimmering gold thread holding the flowers together. It is sleeveless with a deep neckline. There are no flowers at the waist, then they start again on the short billowing tulle skirt. At hip level the flowers stop and the rest of the skirt is pure black tulle.

I take off my jeans and notice that my legs are full of tiny gold hair. Hmmm ... I stand in front of the mirror undecided. It'll be a bit embarrassing to get a shaver off Cash, but what the hell? I'm not going to spoil such a magnificent dress with unshaven legs.

Chapter Twenty-four

Tori

I leave the room I am in and go past the living room to the next bedroom. The door is open and I walk in. The room is empty, but it must be Cash's bedroom because there are clothes laid out on the bed. I go towards the en-suite bathroom and stand at the doorway.

Cash has had his shower, his hair is wet and he is standing in front of the mirror with only a smallish towel around his hips. His face is full of shaving cream and there is only one strip that he has carved through the cream.

He freezes and we stare at each other in the mirror. It could have been really awkward me asking to borrow his shaver, so I smile and say, 'Let me do that for you.'

I walk up to him and slide between him and the basin. There is a small smile tugging at his mouth. 'I wasn't planning on donating blood tonight,' he says.

I take the razor from his unresisting hand. Very slowly I drag the razor down his cheek through the white foam.

His eyes never leave me.

'Sometimes it's a good idea to let someone else do the work,' I whisper, as I dip the razor head in the sink filled with warm water and shake it to dislodge the cream and bits of hair. I run the razor down his face carefully, meticulously until every last hair is gone. Then I whip the towel from his hips, an act which makes his eyes widen, and use it to gently dab at his face.

'See,' I say softly, looking at his erect glory. 'I was never after blood.'

His eyes are infused with lust. I feel wetness pool between my legs. He curls his large hands around my butt and lifts me up to the rim of the sink. He rips my panties off my body and opens my legs. Holding onto the thick knots of strong muscles in his shoulders, I bring my spread knees up almost to my shoulders.

He looks down between my legs, his eyes hot and hungry, and draws his fingers along my crack, already slick with juice.

I whimper.

He inserts a long finger into me.

'Oh,' I cry.

Laughing softly, he grabs my hips and thrusts so far into me my eyes widen and my mouth opens to a shocked O.

With his eyes blazing into mine he fucks me hard. The meaty sound of our flesh slapping, the sink creaking, and our grunts hit the marble tiles and echo around us. He pounds me relentlessly until I feel as if an enormous engine is being switched on inside me and its blades are starting to turn. Faster and faster they go until I am practically vibrating with the intensity of the coming climax.

'I'm coming,' I cry as the machine starts throwing out sparks. Trembling, twisting and jerking, I fall into the same fantastic void he plunges into.

Against my ear, he laughs, a lovely deep rumble. 'That was the best shave I ever had.'

He pulls out and his seed trickles out of me. He leans forward and bites my lower lip.

I lean back and look into his eyes. They are heavy-lidded and dark with sensuality, and I feel suddenly sad. This should be my man. I already know that I'll never get over him.

'What's wrong?' he asks.

I shake my head. 'Nothing,' I whisper. Twisting my body around, I pick up the razor from the ledge where I left it. 'I was actually after this,' I say.

'Nicely done,' he says.

His laughter warm and rich, follows me until I close the door of my room. Without wasting any time, I go directly into the en-suite bathroom. Sitting on the edge of the bathtub I shave my legs. Then I go back into the bedroom and get into the beautiful gold and black dress. It fits like a dream.

I stand in front of the mirror and gape at myself. Wow! Incredible. I almost cannot believe what I look like. Who'd believe that I could look like a movie star on a red carpet?

I run to the shoe boxes and open them all. I could have gone with a gold pair or even with the inferno booties that I have seen in a magazine, but I fall in love with a fabulous pair carrying a label I have never heard of. Sophia Webster.

They have heels made out of shiny poppy-colored balls, and are the closest shoes can get to a true confection. They wouldn't have looked out of place in one of those old fashioned sweet shops. I secure the gold strap around my ankles and feel like a million dollars.

Quickly I open the other boxes. I find new cosmetics in one and in another I find hair accessories. I apply some smokey make-up to my eyes, a touch of blusher to the apples of my cheeks, and a slick of nude lip gloss. Then I put my hair up with some of the gold pins I find in the accessories box. I pull out a few loose tendrils to frame my face and neck. Then I walk over to the mirror and look at my reflection. The woman in the mirror doesn't even look like me.

I take out my mobile and snap a couple of photos of myself to show Mom and Leah. There is a small black purse amongst the accessories. I drop the lip gloss, my credit card and my mobile into it and snap it shut. Picking up the black wrap that goes with the dress, I leave the room.

Cash is already in the living room. He's wearing a cream dinner jacket with shawl lapels, a white dress shirt, a black silk bowtie, and slim cut black trousers. Everything is perfectly cut and gives him a rakish, devil-may-care appearance. At the sound of my arrival he turns, the bottle of beer on its way to his mouth stays suspended in the air. He doesn't smile. Just stares at me as if even he can't believe his eyes.

I feel myself start to flush.

He puts the beer bottle down on a counter and walks towards me. 'Christ,' he whispers.

I can see myself reflected in his eyes, an odd shaped pixie. I touch my hair self-consciously. 'Am I overdressed or something?'

He smiles. A strange smile. 'You're not overdressed. You, Tori Diamond, are heartbreakingly beautiful.'

Time stands still. The world stops spinning. I even stop breathing. *Cash Hunter thinks I'm heartbreakingly beautiful.* Then I reach out a hand and pretend to straighten his already straight bowtie.

He holds out his elbow. 'Shall we?'

I slip my hand through it.

'I can't get over your transformation, Wildcat,' he murmurs, his eyes raking me from head to foot.

A stretch Mercedes with blacked out windows is waiting for us outside. As soon as we appear at the doorway, Cash's security men — four enormous military types with sharp cold eyes — nod at him and snap into action. They rush towards the Mercedes and hold open the passenger doors. Cash settles me into the car, then goes around to the other side. As he slides in beside me, two black SUVs screech to a stop in front and at the back of the Mercedes.

I watch the burly men quickly pile into the two SUVs. They give the all clear signal and the Mercedes starts moving. We travel sandwiched between the two SUVs.

It is not a long journey to Brewer Street, right in the heart of Soho.

Chapter Twenty-five

Tori

https://www.youtube.com/watch?v=6oIt
HLz5WEA

If not for the long queue of people waiting to go in and the remarkably large bouncers gathered outside the wooden doors, I would never have imagined that those bland doors are the entrance to London's ultimate in naughty burlesque and fantasy cabaret. A place that is supposed to give one of the strangest nightclub experiences in all of London's night life.

Even before the Mercedes comes to a halt, Cash's security detail jump out of their vehicles and head quickly towards our car. All eyes immediately turn curiously in our direction with the knowledge that a celebrity is about to emerge from it.

Both Cash's door and mine get opened at the same time. I take a deep breath and slide out nervously. So many eyes are on me. Then Cash steps out on the other side and instantly there are shouts, whistles and wild screams. People start calling out his name. Cameras start flashing.

Surrounded by his menacing team of guards, Cash looks to me, smiles and thank God, takes my hand in his. Then we are quickly escorted towards the entrance doors.

Suddenly a bunch of girls leave the queue and rush forward squealing Cash's name and stretching out their hands to touch him. I immediately feel intimidated by the surge, but Cash seems to take it all in his stride. He lets go of my hand and stops. He even shakes some hands. A girl begs for his autograph and suddenly thrusts her arm to him. Immediately Cash's security team form a wall to block her.

'Hey, it's cool,' Cash says, and taking a pen from one of the security team proceeds to sign her arm.

'I love you,' she screams as the red ropes are lifted and we are ushered quickly into what looks like a large theatre with two stages and meters upon meters of luxurious red velvet, exquisite gold embellishment and candles everywhere.

Oiled-up naked beauties hang from the ceilings and dance on top of bathtubs. I know, weird, but wonderful. A woman named Ashleigh, one of the hostesses, comes to show us to a cordoned off private party area. There is red banquette seating and it is already crowded with people. The only people I recognize are Octavia and Gavin and two other members of Alkaline. Octavia smiles tightly at me, and Gavin gives me a slow smile.

Cash starts introducing me to them. There are too many for me to remember, but the thing I notice straight away is how quickly the other women eye me up and down, then immediately set out to completely ignore me. As we mingle I even find myself being deliberately elbowed out of the way. Disgusted, I let go of Cash's hand and almost instantly other people push me out of the way, like water closing on something. I turn away to go back to the table and a pair of strong arms catches me by the forearms.

'Hey,' Cash says, turning me around. 'Where do you think you're going?'

'Look. I know everybody wants to talk to you. I don't blame them, you're the star. I'll just go back to the table and wait for you there.'

He frowns. 'Fuck off, you will. You're with me. If I wanted to spend the night with them I would have come on my own.'

'Cash,' someone calls.

'See,' I say softly.

'No, I don't see,' he says, and putting his arm around my waist turns to the person who called him. Now that it is clear I am to be part of the conversation and cannot be pushed away, some of the group reluctantly include me in their discussion.

I understand that my voice is not welcome so I don't say much. I just listen to what everyone else has to say and I try very hard not to watch Cash avidly or not to be distracted by his thumb slowly rubbing the small of my back.

Thank God for the shows! I watch them with something akin to astonishment. No wonder they have a ban on phones and cameras. Nobody back home would believe the 'cabaret' shows at The Box.

Two naked pre-op transvestites suck up the contents of a bottle of champagne into their butts and then spray it on the audience. No, you didn't get that wrong. I did say butt and not mouth. Cash laughs at my shocked expression and tells me that is what it means to transcend the concept of indecency! There are also strip shows and a rather impressive fire eating stunt.

Eventually food is ordered. Everyone has burgers and fries since it seems to be the only thing on the menu. After the show, the DJ plays plenty of dance hits and the dance floor fills up. When Cash excuses himself to go to the toilet, Robbie, one of the other band members who is very drunk, turns to me and says, 'Hey, Yoko.' There is something nasty in his voice. That gets the attention of the whole table.

'What did you call me?' I ask.

'Are you planning to be a Yoko?' he says again, this time louder.

I feel my face start to burn. What the hell is a Yoko? All eyes at the table are on me. Some of them are openly sneering.

'Leave her alone, Robbie,' Gavin says.

'No, let her answer,' Octavia says, her jaw tight.

I sit forward, anger storming at my gut, but I keep my voice even. No way in hell am I going to let this bunch of spoilt, entitled, green-eyed, immature shits get to me. 'I'd answer if I knew what you were talking about.'

'You know Yoko Ono. John Lennon's big mistake. The bitch split the Beatles up.'

With the exception of Gavin everyone at that table is hostile to me. The women are bubbling with jealousy and the men feel threatened that I will lure their precious superstar away from them. Cash and I have hardly started our relationship, it is at the just sex stage, and yet all these people see me as some kind of jezebel.

'I have absolutely no intention of breaking the group up,' I say clearly.

'Let's hope so,' a man in a suit says sarcastically.

Octavia says nothing. Just looks at me with hatred glowing in her eyes. The intensity of her animosity shocks me and I turn blindly to the only person who seems to offer any kind of support.

Gavin winks at me as if to say I did OK, and I mouth thank you.

Everybody is deliberately watching me and trying to make me feel unwanted and unwelcome, so I casually pick up a cold fry from my plate and slip it daintily into my mouth, as if I don't feel the waves of loathing coming at me. I chew it slowly, it tastes and feels like a wad of cold newspapers in my mouth. Then, without warning, everyone starts talking and laughing normally, I stare at them thinking I must be going mad when I feel a warm hand on my shoulder. Ah, they saw him arriving. I look up at him with relief.

'Want to dance?' he asks.

I can't even speak. I just nod and get to my feet. He leads me to one of the little raised platforms all around the club that are being used as mini dance floors. Faded is playing when Cash takes me into his arms. He doesn't dance like anyone else. He just holds me close to his body, his hands enveloping me, and moves slowly so the only thing between us is the music swirling around us. He looks into my eyes and smiles so long and slow and I think my heart will stop. All the while I can feel his erection press into my stomach.

'That's what you do,' he whispers.

'What?' I whisper back.

He puts his forehead to mine. 'You make me fade away.'

My brain refuses to believe. Impossible. 'Not the adored, famous, sex god, Cash Hunter?' I croak.

His lips are an inch away from mine. 'Do you always have to be this annoying?' he asks.

'I call out bullshit as I smell it,' I say.

He chuckles. 'You're right. The truth is you make me so fucking hard I can't even think straight anymore,' he says and takes my lips.

My heart pounds and I actually feel as if I am drowning in Cash Hunter. When he takes his mouth away I stare up at him, dazed, my legs like jelly, and my head spinning.

'Excuse me, can we have an autograph please?' a voice says and I jump.

Startled out of my world, I swing my head towards two young women not much older than me, their faces animated and filled with excitement. They are staring at Cash as if they can't believe their eyes. I turn my head back to him and unlike how he had been outside, there is now an expression of extreme irritation on his face. He closes his eyes, takes a deep breath, and turns to them. 'Not right now,' he says tightly.

They look so utterly crushed I feel sorry for them. I see myself in them. Once that was me. I would have killed for an autograph. OK, maybe not killed, but I could have not eaten for days, or something equally difficult. I turn back towards Cash and smile. 'Go ahead. I don't mind.'

An expression crosses his face. He looks suddenly tired and older. He lets go of me and as he turns towards them, the public face of Cash Hunter drops into place and he flashes one of his superstar smiles.

One of them hands him a paper napkin and the other a piece of paper with the club's logo at the top. The girls gaze at him adoringly while he signs. They clutch their prizes to their chests and thank him profusely.

He turns to me. 'Are you ready to hit the road?'

I nod.

He takes my hand and we start towards the entrance.

'Don't you have to tell your friends first?' I ask curiously.

'Nah, they'll figure it out soon enough.'

Chapter Twenty-six

Cash

'**I**f you don't take that dress off right now I'm gonna rip it off you,' I tell her, as I close the front door behind me and lean against it.

She turns around, her eyes flashing—she doesn't like being ordered about. Nevertheless, she reaches behind for the zip. I watch her slip the little black pieces of material covered in gold flowers down her arms. She is not wearing a bra and her nipples are already hard, ready little stones. Carefully, she steps out of the dress. I watch her hang the dress over a chair. There is something insolent about the way she deliberately takes her own sweet time, even though I know she is wild for it and sopping wet.

It makes me want to punish her.

To fuck her until her pussy is raw.

'Go into my bedroom and sit on the bed. With your legs wide open.'

For a second she stares at me defiantly then she turns around and obeys. I tug at my bowtie and watch her sexy ass as she walks naked, but for those sexy heels, towards my bedroom.

I start unbuttoning my shirt. 'And don't fucking take those shoes off,' I call.

She doesn't reply.

Fuck the girl is begging to be punished.

I give her a few seconds more before I turn up at the door, sans jacket, shoes and shirt. She is sitting propped up against the pillows and as instructed her legs are wide open. Her pussy is puffy, the glistening folds protruding invitingly out of her sex lips. And that small tight hole. It gapes and begs to be filled, and my cock throbs to enter it.

I smile slowly as I yank the last of my clothes off and advance.

Her eyes are riveted on my cock and her chest rises and falls fast. When I am close enough, the heady scent of her arousal fills my nostrils and that unfamiliar and beautiful thing happens again. The rest of the world ceases to matter. I lose control.

Like a hungry man, I swoop down on that deliciously sticky sex of hers. I stick my tongue into her hole and she gasps my name. Watching her face, I keep my tongue pushed deep inside her until I feel her heartbeat inside her pussy. Fast. Excited. Amazing. Then I suck her clit like a man sucking the flavor out of a piece of toffee until she comes with a force that shakes her to her very core.

I lift my head and watch her.

Spread out on my pillow. Her angel hair tangled, her mouth parted, her eyes glazed, and her ripe breasts flushed. I let my eyes travel down to her sex, open, helpless, and throbbing for me ... and I feel that wild and feral urge to brand her.

To call her mine.

To fucking make her mine.

Putting my hands on either side of her body, I mount her. She whimpers and her hands grip my upper-arms tightly as the thick, mushroomed head of my cock stretches her.

'Oh Cash,' she trembles as I force my way in until her pussy has swallowed my entire cock. Her whole body jerks while I pound her ferociously. It is not long before I explode inside her, my seed spilling everywhere, coating her insides.

I pull out of her and walk to the cupboard. I open it and rummage around inside a drawer. I lay my hands on a red dildo. I bring it back to the bed. She is still lying there, her legs open and my cum trickling out of her.

Tori

I stare up at him silently.

He holds a fire-engine red dildo out to me. 'Put it inside you and make yourself come,' he says.

'I'm tired. I don't want to come anymore.'

'Do it for me,' he cajoles softly. 'I want to watch.'

I hold out my hand and he puts it into mine. It is made of rubber and it's cold. I have never had a dildo inside me before. 'Put it in for me,' I say.

He shakes his head. 'I want to see you pleasure yourself.'

'Please,' I beg.

He takes the dildo and hunkers down between my legs. The head is quite thick and he places it at my entrance and pushes it into me while he avidly watches the red thing enter me.

'Play with yourself while I fuck you with this,' he says.

I circle my clit while he thrusts the thick instrument into me. As I climb higher his speed increases until I finally climax so hard I am sobbing his name. He sits there watching me. I reach for the dildo to pull it out.'

'Don't take the toy out,' he commands.

I let go of the toy and allow my hand hang limp over the side of the mattress. Unable to bear his eyes on me anymore, and with the toy still lodged inside my sated pussy, I turn over on my side. He circles one ankle with his hand and lifts my legs so they make a wide V. I see him watch my pussy with the bright red toy sticking out of it.

'Beautiful,' he says softly.

He reaches for the toy, pulls it out of me with a sucking sound, and puts it between my lips.

I draw in a sharp breath and at first I refuse to open my mouth. I stare at him defiantly. Then slowly I open my mouth and the toy slides between my lips.

'Suck it,' he orders.

I obey him.

He smiles slowly. Then he bends down and sucks my pussy. Laps up all the juices.

I enjoy the sensation of his gentle licking. When he lifts his head I sigh.

'That was nice,' I whisper.

'This will be better than nice,' he says, and thrusts his cock into me again. He pounds me until he comes, his hands possessively gripping my hips and with a triumphant roar. He lays beside me, the scent of sex all around us.

'Cash?'

'Mmmm ...'

'Why didn't you want to give an autograph to those two girls in the club? It seemed a bit mean. It was so little to ask and it was obvious how important it was to them. It would have been something they would have treasured for a long time, maybe even for the rest of their lives. Years from now they will be talking about the time they met Cash Hunter.'

For a few seconds Cash doesn't say anything and I think he is not going to answer me, then he sighs. 'The fans think they own you. They have the right to walk up to you anywhere they see you and get their little piece of you. For the most part I can put on my 'play nice' face and sign their CDs or little scraps of paper or body parts, but sometimes, like tonight, when they want to intrude even in my smallest moments of privacy and beauty, I lose it.'

He turns his head to look at me.

'Fucking hell, Tori, some of them are so crazily hooked they simply can't get enough of you. They're so mad they actually come up to me and tell me their rooms are shrines to me! Can you believe that? They own every Cash Hunter record, mug, spoon, pillowcase, doll. Because they watched every video and documentary and read every magazine article on me, they think they know who I am. How I think. How I feel. They think that they know the real Cash Hunter. The fuck they do!'

He gets up on his elbow.

'Cash Hunter is a fantasy. Created in part by myself, but mostly by the record company's PR machine, and enhanced by a mercenary media's ravenous hunger for celebrity scandal. The irony is even I don't know who the fuck Cash Hunter is anymore, babe.'

He lays his palm on my belly and strokes it absently.

'The worst ones are the ones that stalk you and try to pass their number to you through any means possible. They'll bombard the record company with messages of love and whatever else. They'll come to gigs and they'll lie, cheat and do anything to get backstage. Those are the ones who want to get with me. Like being fucked by me is going to change their lives in some meaningful way. There are some who promise never to wash again. I mean can you believe that shit!'

He shakes his head and I feel the coldness seep into my heart. I see me from his point of view. The crazy mad fan he is describing was once me. My room was a shrine to him. I read and watched everything about him and convinced myself that I was in love with him.

'Isn't it wonderful that your fans love you so much?' I whisper.

'No, it's not wonderful to be mobbed, or have your clothes torn off your body, or have girls befriend your sister just to get to you. It was definitely not wonderful when one of them climbed the gate, broke a window and ended up inside my house. She told the police she didn't mean any harm. She was in love with me and was only looking for memorabilia.'

'Well, I really should be going back,' I say, and my voice shakes. My heart feels hurt. What will he think when I tell him about me? About the real me? The me that was crazy about him? The me that travelled across half the world to close the door on my crush? Will I too become that person he holds in so much contempt?

'Are you OK?' he asks with a frown.

I force a smile. 'Sure. Just don't want to accidentally fall asleep here.'

'When do you plan to tell my sister? I don't like this sneaking about?'

'Soon,' I promise.

But first I have to tell you about the real me and then you might not want to be in a relationship with me anymore.

Chapter Twenty-seven

Tori

Since Britney's birthday party is no longer to be a surprise, she decides to hold it a week later. Right after Alkaline's concert in Milan, in fact. The concert is on a Friday and the party will be that Saturday night at the Hunter residence. The plan is for everybody to fly back for it.

The days leading up to the concert are a busy time for Cash. He is at the recording studio a lot working on their new album. He works from mid-morning to late at night or even the early hours of the morning, so he sends a car around to take me to his apartment to make sure that I am already there by the time he comes in.

Even though he would have been working all day and sometimes looks dead on his feet, he will still be full of pent up energy. Most nights he falls on me like a starving animal. After that he is always hungry.

'Feel like some Chinese food?' he asks that day.

'It's already one o'clock. I'm going to get fat eating so late every night,' I grumble.

'No way. You eat barely enough to exist.'

'I eat a lot during the day, thank you. It's all right for you. You're practicing dance moves all day long and burning up energy performing at concerts, but eating at this time of the morning is bad news for someone whose idea of exercise is dipping a couple of chicken nuggets into barbeque sauce.'

He grins and hands me the leaflet menu from Green Jade Royal Cuisine. In the front it bears the caption in red letters.

'Eat more! The heavier you are the harder it will be to kidnap you.'

'Thanks for the suggestion Green Jade Royal Cuisine, but I have absolutely no intention of foiling my kidnappers by letting myself get fat.'

Cash laughs. 'Fine. You can watch me eat.'

He calls them on his mobile and puts through an order that would feed a football team. After he ends the call, he drops his mobile on the table, and walks over to me. 'The food will be thirty minutes. Want to have a shower with me?'

'Midnight feasts and showers. All dangerously tempting offers, but I think I'll pass.'

He cocks his head. 'Strange how that came out as a question. It was meant to be an order.'

I giggle. 'I don't know what kind of girls you have been hanging out with, but all this macho caveman shit doesn't work with me.'

'No?' he asks as if giving serious consideration to my statement.

'No,' I say firmly.

He nods, bends down, and scoops me up still laughing and protesting.

Yes, we have a shower, a very interesting one. One that actually gives me an appetite. Flushed red and wrapped up in one of Cash's big toweling robes, I sit in the living room next to him with all the food spread out on the low coffee table.

I watch his large, wonderfully masculine hands peel a pancake, spread a thin layer of plum sauce on it and load it up with shredded duck meat. Then he lays julienned cucumber and spring onion on top of the meat, rolls it up, and takes a healthy bite.

'So what did you do at work today?' I ask.

'You seriously want to know?'

I pick up a prawn cracker. 'Uh huh.'

'We were laying down vocals for the new tracks.'

I bite into the cracker and let it melt on my tongue. 'How's it sounding?'

'They have to mix it further of course, and the finished product will sound totally different, but so far, it's not bad.'

'Good,' I say and casually pick up a crab claw and dip it into a container of sweet chili sauce. 'So ... was Octavia there?'

He starts building another pancake. 'She popped in for a bit, yeah.'

I drag the claw in the dip. 'She didn't stay?'

He stops chewing. 'Octavia in the studio? No. She just books the studio times for us.'

'Doesn't she stay to make sure that everything works and stuff?'

'Octavia has many talents, but she's no sound engineer or music producer.'

'But she is a good manager, isn't she?'

He picks up a pair of chopsticks. 'She's a formidable PR agent. She can make the public think black is white and white is you.'

I let my finger trace the edge of the table. 'Cash, have you ever, I mean, have you ...um.'

He uses his chopsticks to pick up a piece of chicken. 'What? Spit it out.'

'You know, have you ever, well, slept with Octavia?'

He gives me a narrowed look. 'Fuck, Tori. What do you think I am? The woman's my manager.'

'It's just the way she talks to you. Like she owns you, or has some kind of hold on you.'

He looks at me incredulously. 'So you think I fucked her?'

'I'm just asking.'

'Well, the answer to your original question is a big, fat never. She's the last person you have to worry or be jealous about. She has nothing I want.'

I nod, relieved but trying not to show it. 'I'm not jealous or anything like that,' I deny primly.

He grins suddenly. 'You're not jealous? You're totally jealous.'

'I'm not.'

'So why all the questions then?' he challenges.

I shrug. 'I just wanted to know where I fit into the scheme of things.'

He puts his chopsticks down, moves back on the seat, then curls his hand around my wrists and tugs me so I fall into his lap. Slightly breathless I look up at his face. 'Where you fit in? You fit in because I kind of like fucking my sister's little PA.'

I slide my hand underneath his shirt and lightly scratch the skin of his bare chest. 'Kind of?'

'Erase that. I fucking cannot get enough of my sister's little PA.'

I giggle. 'Yeah?'

'Yeah, she's got me all knotted up and twisted around her little finger.'

'Right. I'll just file that under Fiction, shall I?'

His eyes are suddenly serious. 'Why? Does it not seem like that to you?'

I stare into his eyes. 'You want to know what it really seems like to me. The real truth?'

He nods slowly.

'You have so many choices. You'll play with me for a while then you'll drop me. If I think it's just sex then I'll be OK when that day comes. If I think it is anything else I'll be hurt.'

He strokes my hair. 'I don't know what the future holds, Tori, but I know this. I never felt this way about any girl before you. I can't even bear it when you talk to other men. I feel like ripping their fucking heads off.'

I feel a rush of pure joy fill my heart. My lips widen and I can't stop grinning like an idiot. 'Really?'

'God's honest truth.'

At that moment I really want to confess about my childhood crush, why I got the PA job to his sister, basically everything, but he takes a prawn and puts it in my mouth. 'No more talking. I have other things planned for that mouth of yours.'

Chapter Twenty-eight

Tori

Sometimes Cash looks at me with something more than lust in his eyes, but some part of me holds back and I never reveal that I'm in love with him. I can never get past what he said about those crazy mad fans that build shrines to him. I know I should tell him, but every time I try to I just can't bring myself to do it, and the longer I leave it the harder it is becoming to tell him the truth. I promise myself that I will tell him. Soon. Very soon.

On the Saturday night before Britney's party, I meet Cash at the front door in a racy black crop top that leaves my midriff bare, a leather skirt, and black patent leather boots.

His eyes widen. 'Well, well,' he drawls.

But I shake my head and, taking him by the hand, sit him down at the dining table where I have laid out my surprise.

'What the—'

'Shhh,' I say and set about fixing a dark brown wig on his head. Then I glue on a fake, but surprisingly real looking nose on his face. Using a square of sponge, I apply a slightly darker foundation than his complexion onto his whole face and carefully blend it into his hair, then put some on his neck too. The rest is easy. I stick on a moustache and small beard and voila he is pretty unrecognizable.

I lean back to admire my efforts.

'Where are we going?' he asks, his eyes alive with excitement.

'The Ministry Of Sound,' I say with a grin. I've been wanting to go there ever since I arrived in this country.

We sneak out the back of the building and hail a passing black cab. There is a long queue of people that snakes around the building and we join it. Cash looks impatient. I realize he never has to queue to go anywhere. No matter where he goes, he is ushered in immediately and taken to the roped off VIP sections.

I don't think he enjoys the experience of waiting in line. Welcome to the real world. Even worse, when we get to the entrance I drop my bag and while I am on the ground picking up my lipstick the bouncers tell Cash that he cannot come in. They don't consider him hip enough to enter their club! But when I straighten they tell me I can go in.

I tell them I am with Cash, and after a brief hesitation they let us both in. I cannot stop laughing at the expression on Cash's face. He looks shell shocked. He has NEVER been refused entry anywhere. Inside it is the same, no one rushes to serve him, hangs on his every word, or pesters him for autographs. I think he might have secretly hated it at first being so thoroughly ignored, but after a while he really gets into his anonymity.

He can behave any way he wants without worrying about it getting into the news, and the way he behaves is to almost have sex with me on the dance floor. We drink, we dance, we laugh, we talk and simply enjoy being with each other. Just like any other normal couple in a club.

When we get tired we sit on the massive speakers with a group of other revelers. We sit with our shoulders touching and our legs dangling as we talk to the others. They are ordinary people, really nice and without airs. The talk is light and easy.

They offer us pills they claim are 'fantastic' but both of us refuse. We are on a natural high that is difficult to beat with chemicals. They seem pretty out of it, but they are friendly. They tell us they are from Italy and that they are working in one of the restaurants in Chelsea. One of the girls actually tells Cash that he should shave off his beard because he looks a bit like Cash Hunter.

'You know what? I think she could be right,' I say peering intently into Cash's face.

'No,' Cash says modestly.

'Si,' she says. 'You must shave. You will be, how do you say, *un bell'uomo.*'

'A handsome man,' her boyfriend, the chef, supplies.

'Do you like Cash Hunter?' I ask her.

'Siiiiii,' she says. 'I love him.' She shakes her head in admiration. 'He is too beautiful.'

Her boyfriend catches my eyes and twirls his index finger at the side of his head. 'She is mad,' he says.

'Why is she mad? I like him too,' Rosella, the waitress, admits defiantly.

Her boyfriend shakes his head in exasperation.

I look at Cash. 'Me too. I'm crazy for him too.'

'Are you trying to make me jealous?' Cash asks.

'Yes,' I say.

Then Stefano, the single guy in the group, comes up to us with seven bottles of beer and the conversation moves to other things.

When we are leaving, Cash pulls four tickets to his concert in Milan from his back pocket.

'Best seats in the house. If you don't want to go, sell them on the internet. They're worth £200.00 each,' he says.

While they are still staring at the tickets dumbfounded, we slip away. Outside it is already light. It is four in the morning but we are both wide awake. Taxi touts call out to us.

'Should we take one of them?' I ask.

'Yeah, let's go eat something in Soho,' he says with the excitement of a little boy.

I gaze up at him, so happy I think I will burst.

We sit in a Chinese restaurant eating lobster with ginger and egg fried rice. We smooch and his moustache falls into his rice. He picks it up with his chopsticks and puts it back on his face covered in rice and makes a funny face. I laugh so much my stomach hurts. In the taxi back I fall asleep on Cash's chest. He wakes me up just around the corner from the Hunter residence. I open my eyes, look into his eyes and breathily whisper his name in surprise. 'Cash.' Then I remember where I am.

'Come on, I'll walk you to the front door,' he says.

I stand for a moment on the sidewalk. It is nearly half five and there is a man walking his dog. I think neither of us wanted the night to end. I look around us. Then I say, 'Sleep well.'

'Go on. I'll wait until you get in and close the door.'

I stand in front of him, desperately not wanting the night to end. I never want to forget this night.

'It's been a beautiful night. Can I take a picture of you like this?' I ask.

He gets into odd poses for me and laughing I snap a few shots.

'See you tomorrow,' I say.

'See you later,' he says.

I peck him on the cheek and run up the stairs. I open the door, step inside, and wave to him.

'By the way I forgot to tell you your nose looks ridiculous,' I say.

He touches his fake nose and laughs. I close the door and lean against it. Christ, I am so in love.

Time seems to pass so quickly. Before I know it, Cash is telling me that he is leaving for Milan in the morning.

'I would have preferred if you were coming with me,' he says.

'I'll come with Britney later in the morning as we agreed. Anyway, you'll be at rehearsals and sound checks and you won't have time for me.'

He scowls. 'I'll allow it this time, but I swear if you don't' tell Britney soon I'm going to

have to tell her myself. A) I think it's bullshit that Britney will care either way. B) if she does care she'll just have to get over it. I love my sister, but there's no way I'm going to let her meddle in my affairs.'

'I'll tell her after her birthday party, OK?' I promise.

He doesn't know that I'm just buying time. I need to tell him about me, but I'm afraid it would ruin everything so I keep putting it off.

'You better,' he says with a frown, 'because I want everyone to know you're mine.'

'Really, I'm yours?' I ask innocently.

'All mine. Every last inch.'

'Act like it then,' I say with a wink.

So he does.

Chapter Twenty-nine

Tori

'**A**re you ready, Brit?' I ask, knocking on her bedroom door. Britney is always late. I hope she has at least finished packing.

'Come in,' she calls. Her voice sounds stressed.

I turn the handle and go in. Her room looks like a bomb hit it. There are clothes and shoes all over the bed and floor.

'What the hell, Brit? We're going for one day!' I exclaim incredulously.

'I know. I know, but I couldn't decide what to wear. If I take all the clothes and shoes I could conceivably want, then I eliminate the possibility of being devastated that the thing I want to wear is actually back in England,' she explains with mind-boggling logic.

'Right,' I say, blinking slowly. 'Can we establish that you have got everything you could conceivably want, and that it is safe to close your suitcase and take it downstairs?'

'I believe so. However, I've still got to dash into the shower first.'

'OK, quickly, please. Victor will be here in ten minutes,' I appeal, deliberately increasing the urgency in my voice.

'Don't worry, he'll wait,' she says coolly.

'I'll be in my room,' I say and leave her.

On my bed is my knapsack. I have only packed two changes of clothing and I haven't taken anything for the concert since Brit and I are going shopping as soon as we get to Milan.

I walk to the window and look out. The street is unusually quiet and I suddenly feel a little sad. I've not heard from Cash since last night as he caught his flight whilst we were all asleep. I sent him a warm text when I woke up this morning telling him how excited I was, how much I looked forward to meeting him in Milan and seeing him perform. I guess I expected a text back, something, anything, but nothing.

I feel a dull unease in my stomach, but I tell myself obviously, he would have been terribly busy. Maybe he slept on the flight, and then he will no doubt have been mobbed at the hotel by hordes of screaming teenage girls. From there the band members would have been driven to the stadium for their rehearsals.

A horrible thought suddenly enters my head.

What if it is not the wonderful, funny, beautiful man who seduced me so wickedly who meets me in Milan, but Cash Hunter the Sex God and Bad Boy? What if he is different? What if I am just another girl he had sex with and he has already moved on? The thought disturbs me, but I quickly reassure myself that all will be fine. I shouldn't be so insecure.

I turn around quickly when I hear Britney's voice split the still air of the house. Mr. Hunter is out and only Cora is in.

'I need help Tori, I can't close my suitcase,' she cries, standing in her bathrobe, her hair still wet.

'Don't worry. Leave it to me,' I say automatically.

A real struggle ensues, but I overpower her suitcase by sitting on it and pressing down the edges and getting Britney to push down on the locks. She claps her hands in appreciation.

'Come on, Brit. Dry your hair and get dressed,' I urge.

'Yes, mam,' she says cheekily.

Just as she switches on the hairdryer, the doorbell chimes. I run to the window and see the car parked on the street below.

'Victor is already outside,' I shout over the sound of the hairdryer.

'Your ride's here. Are you girls ready?' Cora yells from the bottom of the stairs.

I quickly run to the top of the stairs and scream, 'Coming,' and return to rush Britney along. Finally, after her hair is dried and she has flung on some casual clothes, she stands over her suitcase moaning that the case is too heavy to carry. I have a go and even I can barely shift it.

I tell her to wait in the bedroom whilst I quickly take my stuff downstairs to the car and ask the driver if he'd mind carrying Britney's suitcase from upstairs as it's too heavy for us.

Immediately Victor leaves his seat and goes upstairs.

'Have a lovely time, won't you?' Cora says to me.

'I'm sure I will,' I reply as Britney comes down with the driver who looks like he totally underestimated the weight of the case as his face is beetroot red and he's breathing rather heavily.

'Thank you so much,' Britney says as he opens the boot.

I offer to help but, being a man, he refuses and manfully manages on the second clean lift to get it to his chest and into the boot. I wave bye to Cora who's standing at the door, arms folded and smiling. Britney has already taken her seat inside as the driver goes to the front and I jump in the rear next to Britney.

'I hope I haven't forgotten anything?' she says in a questioning voice.

'So what if you did?' I say, turning to her. 'That would only make our trip into an adventure,' I say with a grin.

She wrinkles her nose. 'An adventure? How quaint, but yes, I suppose it could be an adventure.' She touches my arm. 'I'm really glad you're not jaded, Tori. Everybody I know would have made a point of pretending how tedious it all was, but you, you just see everything as if it is an exciting gift.'

'To be honest I still can't believe I'm going to Milan on a private jet,' I say excitedly.

'Oh, you'll enjoy it, Tori, it's really quite the biz. I've flown a few times with Cash on his jet and flying commercial simply doesn't come close after you've flown private,' she says, her voice animated and cheerful.

I grin happily at her. It is wonderful to see how much she has changed, from spoilt and childish to this happy, joyful young lady.

An hour later we arrive at Docklands city airport and our driver pulls up alongside a gleaming silver Embraer Legacy 500 private jet with its door open, a smiling air hostess standing in it. Just like in the movies.

Britney giggles when she sees my gobsmacked reaction. 'It's just a plane Tori.'

'Just a plane?' I exclaim as Victor opens her door.

'Close your mouth,' she says and yanks me out after her.

A man takes our bags and Britney runs up the steps pulling me along as a gust of wind almost blows me off the last one. Inside we are welcomed and shown into the sumptuous cabin. I drop my body into the plush seat and it's like falling into a luxurious bed. Britney has taken the seat opposite me and she's laughing at the dazed shock on my face. I laugh at her and then the star treatment starts. Hot towels, followed by pink champagne and a platter of delicious canapés.

'My God, Britney your brother is a gem. This is just so awesome.'

Britney raises her glass. 'To us having a fabulous time.'

We clink glasses. 'To a fabulous time,' I echo.

'Yay,' she yells happily. 'We're going to have a brilliant time. I just know it.

I take a sip of the chilled bubbly and lie back. 'Mmmm.'

Soon the champagne and the fantastic service put me in a relaxed mood. Brit is playing Candy Crush on her mobile and I close my eyes and let my mind wander away to Cash and wonder what he's doing now. The next thing I know Britney is shaking me enthusiastically. 'We're here Tori! We're here!'

'What?' I ask, confused.

'Look out, we're above Milan,' she says.

I pull back my shutter and the bright sunlight temporarily stuns me before I see that she is right, we are just over Milan.

'It looks amazing,' I say as the pilot announces that we're preparing to descend. Britney reaches over for my hand and holds it tightly in hers. A few minutes later, touchdown. Milano.

Chapter Thirty

Tori

As we are about to disembark, one of the cabin crew comes to talk to us. 'You have had a message from Mrs. Knowles, Mr. Hunter's secretary, to let you know that she has arranged for a driver who speaks English. He'll take you wherever you want to go and will wait for you. Please don't go anywhere without him.'

'Cool,' I say.

We thank the rest of the crew as we exit the plane and step into the glorious sunshine. Even though it is only eleven in the morning it's already very hot. Our passports are checked then we walk to a black Mercedes idling on the tarmac.

'Welcome to Milano,' the driver says as we reach the car. 'I am Fabio and I will look after you during your stay here.'

'Ciao, Fabio,' Britney greets cheerily and slips elegantly into the door he holds open for her. I get in on the other side. He walks over to the front, gets in, and turns around to pass us both cards with his cell number. 'Telephone me when you wish to go anywhere or if you need me, Signorine,' he says.

We murmur our thanks, and he puts the car into motion. It's only then I hear my phone ping and eagerly retrieve it from my bag. My heart races as I read the text.

Hey Wildcat. Been thinking about u nonfuckingstop. My dick's going wild & I'm feeling cocky. So consider yourself warned. Buy something dead sexy for tonight. C u later. x

Britney sees the wide smile on my face and turns to me with an inquiring look. 'Someone's made you happy,' she says.

'Yeah,' I say.

Barely able to contain my happiness, I lie back and watch the sun-drenched countryside pass us by. An hour later we turn into the fabulous pillars that straddle the entrance of the Hotel Principe di Savoia.

'Wow, it's breathtaking,' I gush.

'I know and I can't wait to see our rooms.'

The driver drops us off at the main entrance and we go inside the massive foyer with its fabulous centerpiece waterfall. At the reception desk we are welcomed by a sultry Italian brunette and told that we have a suite on the top floor. She also passes a white envelope with both Britney's and my name on it.

'OMG! It'll be so much fun, we have our own suite together,' Britney squeals as I open the envelope.

'What's in the envelope?' she asks.

'Our stage passes and ... a letter,' I reply.

'What does it say?' she asks peering over my shoulder and reading the letter.

'For a few seconds there is silence as we read the letter, then Britney is doing a happy dance right there in the posh foyer that positively smells of big money.

'Ha, ha, ha, I can't believe it. Cash asked Mrs. Knowles to open accounts for us in Fendi, Prada, Moschino, Gucci and Versace. We can buy whatever we want to,' she sings.

'Mrs. Knowles is really efficient,' I say in a hushed voice. I've never been so spoilt in all my life.

'Brilliant, brilliant, brilliant we're all organized,' Britney says as a bellboy approaches us and takes us to the top floor. Our suite is a to-die-for mixture of classical elegance and modern contemporary. Britney claims the bedroom overlooking the street and I take the one overlooking the garden and pool. The bathrooms are stunning with pink marble and Jacuzzi whirlpool baths. I throw myself on the bed and think of Cash. I can't wait to see him later.

'What do you want to do now, Brit?' I shout across the room. 'We have six hours before we need to leave for the stadium.'

'Shopping obviously,' she says appearing at my doorway. 'What else is there to do in Milan? We'll hit the shops on Mrs. Knowles' list.'

I call the driver and we find ourselves in the Quadrilatero d'Oro (Rectangle of Gold). We visit so many shops that I lose count. For the most part I stare in awe at the beauty, the design brilliance, and the incredible choice I see on display in Milan. Bright colors, classic lines.

Britney buys a striped trouser outfit at Fendi and a really cute dress at Moschino. She also finds a luscious snakeskin bag at Gucci and a pair of boots at Prada. I find the perfect buy in Versace. A leopard print, tight, velvet mini-dress with a high collar. The sales assistant, a gay man with very beautiful eyes, then suggests a pair of shoes that I would never have thought of wearing with my print dress. A black Medusa tri-strap platform. I put them on and stand.

'Very sexy,' he says in his thick Italian accent.

'They're perfect. Get them,' Britney says very firmly.

I walk up and down the shop. *He wants wild cat. He's got wild cat.* 'OK,' I say.

It is nearly two o'clock and we are very hungry so we stop for lunch at Caffè Baglioni across the street. Between us we polish off plates of eggs and truffle, steak tartare, smoked salmon, and wash it all down with a bottle of champagne.

We arrive back at the hotel quite merry, a teeny bit tipsy, and with about two hours to go before we leave for the stadium. Already the adrenaline is flowing in my blood. I can't wait to see Cash. It's as if we haven't been parted for just a few hours, but weeks.

Britney is in her room with the music at dance level decibels and is busy trying on various outfits for later, so I decide to avail myself of the Jacuzzi. I lie back and close my eyes. As the lovely sensation of jets of water gently blast my body, an image of Cash the first time he cheekily came into my bathroom with his mouthwatering wares on display comes into my head.

I remember his manly smell, his tanned muscular torso, his large hands as they spread my legs, and instantly my body starts aching for his brand of pleasure. My hands move of their own accord and start squeezing my breasts and caressing my nipples, anticipating how it will feel to be taken and fucked hard by Cash again.

It seems an impossible dream that I will stand in the audience watching the hero of so many of my teenage wet dreams, and I will not scream or cry his name, but will go home with the real thing, Cash Hunter.

I stand in front of the mirror, my hair loose and shining down my back, my eyes alive with excitement, my skin pink with all the blood rushing madly around my body, and with only one way to describe my dress: sexy, sexy, sexy.

I just hope to God that Cash doesn't think it's too slutty.

I go into Britney's room. She is zipping herself up into a long sleeved shift dress with an A-line skirt, complete with black lace trim. I sit on the bed and tell her she looks amazing, but she takes it off and tries on two more outfits before I look at my watch pointedly, telling her if she carries on in this way much longer we will miss the concert.

'Right. Be a devil and open the champagne bottle and I promise I'll be ready in fifteen minutes.'

I open the bottle that has been sitting on ice since we came in and grab two glasses, then return to her room. I pour the champagne and offer her a glass.

'To a fabulous time tonight,' Britney says.

'To a fabulous time,' I toast.

'I'm so happy I am with you, Tori,' Britney giggles.

'And I'm so happy, Britney, to see you happy,' I say. I almost can't believe how the girl is changing. I barely recognize this good-hearted, warm girl.

Fifteen minutes later she is all dolled up to the nines in the black and pink Moschino dress we bought earlier and we're ready to roll.

I call Fabio who says he's already downstairs.

She jumps to her feet. 'Will I do?' she asks doing a quick and slightly unsteady twirl.

'I'll have a hard time keeping the guys away from you tonight,' I tell her.

'Don't you bloody dare,' she warns and bursts out laughing.

We leave the suite and go downstairs. In the foyer a group of Italian young guys blow kisses and call out, 'Bella, Bella.'

We smile and keep moving. Fabio is right outside the entrance, smoking a cigarette, looking cool and relaxed.

'Mediolanum Forum, Assago?' he asks.

'Si,' I confirm.

As we exit the hotel's forecourt, I realize that I can barely wait to get there, but I dampen my enthusiasm next to Britney.

'Vaffanculo,' Fabio yells furiously as he slams on the brakes.

Both Britney and I jump and brace ourselves on the seats in front of us.

He meets our eyes in the rear view mirror. 'Sorry. Every time big concert, very bad traffic,' he says.

'Will we make it in time?' Britney asks in a panicked voice.

'Don't worry, Signorina. I know all the side roads. We beat the other cars.'

Chapter Thirty-one

Tori

In the end it takes only half an hour before we are driving along a tree lined boulevard and catch sight of huge billboards advertising Alkaline on either side of the road. The band looks fabulous in the billboard photo, but my eyes are drawn to the larger-than-life image of Cash. He looks awesome. Fabio avoids the huge crowd that's queued as far as my eyes can see and drops us off at the VIP entrance.

We show our VIP passes to two burly security guards.

'You're with the band?' one of the men asks.

Britney cuts in before I can answer. 'Where are the dressing rooms for the band? My brother's the lead singer.'

'The dressing rooms are on the other side of the Arena,' the guy says with a shrug. 'We're on the South section and they are on the North.'

Both of us look at each other in dismay. After what seems an awfully long way we finally reach the North side. We then have to climb a large flight of steps up another floor. My heart beats as hard from exhaustion as it is from the thought of seeing Cash.

At the top of the stairs more security awaits us and more showing of our passes. It's an absolute hub of activity now with people running around speaking into walkie-talkies. We stop outside a door that says: Band Dressing Room - Private - Do Not Enter. On a cardboard underneath the sign it reads: Cash Hunter. I feel my breath hitch suddenly and I tug at the hem of my tight dress. Britney raps on the door and shouts, 'Are you decent? We're coming in.'

Cash calls, 'Come in,' and Britney turns the handle.

Inside, Cash and Gavin are shirtless and sitting on chairs next to each other strumming their guitars. A number of empty beer bottles stand on the floor. They both look up and their eyes run down my body in my very revealing dress.

'Hey,' Cash says, smiling slowly.

'Hey,' Gavin echoes.

Cash puts his guitar down and stands up. Strangely Brittany doesn't run to him or throw herself at him. Instead, she bites her lip and says, 'Sorry, I didn't realize you weren't alone.'

'As if that's ever stopped you before,' Cash says, and beckons her with his hand. She goes to him and formally presses her lips against his cheek.

'What's come over you? Have you finally grown up?' he asks, surprised and amused by the restraint she is showing.

'Stop embarrassing me,' she hisses.

Cash flashes me a wickedly sexy smile and I suddenly feel very awkward with both Britany and Gavin around. I don't want either to sense anything, but every primal instinct screams to me to run into his arms.

'Want a beer, Tori?' he offers, his eyes alive with sexual lust.

'No thanks. We drank the champagne that was in the suite. It said compliments of the house,' I say.

He laughs.

Gavin turns towards Britney. 'How was your trip and hotel?' he asks conversationally.

'Everything was perfect,' she says.

'That's great.'

'And for you, Tori?' Cash asks softly.

'I've never been so spoilt in my life,' I reply truthfully.

'Yeah?'

I look deep into his eyes. Sexual chemistry throbs between us. 'Yeah.'

'Where are the rest of the band?' Britney asks.

'In their dressing rooms further along,' Gavin replies.

'And when do you go on stage?'

Cash drops his eyes to his watch and shrugs his shoulder. 'Less than forty-five minutes.'

He fixes his green eyes on me again and comes across the room, and with his hands in the front pockets of his jeans, leans his muscular frame against the wall. What a gorgeous hunk he is. He is so close I smell his skin. 'First time you'll be seeing me perform live, eh? Are you excited?'

I feel my face blush at the lie I am living. I will tell him the truth. Soon. 'Very,' I reply as coolly as possible.

'How are you feeling?' I ask, shifting the focus.

He grins and leans a little forward. 'Fantastic. Bring on the bright lights.'

'No nerves?' I ask, my skin tingling with his nearness.

'We drank those away earlier,' Gavin says.

My eyes move to the empty bottles. He doesn't seem drunk, but there is a kind of tension in him.

'Anyhow, you girls have a great front row seat with your own balcony right above the stage. Sean, my roadie, will take you there just before we come on,' he says as he walks back to his chair.

There is a rap on the door and then Octavia walks in. She takes in the scene in a glance and her mouth tightens. Cash casually reaches for his guitar and strums some chords.

'Let's move it guys. It's time for your make-up and wardrobe check. You're on in thirty minutes.' She turns to Gavin. 'Gav, isn't it time you were back in your own dressing room?' Her stern voice turns the chilled, sexually charged atmosphere, into one of turbulence and activity. A girl carrying two black make-up cases walks quickly into the room and starts opening them.

Octavia turns to me with a fake smile plastered on her face. I realize she is enjoying her position of power. 'What's your name again, honey?'

'Tori,' Britney innocently supplies not realizing that Octavia knows exactly who I am.

'Right. Sorry Britney and Tori, but I can't have my stars distracted so close to the gig, so I'm going to have to ask both of you to leave now,' she says, as a crackly voice comes through on her walkie-talkie.

'For fuck's sake. I'm fucking coming,' she snaps into it.

'Leave them alone, Octavia. They're just getting a bit of behind the scenes. Not doing any harm at all,' Cash says as he repositions his chair so he is facing the mirror.

She seems to burst a gut at this statement. 'Really, Cash! I have enough on my plate without this bullshit. You know the rules. No one other than the artists, make-up team, and management are allowed in the dressing rooms one hour before the show starts.'

She is talking to Cash but her eyes are focused on me and clearly the irritation on her face is all for me.

Cash looks like a thundercloud and I sense she has pricked his pride a little too much and he is about to let rip.

'I'm off,' Gavin says to no one, and hastily leaves the room.

'Come on, Brit. Let's go get comfortable in our front row seats,' I say, hoping to defuse the explosive situation by making a quick exit. After everything Cash has done for us, the last thing I want to do is cause a scene just before he goes on stage.

'Have Sean come and show the girls to their seats,' Cash tells Octavia coldly.

She speaks on her walkie-talkie and no sooner has she finished speaking when there is a knock on the door. It is a young man who must have been in the corridor. As he takes us out, I hear Cash say, 'Not so fast, Octavia. I want a word with you.'

Chapter Thirty-two

Cash

'I've got a million things to do. So this better be good.' Octavia gives me a ferocious look, but that's not going to fucking wash with me. Not when my blood is boiling.

'I think you may have misinterpreted the job of band manager, so let me spell it out for you. You get to organize, arrange, and book everything that involves this band. Recording, publicity interviews, live tours, parties, and hotels. What you don't get to do is talk to me in that bullshit condescending way you just did. I can tell you now, the next time you do it will be the fucking last time. You're out on your ear,' I tell her.

She licks her lips and looks at the makeup girl who pretends to be very busy cleaning her brushes. 'Look, Cash. I'm just trying to do what's best for the band, OK? Sometimes I'm a little rough around the edges, but it's my high standards that have brought this band to where it is today.'

I fold my arms across my chest and stare at her with raised eyebrows.

'I'm sorry I spoke to you in that way,' she says with a forced smile.

'Apology accepted.'

She widens her smile. 'The most important thing now is that you guys go out there and slay them.'

'We're on the same page there.'

'OK, great. I've got a couple of things to sort out, I'll see all of you before you go on.' She puts her hand on the handle and turns it.

'Oh, one more thing. Don't take that bitchy tone with Tori again or you'll be looking for a new band to manage.'

She is not quick enough to conceal the hatred that crosses her face at the mention of Tori's name. Why she should hate her so much is a mystery to me. She's never hated any of the other girls I've been with. She nods once tightly and walks out of the door.

After she is gone, the makeup girl moves forward with her container of foundation. I stare at my reflection in the mirror and think of Tori. Fuck, she knocked me for six when she came through the door in *that* dress. Hell, I wanted to slam her against the wall and take her there and then. Just thinking about it makes me hard.

The only problem is, I was not the only one lusting after her.

I saw something in Gav's eyes that made my blood boil. I've already warned him off once so I hope it's not what I think it is. He fucking knows better than to try it on with Tori. Challenge me and fuck with what's mine and you're on a collision course, dude. Sooner or later I'll meet you head on and it ain't going to be pretty.

'Look down please,' the girl instructs.

I drop my eyes and she starts painting black eyeliner on my eyelids.

I divert my attention to the only thing that matters right now. Pleasure. I'm going to give that tight, sweet, eager, little pussy all it can handle.

Chapter Thirty-three

Tori

https://www.youtube.com/watch?v=YgFyi74DVjc
Written In The Stars

'**S**hit. I've never seen Octavia act that way. What a witch. She had no right to make us leave. The cheek of it. I'm his sister for God's sake,' Britney grumbles furiously as we make our way to our seats. 'Bloody hell, she wouldn't even have a job if not for my brother.'

'Look,' I say, 'I wanted to slap her too, but Cash has taken so much trouble to organize everything for us that the last thing I wanted to do was cause a scene just before he went on stage.'

'But Cash wanted us to stay,' she insists.

'I know he did, but does it really matter in the bigger scheme of things? You've had an amazing time so far and it can only get better. Remember the twin with dung?'

She grins. 'You're right. We'll have a wonderful time.'

Cash was spot on, we have one of the best vantage points in this arena reserved entirely for us, and Sean has arranged for drinks and snacks to be brought to us as well. The excitement is mounting in the stadium and everyone is full of expectancy and energy as the time moves closer to the band's appearance. Eventually the entire audience of more than 15,000 people is chanting for the band.

The chanting stops and the crowd erupts into a loud roar of excitement as five figures, more shadow than real, saunter out on to the darkened stage. Flashbombs explode around them as the driving beat of the band starts and stage lights bathe the band in a breathtaking kaleidoscope of fast moving color. Huge screens surrounding the arena catch every move they make.

'Bonasera Milano,' Cash shouts, his hand lifted high above his head.

The fans scream the greeting back to him, and the air literally vibrates.

'Are you ready to get down and dirty?' he asks.

The applause and shouts of *si* is instant and deafening.

Gavin says something to the audience too, but I don't hear it because Cash is looking directly at me. My heart stops beating. I can't move. I just stand there transfixed and staring until he winks and turns away from me. I watch him energetically run to the other end of the stage as the intro to the first number, *Let's Hang Out,* starts playing. The crowd goes crazy. Cash's deep rich voice sparks more wild screaming.

Britney, like most of the fans, has jumped to her feet clapping, cheering, and dancing to the beat. The atmosphere is so electric with the throbbing of the powerful beat and the grinding of all the people below that it is infectious and I find my body reacting to the vibe too.

I remember that first time in Atlanta being there right in the heart of the energy and how good I felt, seeing Cash up on that stage, so close but so unobtainable. Now here I am with a VIP seat right at the front of the stage and he's just as gorgeous as ever, but this time around he's mine.

At least for tonight.

I look around at the sea of young girls swaying to the beat and filled with wild excitement at the sight of these handsome, virile young men and for the first time I understand what it must be like for these performers. Out on that stage they are larger than life. Heroes. Buzzed up with alcohol and out of control hormones, they look out across the arena at the adoring fans and see prey.

Although the band members are all handsome and have good voices, Cash has that something extra. He exudes confidence, presence and raw sex appeal. He's also the most gorgeous. Hearing Cash's name being screamed by so many beautiful girls makes me slightly insecure and I have to remind myself it's me he has chosen to be with him tonight.

For one hour the band struts and performs dance moves with seemingly unlimited energy, lapping up all the love coming from their fans, as hit song after song reverberates across the packed arena. Britney is still boogieing next to me, trying to encourage me to join in using various facial expressions, but the heat all around is so intense I have to sit to cool down a little.

Then it is time for the finale and Tinie Tempah dressed all in black with a red jacket joins the band on stage. To Britney's delight Tinie wishes her a happy birthday. I look at her with a grin and she is red with exertion, pleasure and excitement.

A girl brings some boxes to the stage. The band members take the boxes and sit with their backs turned away from the audience. When they turn around they are all wearing red shoes that match Tinie's red jacket. Together they sing *Written in the Stars* and I feel the song in my bones. Like the lyrics of the song seasons come and go but I will never change. My love for Cash is written in the stars.

Afterwards they all do Dizzee Rascal's famous jump routine and the crowd becomes an enormous heaving mass of people jumping up and down while they scream, 'Jump, jump, jump.'

Panting, the band announces how much they love their audience and thanks them all. 'Grazie a tutti. See you all next year,' the guys say before the notes for their biggest hit ring out. *The Girl Who Can't Say No.* For the chorus the band lets the audience sing the words.

Two encores later, the crowd is clapping persistently, begging for more, but the guys say their final farewell. 'Buona notte Milan.' They bow in formation and run off the stage.

Even as they disappear from view Sean is already there to fetch us back to the dressing room. The cool air along the dressing room corridor hits my face and I welcome it after the steamy atmosphere in the arena. Britney is still buzzing and smiling happily when a boy with red hair and freckles comes up to us.

'Britney?' he says with an English accent.

'Yeah,' she says cautiously.

'Your brother has arranged for you to meet Tinie Tempah.'

'What?' Britney exclaims.

'Yup, I'm supposed to take you to him. The man has a birthday gift for you.'

'A birthday present, for me?' Britney repeats in astonishment.

'If you want to come with me I'll take you to him and bring you back.'

She turns to me. 'Come with me?'

I shake my head and smile at her excitement. 'You go ahead. I'll wait for you in Cash's dressing room.'

Smothering the squeal that threatens to escape the back of her throat, Britney clasps her hands to her face before planting a big kiss on my cheek.

'This is the best birthday ever,' she tells me and goes off with the man.

I am still smiling as we walk down the corridor when I spot Cash walking towards us.

'I'll be off then,' Sean says. Lifting his hand in a wave, he starts walking back to where we came from.

I stand where I am, frozen, and watch Cash stride towards me. He seems so different. When he reaches me I look into his eyes and I can see that he is wired up. The performance has left him with an adrenaline high.

I feel my body responding to his. I can almost hear his heart thudding hard in his chest. There is a sheen of sweat on his face and body. His T-shirt is drenched and clinging tightly to his body and every muscle is prominently on display. His skin is tingling as if he is full of static electricity.

His eyes drop from my face to my chest. Then he takes my wrist and pulls me along the corridor until we get to a door. He kicks it open and yanks me into a small toilet. He locks the door and turns to me, breathing hard.

He grabs me by the waist and pulls me hard towards him so I slam up against his body. Then he swoops down on my mouth and fucking devours me. Eats me alive. It's like the Fourth of July fireworks. My hands come to entwine in his dripping wet hair. I suck his tongue when he sticks it in my mouth.

'Fuck me, Tori,' he growls.

'What, here?'

He shakes his head slightly.

'I thought fucking in the toilet lost its charm after a while,' I say.

'When you come to me looking like this, I'll fuck you anywhere,' he says roughly. He pulls my skirt up so it bunches around my waist, rips my panties right off my body, and chucks them to the ground.

'Oh,' I gasp, aroused by the violence and urgency in his action.

He swivels me around so I am facing the cistern and my feet are planted on either side of the toilet.

'Hands on the wall,' he orders.

I obey immediately and hear the sound of the metal teeth of his zip, and the rustle of his clothes being hurriedly yanked down. Seconds later he pulls my ass upwards and plunges his cock all the way into me, the entire length in one single movement.

'Oh God, Cash,' I grunt.

Holding my hips tight he powers into me energetically. Thrusting deeper and more powerfully until it feels as if the whole bathroom stall is vibrating and shaking with his thrusts.

'This feel good to you?' he snarls, slamming even harder into me.

'Yes,' I gasp.

'Yeah?'

'Yeah,' I pant.

'You're going to let me fuck you in the toilet again?'

'Yes,' I cry.

'After every concert?'

'Yes. Every. Concert.'

'Good.'

'No more groupies?' I ask.

He doesn't pause or still. 'No more groupies.'

'Only me?'

'Only you.'

And then I find myself climaxing. It's so powerful it stuns me. My body vibrates uncontrollably. Through the waves of ecstasy, I feel Cash's cock grow inside me. I feel him explode and maybe I even feel his hot seed flood into me. Panting hard and with him still buried inside me, he places his hands over mine on the wall. I turn my head and he kisses me.

'You're a bad boy,' I whisper.

'You're a dirty girl,' he whispers back.

I smile.

Chapter Thirty-four

Tori

https://www.youtube.com/watch?v=X9_n8jakvWU

We are all at Just Cavalli club. It is extravagant and opulent with purple neon lights and girls dressed in angel wings dancing next to metal pillars. The Alkaline party is spread over a large area, some of it flowing into an outdoor area with a huge dance floor and torches. I stand at a little cove and watch the crowd that surges around Cash everywhere he goes. Everybody wants a little piece of him. He looks at me and waves me over, but I shake my head.

'Going to the toilet,' I mouth, and point in the direction of the toilets.

Someone calls and he turns away from me after mouthing the words, 'I'll be waiting here for you.'

I turn towards the toilets and walk into Gavin.

'Sorry,' I apologize.

'You're cool,' he says with a lazy smile.

'That was a great performance today,' I say.

'Thanks. I'm very good at playing the second fiddle.'

My eyebrows rise. 'You don't believe that. You have just as many fans as Cash.'

He grins. 'I suppose you're right. I definitely have more than I can get through, anyway.'

Not sure how to react, I smile politely.

'How are you getting on with the others?'

I scowl. 'Not good. They seem to hate me even before I open my mouth.'

He laughs. 'It's not you, babe. Come on, I'll buy you a drink and tell you how it all works in this business.'

I glance in the direction of Cash and see that he is occupied and will be for some time to come. Besides, I badly want to know what I am doing wrong and Gavin is the only one who seems to like me at all. I smile gratefully at him. 'Thanks. I'll really appreciate any pointers you can give me.'

We go to the bar and Gavin taps the bar.

'Tequila OK with you?'

I nod and he orders two shots of tequila with lime and salt and two bottles of beer. We do the tequila, lime and salt thing quickly. I notice his eyes linger on my mouth when I put the lime between my lips and suck it. Then he picks up his bottle and so do I. He points to a sofa a couple have just vacated.

'Let's be comfortable,' he says.

I follow him and we sit at the table. A waitress brings two more tequilas and we down them immediately.

'Hoo,' I exhale. 'That's me done.'

He grins. 'Lightweight huh?'

'I haven't got hollow legs like you,' I retort.

He laughs.

'So,' I say leaning in. 'Tell me, what am I doing wrong? Why does everyone hate me so passionately?'

'You're not doing anything wrong, love. Long, blonde hair, big lips, and seductive, secretive cornflower blue eyes. What's not to like?' he asks cheerfully.

I frown at the sexual description, but I have noticed that this is the way all the band members talk. They always seem to be coming on to you even when they're not.

'If Cash had taken Ke$ha or Selina Gomez or any other celebrity as his girl, there would be no problem,' he explains. 'But because he took an ordinary girl, it turns everybody into green eyed monsters thinking that you have risen above your station and taken what you don't deserve. As long as you are with Cash you will have to put up with it. It will never stop. They'll always hate you.'

I stare at him unhappily. 'That doesn't sound very hopeful. Isn't there anything I can do to make the situation better?'

'Nope. The nicer you are to them the worse they will be to you. Your best bet is to just ignore them and enjoy your time with Cash. Soon enough it will be all over.'

My eyes widen. He sure didn't pull his punches. I pick up my beer and take a small sip. It's one thing for me to tell myself that obviously my relationship won't last. How can it possibly? We are from different worlds. But it is quite another thing to hear it spelt out so succinctly by someone else. I swallow the beer and the lump in my throat and to my horror my eyes unexpectedly fill with tears. Why I am crying I do not know.

'Hey,' he says, his face creasing up, and puts a hand on my shoulder.

'Oh, God, I feel like such a fool,' I say, gently pressing my knuckles into the corners of my eyes so I don't spoil my make-up.

'Come here,' he says, and suddenly drags me to him. Before I know it he has pulled me to him and is kissing me. On the mouth! It takes a second for me to get over the shock of the fact that I am in his lap, his hands are around my waist, and his hot mouth is on mine. I turn my face away and placing both my hands on his chest I push away from him. I push away so hard I feel myself falling backwards. I land on the floor humiliated and furious. From my prone position on the floor I see Britney is standing over Gavin. Her face is twisted with anger, or perhaps even hate.

'Get up,' she snarls.

'What the fuck?' he says.

'Get up you little worm.'

'Calm down, Britney,' he says, looking around him worriedly.

'If you don't get up I'm going to tell my brother what you did.'

He flies up from his seat and looks at her with shifty eyes. 'Listen,' he starts to explain, but he gets no further.

'That's for what you did to me,' she says, and delivers a vicious karate chop to the side of his neck. He goes white, his body arches, and his mouth opens and closes like a goldfish.

'This is for Tori,' she cries ferociously and aims two blows in quick succession into his midriff. He clutches his stomach and bends double. His face is contorted and a hoarse rasp struggles out of his mouth.

'And this one is for messing with my brother's girlfriend,' she says, and executes a sideways kick into Gavin's nuts just like Rita Ora does to the bad guy's belly in her Black Widow video.

His eyes bulge with the agony and shock, then he blinks and crashes to the right, knocking down a stool. He curls up on the ground, odd choking sounds crawling out of his open mouth.

'Oh, and just in case it's not perfectly clear yet, you are uninvited to my party, tomorrow,' Britney spits. She turns to me. 'Come, Tori. Let's go.'

I am too stunned to do anything so Britney holds her hand out and helps me up from the floor. I take one more look at Gavin writhing on the floor before I turn away. All around us people are staring. As we take our first step we come face to face with Octavia. Her mouth is open in astonishment. She snaps it shut, and throwing a furious glare at us, she dashes forward to help Gavin.

We walk to the toilets without saying a word. I turn to face Britney. 'What did he do to you?'

She takes a shuddering breath. 'You know that night at the party in Cash's house.'

'Yeah,' I say.

'He pushed me up against a wall and forced his fingers inside me. I didn't expect it so I was too shocked to do anything, but luckily someone else came into the room and he let go of me. I ran away and came to find you.'

'Oh! My God, no.' I stare at her in horror. Suddenly it all makes sense. That is why she had been crying and in such a state. What a sick bastard. I wish I had kicked his face in too.

'Why didn't you tell anyone?' I ask her gently.

'I didn't want to get him in trouble. I always fancied him and I was afraid that maybe I had encouraged him. I liked it when he first started kissing me, but then he started to get rough.'

'Oh, Britney. It's not your fault. I'm so much older than you and he managed to take me by surprise. I thought he was a nice guy trying to help me. It was all just a pretense.'

'I think he must be very jealous of Cash. That is why he did that to me and you.'

'Hell, Brit, when did you find out about me and Cash?'

'I've known for ages. The two of you are like two elephants roaming about the house at night.'

'We didn't really make that much noise, did we?' I protest, red faced.

'You woke dad up,' she says flatly.

'What?' I blurt out in horror.

'Exactly.'

My jaw drops open. 'Mr. Hunter knows?'

'Um ... I might have told him,' she confesses with a sly grin.

My eyes pop open. 'You did not,' I cry.

'I did,' she admits calmly.

'He's not upset, is he?'

'Why should he be?'

'Oh my God! I'm freaking out right now. Tell me exactly what he said,' I demand urgently.

'Actually he just laughed and said, "Looks like I killed two birds with one stone."'

I look at her worriedly. 'What's that supposed to mean?'

She shrugs. 'You know how dad is. He's always talking in riddles. I asked but he refused to explain further.'

I chew at my bottom lip. 'And you don't mind?'

'Mind?' she asks in a surprised voice. 'I think it's wonderful. I wish he would marry you.'

I stare at Britney, all kinds of thoughts and sensations slam into me at her innocent words. Marry? Cash and me? I was thirteen when I bought a little fake gold ring and pretended to be Mrs. Cash Hunter.

'It's not that kind of relationship,' I croak.

'But wouldn't you like to marry my brother though? It'll be such fun. We'll be real sisters then.'

'It's way too early to tell, Brit. We barely know each other.' I pause for a second and quickly steer the conversation away from this topic. 'Are you going to tell Cash about what Gavin did to you?'

'I don't know,' she says thoughtfully. 'It could break Alkaline up.'

'But you have to tell someone. What he did was wrong. He'll do it to someone else if there are no consequences. Maybe you should at least tell your dad.'

'You're right. I'll tell dad. He'll know what to do. He always does.'

I smile at her. 'You were badass out there. Those self-defense classes sure came in handy.'

'Look at my hands,' she says showing her hands.

They are still trembling with reaction and I grab them in mine. 'I know your dad will be super proud of what you did today. It was very courageous,' I tell her.

She grins at me. 'I'm not the same person I was before. Thanks to you.'

'I'm so proud of you, Brit. You've come a long way in a very short time. Thank you for sticking up for me.'

She looks at her fake nails nonchalantly. 'No problem. I can always fit a little drama into my life.'

I laugh.

'Cash will be looking for you. You should repair your lipstick quickly,' she says.

I look at the mirror and see that my lipstick is smudged and smeared on my left cheek. I pull out some toilet paper and wipe my mouth and cheek clean before I apply a new layer of lipstick. Then I turn around and hug her. 'You do know that I didn't kiss him willingly, right?'

'I know you and I know Gavin,' she says simply.

I smile at her.

'Come on, let's go find Cash,' she says.

We go out. Enrique Iglesias is singing *I Like It*, and Cash is outside looking for us. 'Where have the two of you been? I've been looking all over for you girls.'

We go back to the party and neither Gavin nor Octavia are anywhere to be seen.

Chapter Thirty-five

Tori

'Wake up, you morsel of sexiness.'

I groan and, turning away from the voice, curl up into a tight ball.

'Come on. I've got something really special to show you,' Cash says in my ear.

I open one eye. 'What?'

'Want to see The Last Supper?' He licks along the shell.

My aunt told me she came to Milan and though she desperately wanted to see The Last Supper, she couldn't. She joked tickets to see it were harder to come by than front seat invitations to a Gucci fashion show. I open both eyes. 'You have tickets?'

'Three if I'm keeping it real.'

I stretch luxuriously and yawn. How could this guy have so much energy? He lights up a stage for more than an hour, he parties until late at night, has sex until the early morning hours, and wakes up at first light.

He nibbles my lobe. He's starting something here. 'Unless you just want to stay in bed and we can have sex all morning.'

I pull back slightly. 'As delicious as that sounds, I do want to see The Last Supper.'

He grins. Cocky and confident. 'That's what I thought.'

'What's the time?' I ask.

'Nine.'

'Already?'

'Get in the shower and I'll go wake Brit up,' he says slipping out of the room.

Totally naked I pad over to the shower. Warm water rains down on me, bouncing off my head, face and shoulders. It's a good way to wake up. I'm already out of the shower and getting into my clothes when Cash comes back in.

'Is Britney getting ready?' I ask.

'She doesn't want to come.'

'Why not? I thought she loved art.'

'Yeah, the modern stuff. Her exact grumpy response was, "Go away. I'm not getting out of bed to stand for half-an-hour in front of a painting that's been so heavily restored it's not even Leonardo's work any more."'

I giggle. That so sounds like Britney. 'Did you tell her it's a mural and not a painting?'

'Nope. I didn't think it would make a blind bit of difference.'

'So what does she want to do?' I ask picking up the hairdryer.

'She wants to go to see the Duomo so she'll meet us before we set off for that. I'll arrange for the driver to pick her up and bring her to us.'

I point the hairdryer at him. 'Aren't you worried you're going to get recognized and mobbed?'

He walks over to the desk and picks up the beard and the moustache he used that night we went to The Ministry of Sound.

I laugh. 'Sterling idea.'

We have to pass through a humidity controlling chamber before we enter the refectory where we will only have fifteen minutes before the next lot of people will be let in. We enter, hushed and reverent. There is nothing else in that hall except a painting of Jesus' crucifixion on the opposite wall.

I stand in front of the partially damaged mural and take a deep breath.

The painting is faded and even flaky, yet it is more majestic than anything I have seen before. I'm not a connoisseur of art, and I'm pretty certain I have seen other paintings and frescos with as much attention to detail, but perhaps it is the subject matter which arrests my complete attention. The painting catches the climactic moment when Jesus says, 'One of you will betray me.'

Da Vinci has managed to capture the atmosphere of shock, astonishment, and rage among his disciples. The expressions on the faces of the apostles, their hand movements, and the postures of their bodies tell a mesmerizing story of the awakening of distrust in a tightly knit group of people.

I watch Judas. The bad guy. There is spilled salt before him, and he is clutching a bag of silver in his left hand. His right hand and Jesus' are simultaneously reaching for a loaf of bread.

The guide's voice comes through the device in my ear to say that the vanishing point for the painting is on Jesus' right temple. That is where my eye goes and I'm suddenly moved by the look of gentle resignation and peace in a way I've never seen by him. Poor Jesus.

I steal a look at Cash and he is looking at me. The beard and the moustache make his eyes look as green as spring grass.

'Do you like it?' he asks.

'It's absolutely stunning.'

He smiles.

Then our time is over and all of us exit the convent through a gift shop and file out into the street.

'Are you hungry?' Cash asks.

In the bright sunshine his disguise looks really fake and stupid, but it occurs to me then, I don't even care what he looks like any more. I just love him for what he is. For the things he says and does, and the way he touches my soul without even trying.

'Well ...' he prompts.

 243

I smile up at him. 'I could eat a horse.'

We walk down the pavement hand in hand until we see Fabio's car crawling up the road towards us. We get in and twenty minutes later we are in Via Santa Radegonda. There is a long queue that snakes all the way down the street.

'Must be something pretty special judging from the length of the queue. What is it?'

'It's called panzerotti. It's a pastry triangle stuffed with all kinds of filling. You can have it fried or baked.'

We join the back of the queue with all the other tourists and residents of Milan. It moves pretty fast and soon we are inside a nondescript shop that looks more like a takeaway joint. I have the fried Nutella version and Cash orders two, the classic with tomato and mozzarella and another with salami.

Clutching our beers and greasy paper bags of panzerotti we go to the piazza where we join other people who have the same idea. We find a sunny spot and sit down to eat our pastries.

Cash takes a chunk of his panzerotti and creamy yellow mozzarella oozes out.

'Good?' I ask.

He licks his lips. 'Delicious.'

I bite into mine and chew slowly. It tastes like a cross between a donut and a pizza. The dough is soft and quite sweet.

'Do you like it?' Cash asks.

'Yes. Very tasty.' I take my sweater off. The sun beats down on my head and shoulders. It feels good to be eating out in the open sunshine with Cash.

 244

'Have you ever been betrayed, I mean in a big way, in like Last Supper fashion?' I ask, licking a bit of Nutella from my finger.

'No,' he says biting into his pastry. 'Have you?'

I shake my head. 'I've lead a pretty sheltered life. I mean, my mom and dad would not even have let me come to England if my aunt was not living here. But it's good that someone who has been all over the world and lives the kind of big and bright life you do has never been betrayed.'

He takes a swig of his beer and looks at me expressionlessly. 'I've been betrayed many times, Tori. Not in The Last Supper category, of course, but ...'

'I'm sorry to hear that,' I say sincerely.

'Don't be. It comes with the territory. You want fame and fortune, then don't expect loyal friends as well.'

I stare at him curiously. 'Don't you have people that you trust?'

'I trust my dad,' he says simply.

'No one else?'

He looks at me solemnly. 'I kinda trust you.'

I swallow hard. The lies I've told, they are not a betrayal. They are not meant to hurt him or anyone else. I can sincerely say that I will never betray him. No amount of silver or gold can ever tempt me to betray him. I blush and smile at him shyly. 'Thank you for trusting me. I will never betray your trust.'

The way he looks at me makes me feel as if I have stepped into one of my teenage dreams. My heart quickens as I take a casual bite of my pastry.

He gives a lopsided smile. 'A guy could fall in love with a girl like you.'

His statement is so shocking that I accidentally swallow the food in my mouth. It slides down my throat and lodges at the top of my trachea, and before I can cough it up, my windpipe closes tightly around it.

I've attended life saver class. That death grip is called the drowning reflex. It means if you ever fall into water, the trachea closes in to buy you a few minutes so you can get out of the water. That life-saving reflex has now kicked in and formed the perfect seal. I've stopped breathing because oxygen cannot get in or out of my lungs, and because there is no air to vibrate my larynx with, I can't even make a sound.

For a few crazy seconds my first feeling is not fear but embarrassment. I'm choking. Everybody's going to turn and look. I actually think I can try to cough it up, or surreptitiously thump my midriff.

'What's the matter?' Cash asks, his eyes narrowed.

I open my mouth. Of course, nothing comes out, but black dots suddenly appear in my vision. That's when fear and panic sets in. *Someone needs to do the Heimlich maneuver right now, or I'm going to die here. In a piazza in Italy where no one knows me.*

'Christ. You're choking,' he rasps and, standing up, pulls me to my feet.

He wraps his arms around me, forms a fist below my sternum, and makes a series of hard and sharp (and quite frankly violent) compressions, to try and force the obstruction out.

It doesn't work.

The lump of pastry refuses to budge. The bright day is slowly morphing into a dark narrowing tunnel. So this is what dying feels like. As my knees buckle, Cash roars in my ear, 'Come on, Tori.' He gives a great big heave that lifts my feet clean off the ground and makes me think my ribs are cracking.

The trapdoor opens and I gasp a lungful of clean air before it slaps down again.

'Fuck this,' Cash curses furiously, and heaves again, even harder. This time I cough, retch, and up it comes into my mouth. I spit it out. A slimy lump.

He turns me around to face him.

Tears run down my face. I look up at his white face. 'You saved my life,' I croak.

'What the fuck, Tori? You scared the shit out of me.'

I stare at his eyes, wild with fear and anxiety. 'I'm sorry.'

He grabs me suddenly and pulls me close to his body and I hear his heart racing in his chest.

'You turned blue, Tori,' he says, his voice is almost a sob.

'I'm sorry,' I whisper again.

 247

'It's OK. It's fine. It's all good now,' he croons.

'What's going on here?'

The sudden intrusion jolts us out of our own little world. We turn towards the voice and see Britney looking at us with an enquiring expression.

'Tori nearly choked to death,' Cash answers, his voice hoarse.

'Really? Oh my God. I've missed everything then.'

We walk to the Duomo together. Cash never lets go of my hand. Sometimes I catch him looking at me almost anxiously.

Chapter Thirty-six

Tori

https://www.youtube.com/watch?v=bpOR_HuHRNs
(Wild ones)

We arrive back at 2.00pm on Saturday and Cash and I part at the airport. He has things to do and I have to go back to the Hunter residence to make sure that everything goes smoothly for the party tonight.

'See you this evening,' he says, kissing the tip of my nose.

'See you then,' I say.

In my heart I know that I can no longer delay telling him the truth about me and I promise myself that I will tell him tonight after the party. Come what may. I don't know how he will react but he must care a little. It's not so big, my crime.

So I was a fan. Fine, I was the crazy mad fan he described, but that still doesn't make me a bad person. I didn't harm anyone. I was just young. Surely he will see that, unlike the other crazed fans, I came to his father's house not to steal memorabilia but in an attempt, no matter how misguided, to heal myself.

I made a mistake by not confessing at the beginning of our relationship that I was a fan, but I was embarrassed. Who has never made a mistake in their lives? I am very nervous about the task ahead, but I will have a few shots of vodka, and I'll be brave.

I dress in the loose-cut, tiered, cobalt blue mini dress that Britney and I bought before we left for Milan. With its high, squared-off neckline that connects to spaghetti straps framing a V back, it is fun and flirty. I team it with cross-strap platform shoes in tan suede and go to Britney's room. She is standing in her bra and knickers and looking at the mountain of clothes on her bed.

'Help me,' she says.

'I thought you were going to wear the off shoulder sequined dress ala Taylor Swift?' I ask.

'I'm not sure anymore.' She lets her eyes run down my figure. 'You look real cute, by the way.'

'Thank you,' I reply and walk towards her. I go to the pile of clothes and start putting them back on their hangers. I spot the maroon ala Taylor Swift dress under the third dress and pull it out.

'How could you not wear this? It's so beautiful?' I say holding it up.

She grins suddenly. 'You're right. It is gorgeous and I *will* wear it.'

'It's so tight you won't be able to kick anyone's balls in it though,' I tell her as I help zip her up.

She laughs and gets into a pair of Dolce & Gabbana black boots.

'Wow,' I say.

'You're not just saying it?'

'Cross my heart and hope to die.'

While Britney starts on her makeup, I go downstairs and find people are already beginning to arrive. Lara, the party organizer, is ticking their names off her list. I go through the hallway and see that the caterers have set up their tables out in the garden, and all the furniture in the big living room has been moved into the other rooms. There is a DJ with his mobile disco unit. I go out into the kitchen where Cora is fussing over her version of jello shots. Hers have a mixture of rum, cognac and lemon juice. I help her put them into bowls half-filled with ice.

'Try one,' she says.

I pop myself on a stool. 'Only if you'll drink with me,' I say.

So we sit and have our first shot together. 'He's a good boy, you know.'

'Who?' I ask, chewing jello.

'You know who.'

I stop chewing. 'You know?'

She leans closer. 'Everybody knows.'

I sigh. 'I should have told you, but I didn't know if it was even going to last. You know how it is. Cash is a big star and I'm just the hired help.'

She reaches out her veined, waxy hand and covers mine with it. 'You're not just the hired help. Don't you go around saying such stupid things. You're not uneducated like me. You have a great future in front of you. Grab it all with both hands. He's not better than you.'

I take my other hand and cover hers with it. 'You don't know, Cora. It's not as simple as you think. I lied to Cash about something important. I'm going to try and make it right tonight, but I don't know if I can. I don't know how he will react. So tonight might even be my last night here.'

'Don't be so silly,' she scolds. 'I've known Cash since he was a wee boy and he has a heart of gold. Tell him the truth and I promise you it won't be your last night here.'

I chew my bottom lip nervously. 'It's a really big thing though.'

'Then the sooner you get it out of the way the better for both of you,' she says firmly.

I force a smile. 'I'm just so scared I'll ruin everything.'

'Think about it this way. What have you got if you have no trust?'

I nod. 'You're right. I'll tell him tonight after the party.'

'Good girl.' She grins. 'One more shot.'

I giggle. 'I'm going to be drunk before the night starts.'

'To deal with some of the people that hang around this family you need to be drunk,' she says, rolling her eyes.

I laugh and we down two more jello shots.

'Well, can't hide here forever,' I say slipping off the stool. 'I guess I better go and see what Britney is up to. Wish me luck.'

'Good luck, Tori.'

'See you later,' I say and slip out of the door into the corridor that seems to have filled up considerably in the half an hour I spent in the kitchen.

As I reach the stairs I see Octavia. She's coming down dressed in a fabulous calf length black leather dress and white court shoes. I find myself frozen by the look in her eyes. It is vindictive and victorious. She comes down to the last step and stops in front of me.

'Smile. It's a party,' she drawls, and I cannot help the shiver of unease that rises up my spine.

I don't reply and she walks away towards the main room where music has started throbbing. As I stand there watching her figure walk away, a pair of hands envelops my body and all the tension in my body drains away. I relax into his hard body. He runs his palms over the curves of my hips and plants a kiss on my bare shoulder.

'Your whole back is practically naked,' he growls.

I turn around. In a black shirt and dark blue jeans he is 360% of pure gorgeousness. Everything in me is crying out for him. 'It's deliberate,' I murmur. 'I wanted to distract you. It's wall to wall babes in here.'

He looks into my eyes. 'You know me. I wouldn't go anywhere pussy wasn't running free, but lately all I'm craving is your sweet body.' He pulls me close to his body so I can feel his erection. 'Feel that? That's you. I just can't keep my hands off you. You're so fucking hot.'

My breath catches even as I feel a kind of sick terror in the pit of my stomach. How will he react when I tell him the awful truth? Will he still want me? I lay my finger in his chin dimple. 'You look pretty hot yourself, but you already know that, don't you, darlin'?'

He laughs. 'Class, ass, and a whole load of sass, that's my girl.'

'I like to leave a lasting impression,' I say as nonchalantly as I can, but my words feel hollow as if I am pretending, and my heart sits like a stone in my chest.

'Are you wearing panties?' he whispers close to my ears.

I lean back. 'I'm wearing a mini dress, Cash! Of course, I'm wearing panties.'

'Shame. I love the idea of you walking around bare assed and any moment I could meet you in a dark corner and finger you.'

 254

My heart thumps hard at the image he evokes. 'Don't. You're making me wet.'

He grins. 'Shall we nip up to your room for a quick one?'

God, how I'd love to say yes. To go upstairs and just for a while forget that I have this painful task ahead. 'Don't you want to see Britney first?' I ask.

'What do you want, babe? You want me to go see my sister, or you want me to take you upstairs and stick your wet pussy on the end of my cock?'

My breath starts coming in gasps. I shouldn't be doing this. This is wrong. 'Take me upstairs,' I whisper.

He grabs my hand and pulls me up the stairs to my room. The place is so full by now we have to negotiate people sitting on the steps and those coming down. He shuts my bedroom door and locks it. Then he takes two steps towards me and drops to his knees. He lifts my flowing flirty dress and disappears into it.

'What are you doing?' I gasp.

'Spread your legs. I'm going to make you cream on my face,' he says as he yanks my panties down my legs.

I widen my legs and he slips the tip of his tongue between my wet folds and swirls it. I grasp hold of his shoulders and bite my lip to keep from moaning. He continues to swipe his tongue in long, lingeringly luscious strokes.

'Oh damn. You're fucking killing me with your tongue,' I squawk.

'Forget my tongue. It's my cock you have to worry about, Wildcat.'

Someone tries the door and I freeze, but he doesn't stop until I come with a muffled cry of ecstasy and even his cock is completely satiated.

'Shit. I don't think I've ever had so much sex with one girl,' he says.

'Is that a bad thing?'

'Nope. Come on. It's time I bought my girl a drink.'

'My girl?'

'Yeah. My girl. You're mine, Tori Diamond,' he says possessively and opens the door.

Chapter Thirty-seven

Tori

We are halfway down the stairs when I know that something is wrong. The music has stopped and I can hear Octavia's voice coming from the main room. There is no other voice except hers. She seems to be reading something aloud.

Suddenly my blood runs cold. I stand stock still. I can't move. My feet feel as if they are encased in concrete.

Oh, Jesus. No. No. No.

How could it be? This can't be real. Please don't be real.

I turn to look at Cash. There is a frown on his face. Instinctively he knows that something is wrong, but he still has not realized what she is reading. This is just a fucking nightmare. I just have to wake up, but I can't wake up. I'm already awake.

Then my brain goes crazy and I run into the living room. I can see her at the end of it surrounded by people. The voice she is using to read is different than her usual one, and she has changed her accent to an American one. I realize that she is pretending she is me!

'Can you believe it, Monstrosity? I got the job. I'll have to put up with a totally selfish, vacuous, self-absorbed teenager, but it will be worth it. I finally, finally get to meet Cash Hunter. The guy I've been madly in love with since I was thirteen. It's been a long time, but here I am.'

'Stop it,' I scream, my body shaking uncontrollably.

Octavia stops reading and smiles at me. It is the cruel, gloating smile of a winner. The smile of someone who knows she will take everything that you hold precious. At that moment I *hate* her. I actually feel murderous towards her.

Frantically, I look at all the faces of all the people gathered there. Some are looking at me with disgust, others pity and some are jeering. I look at Britney and she is looking at me with so much hurt.

Jesus.

I want to scream that it's not true. That was at the beginning. I changed my mind. I love her like a sister now, but my throat has closed over.

I turn to see Cash standing just inside the doorway and he just looks so shocked. He is looking at me as if he never knew me. As if I cheated him or betrayed him.

Jesus.

It's not like that, I want to scream.

I didn't come here to stalk you. I came here to get over you. I was going to tell you tonight. But when I open my mouth nothing comes out. I am so embarrassed, so humiliated I feel suffocated. I gasp for air to fill my empty lungs and my chest hurts. It literally hurts to breathe. Tears begin to flood my vision and I snap.

With a cry of shame and defeat, I run out of the room, out of the hallway, through the open door, down the stone steps, and out into the street.

Cash

It's like a hurricane that comes in from nowhere. First the shingles are ripped off the roof. As hundreds of them fly off, water starts coming into the house, then the rafters crack and, with a sickening sound, the whole fucking roof flies off.

That's what this instant feels like.

One moment my life is great, my palm is on the warm skin of Tori's back, her smile familiar and sexy, then the next instant, the heavens rip open and unleash this black vortex. It's only purpose was to destroy everything in its path. In seconds it sucks up what I believed was mine. And there is not a fucking thing I can do about it.

I look at Octavia reading from a furry blue book and don't register what is happening. My mind refuses to believe that, that poison dropping out of her mouth could ever have been hatched in Tori's head. Lovely, kind hearted Tori, but one look at Tori's horrified, guilty face and I know it's true.

That *is* her diary.

She did write those hateful words and she *is* that mad stalker that every celebrity fears. I never heard the warning bells. Not once. Her disguise was perfect. She insinuated herself seamlessly into my father's house. An imposter. She's not real. Nothing was real. I thought I put my tongue into her cunt and felt her heartbeat. I know the truth now. I didn't. It was all an elaborate lie.

In strange silence I watch her run away. Strange. I don't stop her. I let her go. It doesn't even feel real. She's left a book sitting face down to mark its page. She'll never finish it now. Then I look at Brit's face and my heart breaks for her. I start to seethe. I stride over to Octavia. How dare she? I'd like to snap her scrawny neck. It's tempting, so tempting. She is six feet away, four, two, one. Zero.

I hold my hand out.

'She was no good. I did you a favor.' Her voice is cold and hard.

I look into her eyes. Funny how I've never looked deep into her eyes before. Malicious. 'You're a bitch, Octavia. You didn't do me a favor. You just got yourself fired.'

I reach my hand out and pluck the book from hers.

'Cash,' Octavia calls.

I ignore her and walk up to Britney. 'Do you want to come with me, Brit?'

Her face is white and her chin is wobbly. She shakes her head. 'No, you go on. I'll be all right. This is my party.'

I stare at her, even in my moment of loss it occurs to me how much she has changed. She used to be so fragile and unstable.

Then she does something strange. She goes up on her tiptoes and whispers in my ears. Her words are like a lightning bolt. The whole world goes red.

Tori

The paparazzi completely ignore me, and I run down the street in my little flirty fun dress and no panties. I don't know what to do. I can't go back. I have no money even to make a phone call. I go down the steps into the tube station. Tears are pouring down my face. I go to the ticket inspector and I tell him I have no money, but if he lets me through the barriers I will come back tomorrow and pay him. He is a kindly, middle-aged black man. He tuts and takes me to the ticket counter where he buys me a ticket.

'Where to?' he asks.

'Virginia Water.' I try to fight back the sob inside me. It's picking up force the way a storm does.

He hands me the ticket. 'Listen love. It's never as bad as it seems.'

'Thank you.' A sob escapes, the sound erupting from deep within my chest. I feel as if I'm breaking apart.

He pats me on the arm and I go down the escalator in a daze. At Waterloo station I get off and find my way up to the train station. I wait for my train and then I go in and sit on an empty seat and stare blankly out of the window. Once someone comes to sit opposite me. I look up confused. A woman in a long grey and white dress smiles kindly at me

'Are you all right?'

'Yes,' I whisper.

All I see in my head is Octavia reading my diary in that strange voice and Cash's face. He looked as if he had been stabbed. I have never seen him look like that. He was white under his tan.

Oh God! Britney.

Her face. Her birthday party was ruined.

God, why did I keep that diary. I frown. How did she get it? The hateful bitch must have taken it out of my room. When I saw her coming down the stairs she must have already taken it. But she wasn't holding it. She must have put it somewhere else temporarily to wait for the best moment. I remember her telling me to smile.

And the award for Idiot of The Year goes to ...

Tears run down my face. I fucked up, and so spectacularly too.

When the woman opposite me leaves at the next station, a man comes to sit beside me. 'Do you need help?' he asks.

I shake my head. I can't talk. The motion of the train has made me feel physically sick. When I get to Virginia Water, I stumble off the train and sit for a moment on the bench before I make a collect call to my aunt. She tells me she will be there in ten minutes. I sit on the steps outside and wait for her. As soon as her car arrives she jumps out and comes to me. I can barely stand. I know my face must be red and my eyes swollen.

'Hey, hey, hey,' she soothes as she takes the last few steps towards me.

'Oh, Aunt Claire. What am I going to do? I've made such a mess of everything.' The words spill from my mouth as I fall into her arms.

'Shhh, it's OK. It's OK,' she croons softly.

She holds me tight while I cry racking sobs. I think people pass by and probably stare at us, but I'm dead to everything.

Eventually my aunt sighs. 'Come on, let's get you home.'

I feel bruised, battered and irreparably damaged, but my feet somehow move forward and I get into the car. My aunt closes the car door and gets into the driver's seat. The tears fall and fall. They refuse to stop. Some part of me won't give up, but I know in my aching heart that he is gone. No more illusions. No more fairy tale endings. This is real life. He's gone.

Chapter Thirty-eight

Britney

https://www.youtube.com/watch?v=y_SI2EDM6Lo

I lift onto my toes, grasp my brother's shoulder and, putting my ear close to it, whisper, 'You can't trust Gavin either. He tried to rape me at your party.'

Of course you want to know why I whispered that bit of venom right at that confusing moment when my brother's heart would have been racing fast enough to explode?

It's not because I'm a trouble maker.

It's because I look at his shell-shocked face (it was glowing less than fifteen minutes ago) and I feel a rush of pity for him. His die has been cast. There he is. A sex God. Everywhere he goes he is mobbed and loved the world over. Almost any woman he wants he can have and yet at that instant I realize he is the loneliest person in the world.

There is not a single person in the world outside my dad, me, and Cora that he can truly trust. I knew then that if I did not tell him about Gavin, all I would be doing is leading him down a path where he would stand shell-shocked by still another betrayal.

It is like I slapped him. His whole body contracts at my words and he looks at me as if it is his fault that Gavin is a bastard. He takes my hand gently as if he is afraid I would break there and then, and I say clearly. I want to spare him the humiliation of being here. Of having his heart ripped out of his chest in front of an audience. 'Go now. I'm all right.'

'But you ...' he trails off as if it is too painful to even say the words.

'I'm a big girl. I can handle this.'

He nods, turns on his heels and walks out of the room. The room is so silent you could have heard a pin drop. I walk up to Octavia. She blinks slowly at me.

'Get out of my house you vindictive bitch,' I growl at her.

There are shocked gasps all around us. No one has seen this side of me. I am the loony little sister. Be nice to me to get to my brother.

She takes a step back. 'What's wrong with you all? Don't kill the messenger. I'm not the bitch here. Tori Diamond is a lying, cheating slut and I just exposed the truth. You should be thanking me. She was about to ruin your brother. Couldn't you see, he was intoxicated by her?'

I look at her. Yes, Tori turned out to be a snake in the grass, but I always liked her, there was something warm and kind about her, but this cold, black-hearted, mercenary bitch, I disliked her from the first second I laid eyes on her.

I let my eyes run down her skinny body in her designer leather dress. 'Tori has more class in her little finger than you ever dreamed of having.'

Her eyes register shock and fury. She always dismissed me as the inconsequential little sister. Well, I'm not. Not anymore. Thanks to Tori. So I'm not going to say a bad word about her.

'You don't mean it,' she says, trying to look dignified, but her face is red with humiliation.

'I never wanted anything more in my life. Get out of my house before I get the bouncers outside to escort you out. With the paparazzi vultures gathered outside that would make very interesting breakfast reading.'

For a second she hesitates, then she lifts her chin proudly, and leaves the room. The sound of her heels clicking on the hardwood floor is loud.

I look at the DJ and smile at him. 'Can we have some music before this party dies of boredom.'

He raises his eyebrows in an impressed way and spins a revved up version of Taio Cruz and Ludacris' *Break Your Heart*. Adrenaline is pumping in my veins, but soon the tears will come. With my head held high I walk away to the kitchen. Cora. Cora will know what to do.

Cash

Clutching Tori's poisonous diary in my hand, I go out through the kitchen door, cross the garden, and vault over the brick wall. I'm halfway up Mrs. Herrington-Little's garden when she spots me through her kitchen window and comes to open the sliding door.

'Wipe your feet,' she instructs as if I'm still thirteen.

I wipe my feet and automatically ask about her son. My voice sounds normal, not like my head is on fire and Tori's name is vibrating in my chest like a fucking cell phone. Cash calling Tori. Cash calling Tori. Cash calling Tori. Fuck it.

Mrs. H chatters about her son as she walks me to her front door. I don't hear a word.

I open the door. 'Thanks, Mrs. H.'

I walk on to the street and stride down it, my head lowered. I take a left at the end of the road and casually walk towards my car. A scruffy man standing near my father's front door spots me. Shit. He raises his long lens camera and starts snapping away. It alerts the others and they begin running towards me. Everybody wanting to get the best shot. They remind me of a pack of hyenas. I get into my car and floor the pedal.

I dial Gavin's number.

He answers on the third ring. His voice is cautious. 'Hey, Bro.'

'We need to talk,' I say, my voice completely normal.

'Yeah, I agree. Let's talk, dude.'

'Where are you now?'

'Home, but I've got company.'

'Get rid of her.'

'Right. Right. Got it,' he stutters.

I kill the connection.

As I'm driving, my mind veers back to Tori. I can still smell her on me. Fuck, I was inside her pussy less than an hour ago. My hand slams into the steering wheel and the car swerves wildly. Someone behind me blows his horn. Asshole. I hit the button that brings the glass of my window down. Cool night air rushes in as I give him the middle finger and accelerate so fast my tires screech.

The security guard at his post nods and lets me through the gates. I stop the car at the front of the house and run up the steps. Before I can put my finger on the doorbell, Gavin's butler, Jeremy, opens the door. He is so pale and still, he always reminds me of what you'd expect to find inside a satin lined coffin.

'Good evening, Mr. Hunter,' he greets formally.

I have no time for pleasantries. 'Where is he?'

'In the Blue room, Sir,' he says, his eyes showing just the flicker of surprise. There is hope yet for him.

I stride towards the room and open the door without knocking. I stand at the doorway and stare at him. I've known him since I was fifteen, but it would seem I've never really known him at all.

He is standing nervously by the great marble fireplace. He has obviously heard me come in and is waiting for me. He has the expression of someone about to bolt. Fucking coward.

'Why Britney?' I ask, the fury in my voice barely leashed.

Gavin shrugs. 'I was drunk, man. I didn't know what I was doing. I would never have touched her otherwise. You have to believe me.'

I stare at him. Fucking liar.

'I was drunk. It was dark. I didn't even know it was her. I thought it was some chick. Come on. You must know I'd never do something like that.'

'Tell me something I can believe,' I tell him coldly.

His mouth quivers as he analyzes his next move. 'It's the truth, man. You gotta believe me. I swear it's the God's fucking truth.' He takes a couple of steps forward, his voice pleading, his expression shifty. 'We're mates. You know me. I can get any girl I want.'

Look at him. How weak he is. I haven't even swung a punch yet and he is shaking like a fucking leaf.

'So why her? All the women in the world and you picked my sister. Did you think I wouldn't find out or when I did, I'd stand back and watch my little sister be hurt by a little, coke snorting, acid licking, waste of skin like you?

What do you think I am? A moron? A coward like you?'

'Oh fuck, Cash. I was so wasted. What'd you want from me? She came on to me,' he cries desperately.

Of all the things his twisting, turning devil tongue could have said. That was the worst. In the blink of an eye I had covered the distance between us and slammed my fist into his face. Pain blazes up my arm as my hand connects with his jaw. He stumbles back, blood flowing from his mouth and spilling down his chin. I don't allow even a brief second for him to catch his breath. I drive back into him and he tries to throw a sloppy blow. I dodge it easily.

Blood hums in my veins as I grab his head in my hands and bring my kneecap to his nose. There is a blunt crack before he screams in pain. I release his head. Two streams of crimson are running from his nostrils and his nose is twisted. He grabs hold of my body in a kind of protective hug. I tilt my head back and smash it into his. Stars burst in my vision, but he sinks to the ground barely conscious.

His mouth moves, no words come out.

'You tell anyone your version of what happened, call her name, or you come near her again and I swear I will fucking destroy you.' I grab a handful of his hair. 'Do you understand me?'

He nods weakly. I open my wrist and his head lands on the carpet with a soft thud. I stand over him watching his chest rise and fall with every shallow breath he takes, then I walk to the bottle of whiskey on the table and I pour myself a generous measure.

Jeremy enters the room. His face is impassive. 'Should I pour, Sir?' he asks.

'I'm good, thanks.'

'Should I perhaps call for a doctor?' he asks as if he is asking me if he should bring in the tea.

'That's a damn good idea, Jeremy.' I down the rest of the drink and walk away without looking back.

I get into my car and I fucking stamp on the accelerator. The car flies until I hear the sound of sirens. I look in the rear view mirror and see the blue flashing light. Fuck them. With the horsepower under me I could have outrun them, but I don't.

Sometimes the future is written in the stars. I pick up my mobile and call my lawyer.

Chapter Thirty-nine

Cash

-That's me in a cockfight, losing to a fucking pigeon-

It is not my lawyer who gets to me first. It is Octavia. She prowls the small utilitarian room at the police station restlessly.

'Forget it, Octavia. You're wasting your time. It's all over for me, anyway. I'm not coming back.'

'Why is it over? What has any of this got to do with the band?' Octavia looks about as malevolent as a scorpion crawling into a baby's crib.

I look her in the eye. 'There's no fucking way I could be in the same room as Gavin after what he did.'

'She was a slut. She came on to him.' Her voice is full of anger.

I stare at her in disbelief. 'What the hell are you talking about? You actually believe *my sister* came on to that brainless waste of skin?'

For the first time since I've known her she looks at me with confusion. 'Your sister?'

The realization is instant. Bile rises up in my throat. My eyes narrow on her. 'You were referring to Tori, weren't you?'

She recovers fast. 'Well, that's neither here nor there now.'

Frustration bubbles up inside me. 'What did he do to her?' I ask with deceptive softness.

She hesitates, then shrugs carelessly. She doesn't care that she's tearing open my chest and ripping my heart out. 'I found her on Gavin's lap. She was kissing him.'

My breath comes out in a rasp. I've never wanted to hit a woman before, but I would love to swing my fist into her pitiless, plastic face.

'She was no good. Look how much damage she has caused. Don't let her ruin everything. Please, Cash.'

'Get the fuck out,' I say through clenched teeth. My stomach burns. *Be still heart. Be still.*

'Fuck this. I'm not having this. I worked around the clock, called in a lot of favors, made threats, and generally fucking sold my soul to keep your shitty story out of the media.'

'Looks like you wasted your time. I'm out.'

She looks at me incredulously. 'Are you really that stupid? Do you really want to throw your career away over a lying psychopath? You don't even know who she is. We've been through a lot and we'll overcome this if we stick together.'

I look at her impassively. 'Fuck you, Octavia. I don't care if they burn me in the headlines. I don't care if the record company drops me and no one else picks me up. I'm through playing this game.'

She shakes her head in disgust. 'You know what your problem is? You've started to believe your own hype. You're nothing but a spoilt, talentless, fuckboy. The lead singer of a boy band singing jingles for teenagers and you're nothing without me guiding your career,' she screeches furiously.

I clap my hands. 'Bravo. Finally, the moment of truth. A little bit of what Octavia truly thinks. I actually prefer this to all the sickening lies. The band can continue without me. Find a replacement for me. Shouldn't be too hard considering how talentless I am.'

'You'll be sorry, but it will be too late. If I walk out of this door, I swear, there will be no way back for you.'

'Bye.'

She clenches her hands into tight fists and grunts with anger. 'I made you and I can break you.'

'Have fun doing it.'

She turns on her heels and walks to the door. She puts her hand on the handle and turns around and smiles. 'I know you are upset now. It doesn't matter. I've taken care of everything. Of course, I'm not going to break you. I care about you. You're like the son I never had.'

I wince. Even the idea of her as a mother figure makes me want to puke.

'You need me,' she adds fiercely.

I shake my head slowly.

'Yes, you do. You're just too immature to realize it. You'll see soon enough how your career nosedives without me.'

I shrug. 'You should go. You're wasting your time.'

She opens the door and goes out. I hear her heels clicking sharply down the corridor.

How on earth did she ever manage to convince me that she was acting for my greater good?

Many years ago while I was in America I went into a diner for a meal and the guy flipping the burgers in the kitchen recognized me. Then I was not a celebrity, but I was a rising star. He came out and told me he was once a one hit wonder. His record sold in the millions. I never forgot what he said.

'This industry is full of leeches. They glue their mouths to your skin and suck you dry. When there is nothing left to drain they drop off and look for the next unsuspecting victim.'

Tori

That night I can't sleep at all. I lie in bed with the curtains open, looking at a starless sky. The whole time my mind is replaying the scene with Octavia reading my diary out and my body is listening for the phone or the sound of a car pulling up on the road outside. He will forgive me. He will call. He has to. The mere thought of being without him gives me heart palpitations.

By six in the morning I finally drop off to sleep, exhausted and defeated. The sound of a car coming up our driveway wakes me up at nine o'clock. I run to the window and look down. For a second my heart stops. It's Victor. Then I see him get out of the car, open his boot, and take out a large cardboard box.

I have to cover my mouth to stop the sobs from escaping. I watch him walk up the path and come up to the house. I hear the doorbell ring and I hear my aunt answer it, but I don't come down from the bedroom. I just stand at the window and watch Victor go back to his car and drive away.

After a few minutes my aunt comes up and knocks on the door.

I go and sit on the bed and say, 'Come in.'

She comes in with the box. 'Your things. It was nice of them, wasn't it?' she says, putting the box on the nearby desk.

My throat feels hot and constricted. I nod wordlessly.

'Do you want to come down for some breakfast?'

'In a while,' I say softly.

'OK, I'll see you downstairs then,' she says.

'OK,' I say, relieved that my aunt doesn't want to talk 'about it'.

She closes the door and goes out. I stand and walk to the box. I pull the duct tape off and open it. The first thing I see is my mobile phone. I switch it on and check it for messages. Nothing. I look at calls received and ... nothing. There is a letter. I recognize the writing on the envelope as Cora's.

Dear Tori,

I'm so sorry, duckie, that it happened the way it did. You didn't deserve that. I still believe in you. There must be a way to work this out. If there's any way I can help you just let me know and I'll do everything in my power to do so.

With love and hugs,
Cora

I feel tears blur my vision. I put down the letter and go through the box. The leopard print dress is in there and so are the Medusa tri-strap shoes. At the bottom of the box I find another envelope with Mr. Hunter's writing on it. Inside there is a check made out to me, the sum equivalent to two months' wages. He has stuck a Post-it Note on it with the words Thank You. I think of Britney's face when Octavia was reading my diary out and I have to close my eyes and breathe slowly and deeply or the blinding regret I feel will make me scream uncontrollably.

If only I had not taken that damn diary with me or if only I had never written those things. If only I had told Cash earlier. I had the perfect opportunity while we were upstairs, but instead I had sex with him. Stupid. Stupid. Stupid. Then I suddenly realize that my diary is not in the box.

I wonder who has it and why they have not returned it. I hope Britney has it, because if she reads it all she will realize that I only felt she was shallow and selfish before we got close that night at the pool party. By the time we went to Milan together she was the sister I never had.

I get dressed, braid my hair — concentrating on the mundane is the best distraction from grief — and go downstairs where I talk to my aunt and pretend that I am not dying inside. My mom calls and I repeat the lie that I am fine with faux cheerfulness.

'Are you sure?' she asks.

'Yeah, I'm sure. It was all a stupid misunderstanding.'

'But your aunt said—'

'Anyway, it's all for the best,' I interrupt, shutting her down with brutal efficiency.

'I love you, Tori,' she says after a pained pause.

'I love you too, Mom,' I say, and my voice almost breaks, but I manage to control it enough to say goodbye.

It is even harder to do when my dad comes on the phone and asks if I want him to send me a ticket home. Then I just want to crawl into his lap and bawl my eyes out the way I used to when I was a little girl and anything went wrong in my life.

However, when Leah calls, the dam bursts. I don't try to hide my pain. I tell her everything. Every hateful detail of my imploded world. 'My heart is broken, Leah,' I sob. I never thought it would hurt this much. Then I cry my eyes out.

Chapter Forty

Cash

The door opens and a man in a police uniform comes in. 'You're free to go now, Mr. Hunter.'

I stand and start walking towards the door.

'Er ... Do you mind signing this CD for my niece?'

I turn to look at him.

'I ... er ... ran out to get it during my lunch break. It's her birthday next month, you see.' He holds the CD and a marker pen out to me.

'What's her name?' I ask.

'Athena Williams, but just Athena will be great.'

I take the CD, sign it, and give it back.

He smiles. 'All right, Sir. Thanks for this. You take care now.'

'No problem,' I say, and walk out of the door.

Outside it is gray. There is not a single reporter or TV crew waiting. I have to hand it to Octavia. She knows her job.

I stand on the deserted stone steps and suddenly I remember that night Tori dressed me up in the mustache, beard, and fake nose. It feels like a lifetime ago. I was happy then. But all of it was a lie. Fuck her. I don't need her.

A woman is coming up the steps, our eyes meet. She recognizes me. As she opens her mouth I let my eyes slide away and, keeping my head down, start down the steps. I've got no wheels. The fuckers impounded my car, but whatever. On the pavement I walk briskly down the road.

When I see a taxi I hail it. I sit at the back of the cab and don't allow myself to think. As the taxi turns into my street I shake my head. Fuck! Both sides of the streets are full of camera crews from all the large TV networks. So she called them.

'The fucking bitch,' I swear under my breath.

The driver meets my eyes in the rearview mirror. 'I can turn around and take you somewhere else.'

I shake my head. 'Just drop me off right outside that black door.'

'Right you are,' he says crisply. 'My youngest daughter loves you by the way. Can I have an autograph?'

I sign a fifty pound note and slip it through the gap in the partition.

'Thanks, mate,' he says.

He stops outside my door.

Pandemonium breaks around me as I run up the steps. Microphones being thrust into my face, flashbulbs going from every direction, people screaming, 'Here, Cash. Look here, Cash? Is it true you were caught having a blow job at the back of your car? Who was the girl, Cash? Turn this way, Cash? Will the police be charging you with reckless driving? How high over the limit were you? Are you going to lose your license, Cash? Give us a smile, Cash. Any comments?'

I slip my key into the keyhole and turn it. The door opens. I walk in and shut the ugly world outside. The phone is ringing steadily. God, what a bitch! She leaked the story that someone was giving me a blowjob when I was stopped.

An excellent example of a 24 karat bitch style revenge.

Well done, Octavia.

Tori

I catch the six o'clock news and I am shocked by how horrendously pained my heart is by the knowledge that a woman's lips other than mine have been wrapped around Cash's shaft. In my mind I must have already claimed it as my own. Then the agony of knowing how quickly he has replaced me.

I go down to the bottom of the garden and sit under the apple tree. The air is muggy and lazy with the buzzing of bumble bees. I pull my knees up to my chest and cry my eyes out. My heart feels like it has shattered into millions of pieces.

In my mind I cannot stop scolding myself. If only I had sat him down earlier. If only I had told him. I'd give anything to turn the clock back. Why did I waste that opportunity in my room having sex? I should have told him then. If only. Oh God. Why? Why didn't I do it? Stupid. How stupid I have been!

I hear the sound of rustling. I look up and my aunt is standing in front of me. She sits beside me, arranges her skirt around her ankles, and turns to look at me.

'I'm sorry, Tori,' she sighs softly.

Fresh tears start pouring down my cheeks. I wipe them away with the backs of my hands.

'Tell me what happened?' she asks, her face concerned.

I know I have to tell her. This is going to take much longer than I imagined to get over. I can't walk around like death warmed over and expect everyone to pretend that all is well. Haltingly I tell her everything.

'I did write those words. It was my diary and it was where I recorded all my frustrations and thoughts, but she took it out of context and made it sound so bad, Aunt Claire. She made me out to be such a conniving bitch. As if I had set out to trap him. I swear it was never my intention. I just wanted to finish my crush one way or another.'

I sniff and blow my nose.

'I thought, I actually thought that I would meet him and in the worst case scenario we'd have sex and he would start ignoring me, and I'd have to draw a line in the sand and move on, or best case scenario I would see him up close and realize that he was a media created, shallow creature and naturally fall out of love. And be free. I didn't mean to hurt anybody. In my plan the only person who might have got hurt would have been me.'

'Oh, Tori,' my aunt exhales.

'And you know what the worst thing is? I hurt Britney. She's the sweetest, most generous soul ever. It was her birthday party and she had so looked forward to it.'

'Why don't you call him?' my aunt suggests gently.

'I can't. He's totally disgusted with me. You should have seen his face, Aunt Claire.'

'I still think you should explain. The man I met wouldn't push you away.'

'He knows where I am, but he doesn't want anything to do with me, and I can't say I blame him. I should have told him.' I pause. 'Anyway, he's moved on. It's not like he's lacking in female company.'

'I find that hard to believe.'

A bark of bitter laughter passes my lips. 'They mentioned him on the six o'clock news. He was caught driving under the influence and ... and ... he was getting a blowjob in his car.'

My aunt frowns. 'Oh dear. Still, you can't believe everything you see on the media. A lot of this stuff is just ... fluff and scandal to sell more newspapers and boost viewing figures.'

'I don't know what to do. I can't believe I have messed up this bad. It's so painful I can't bear it. I can't stop thinking about him. At night I lay awake for hours, tossing and turning, and when I finally fall asleep I dream of him. Everything reminds me of him.'

'I know you are hurting now, but you are young and you will get over him.'

I shake my head. 'No, I won't. I've loved him for as long as I can remember, Aunt Claire. Nothing I've ever done has changed that. I've tried having other boyfriends, I tried cold turkey and I've tried this latest fiasco, and in the end I just fall deeper in love with him,' I sob.

'Oh, darling. What you need to do is leave England, at least for a while. Activity and change. That's what is going to knock him out of your mind. Why don't you take that trip you planned to Europe, hmmm? Isn't Leah just waiting for you to say the word?'

'Yes, but the idea of backpacking through Europe has completely lost its appeal. I can't even bring myself to think of going to the corner shop let alone all around Europe. I'll just be miserable there instead of here.'

'No, you won't. When you're on the move and seeing new things every day you won't have much opportunity to mope around feeling sorry for yourself. Trust me. It's the best thing for you.'

I lean my cheek on my knees and look at my aunt. 'What if I go and I'm still miserable and I just end up spoiling poor Leah's holiday?'

'Honey, you have more chances of winning the lottery than spoiling Leah's holiday. If I'm reading Leah right, she'll drag you right over this slump and bring you out on the side of the living.'

I smile weakly.

'So it's decided then. You'll both go on your holiday. She's coming over tomorrow so we

 284

might as well do a bit of shopping today to get you everything you need for your holiday.'

My jaw drops. 'Leah is arriving tomorrow?'

My aunt nods. 'Be grateful for everything you have, Tori. Because you have a lot. Far more than most people. You have a big family who love you to death and you have Leah who'll do anything for you.'

'She didn't say she was coming and I thought she wanted to save a bit more money for at least the next two months.'

'I lent her the money.'

I look at her in amazement. 'You did?'

'It was worth it to get your cute little butt out of my way,' she says with a smile.

My aunt and I go to the airport to meet Leah. She doesn't say a word. Just envelops me in a big, silent hug and lets me cry my guts out. Never once does she say, 'I told you so.'

Afterwards, bless her, she takes total charge. She is like a whirlwind. In two days we are in St Pancras International. As we pass a newsstand I see the screaming headlines in one of the tabloids.

Alkaline break up.

I can't help but read the subtitle.

Sources close to Cash Hunter say that he is the reason the band is dissolving. He wants to pursue a solo career in music.

Then, before I know it, I am sitting on the high-speed train to Paris. I stare out of the window. Cash Hunter is leaving. He's going to pursue his dream of making the kind of music he wants, and I won't be there to see it.

I feel my heart sigh deeply. It's over. The party's truly over. I've drawn the line in the sand. I'm hurt and shattered and I am filled with regret for the things I did, but I don't regret coming to England. I don't regret meeting Cash, loving him, giving my body to him.

If I had my time over I would make the same decision again today, only the execution would be different. I would tell him the truth on the first day. I'd say. 'Wow, do you know, Cash Hunter, I'm your biggest fan?' Who knows what he'd say. One thing for sure it'd be crude and funny. Maybe I'd laugh. Maybe we'd have dinner. Maybe ...

Maybe my aunt is right. One day I will forget. One day I will stop being so crazy over him. I will glue all the broken pieces of my heart together and I'll find someone else. In the glass I see my reflection. My face is pale and my eyes red-rimmed and blotchy.

'Look, the white cliffs of Dover,' Leah cries, her voice full of excitement.

I turn my eyes towards the majestic sight. 'Goodbye, Cash. Goodbye.'

https://www.youtube.com/watch?v=Ny4izkgnX_k
(To Be By Your Side)

Chapter Forty-one

Cash

https://www.youtube.com/watch?v=NwIZdh6MqIo

It's been a long but good day. I think I did my best work today, but it is good to leave the studio for a bit and spend some time at my father's house. Cora has made chicken pie for dinner. It's delicious and both my father and I polish our plates. Afterwards my father asks if I want to join him for a drink in his study.

'I'll just sit here for a bit on my own and ...' I lift my beer bottle, 'finish this.' I smile and take a swig.

'Right,' my father mumbles, and disappears into his study to wait for Britney to come back. She is out on a date with a guy called Liam Foxgrove. He's probably a good kid, but my father and I treated him to the Hunter ~~interrogation~~ welcome routine anyway. His hands were shaking by the time Britney floated down the stairs.

After a while, strains of music float out of the study. I recognize it. Nick Cave is singing Leonard Cohen's Suzanne. It suits my mood and I sit back and gaze through the window at the garden. I watch the neighbor's ginger cat climb over the wall and crouch by a hole in the ground.

I see her get bored of stalking an empty hole and walk away, her tail swishing. I stay staring out until the solar lights come on.

Cora pops her head around the door. 'I'm off. Can I get you anything else before I leave?'

'Nah, you go on. I know you can't wait to get home and jump your husband's bones.'

'Oh you,' she scolds, but her eyes twinkle.

I finish my beer and go into the kitchen for another. I go to open the fridge and I suddenly see it and freeze. It's a postcard from Italy. It has a picture of David wearing a fig leaf. It could have come from anyone, but I knew even without turning it over that it was from her. There was a time I couldn't stop thinking of her. Now I don't allow myself to think of her.

Like a man in a trance I reach for the card and slip it out from under the magnet. I turn it over and the sight of her writing is like a knife in my heart. There is only one sentence written in purple ink, but I start bleeding again.

He has a small dick. :)
Love,
Tori

She has sent a card to Cora. I stroke the ink and just like that I am by her side. I try to think of her in Italy. Her hair bleached by the sun, her skin golden brown. Her perfect body encased in something summery. She was like a glass of bright yellow sunshine. I didn't drink enough.

I slip the postcard back under the magnet and walk out of the house ...

But I come back often. To look for her cards. I tell myself that I'm just curious, but any fool can tell that's a fucking lie. Every two days once I make the journey to my father's house. Full of anticipation.

They are always funny or cute. I travel with her through Europe staring up at cathedrals and palaces and great monuments, down to Turkey, then Egypt where she sends more postcards than any of the other countries before. Pyramids, obelisks, statues of Pharaohs.

She leads me to India where I watch her break her heart when she is swarmed by a gaggle of baying child beggars. They grab her clothing and clutch her body, and she has no choice but to beat them with a stick to dislodge their clinging hands. She takes me by the hand into the Golden Temple of Amritsar and feeds me round sweets called *Ladhu*.

I follow her down the Ganges River to see the *Aghori,* the mysterious cannibal monks of Varanasi. They paint their unclothed bodies in ash, drink from human skulls, and live their entire lives in cemeteries. Their eyes are red and wild. I'll send pictures when I get back, she writes.

I am filled with longing to be on the same journey.

From India they take the South East Asia route. In Thailand they visit a Buddhist temple where the girls shake a container of sticks until one of the sticks falls out and a monk reads their fortune according to the number on the stick.

'Your Prince Charming is coming,' the monk tells her.

I feel it like a punch in the gut.

But she is mine.

Next stop, Malaysia. She sets out to enjoy the fantastic variety of food, that is, until they get dysentery. It puts both girls out of action for four days. They lie in their cheap hostel room groaning and rushing to the toilet. Weakened, lighter, and wiser, they reluctantly cancel their trip to Indonesia and catch a flight out of Singapore to the last destination of their journey. Australia.

There are three more cards while she tours Australia. From the postcards I know they spent a few days on a friend's farm helping to pick cherries. Then comes the final card. It has the picture of a mother kangaroo with its baby peeking out of its belly.

The holiday is over. We're flying back home tomorrow. A bit sad.

Tori

Don't get me wrong, I'm glad I went on this trip. I've seen so much and learned a lot about the world. Leah and I have witnessed and done things very few people do in their lifetimes. I know it has developed me as a person.

Before this trip someone would have had a very hard time convincing me that there is a dying breed of wild-eyed monks who exist in a state of intoxication and believe that they can reach enlightenment by the very act of turning away from all earthly pleasure and partaking in everything that is disgusting and taboo. Even eating dead human flesh or human waste.

Now I know better.

When we were in Australia I met a cute Australian surfer who chased me relentlessly. Probably because I didn't turn him down flat as I had all the others. In some small way he reminded me of Cash. It wasn't his looks. Maybe the curve of his mouth, but it was enough to endear him to me. Still, in the end I didn't want him. Even drunk on Fosters I couldn't bring myself to go with him.

Leah and I made a pact never to discuss Cash. We never bought a gossip magazine or watched E-news. She is of the opinion that the more you obsess and think of something the more it embeds itself into your heart. She thinks the solution to a broken heart is to never talk or think about that person.

We were on a strict Cash free diet.

I fell off the wagon once. Just once when Leah went into a shop to get us a couple of cans of coke. It was in India. I was standing beside a wooden stall selling magazines and sweets and cigarettes and my eyes fell on a magazine cover. He was on it. My heart slammed into my ribs.

I looked away quickly and then, like an addict, I looked back at his face. There was something different about it. I would have stared more, but Leah was coming back and I hurriedly turned away and smiled at her.

'What's wrong with you?' she asked.

'Nothing. Bit too hot I think,' I said.

She looked at me strangely, then at the Newsstand, and sighed. 'Come on. Let's go find a cool bottle of beer.'

Other than that one time I never thought about him, well, during the day at least, but when I got into my sleeping bag, or into my hostel bed for the night, my mind would replay that scene when he looked at me as if I had stabbed him in the back. With such hurt.

Hurt always turns to hate.

Sometimes I cried silent, bitter tears, thinking of him in England hating me and other times other memories would come back. The ants in his pants, being on the roof, laughing together under the sheets, going to The Ministry Of Sound, our unforgettable time in Milan, having sex, having sex, and having sex.

Chapter Forty-two

Tori

https://www.youtube.com/watch?v=0358xut_JBE

I look around the dinner table. My mom, my dad, even Brad has come home tonight for our family dinner. They listen to my tales with wide eyes. We laugh, we drink, and we talk late into the night. It is gone midnight when Brad leaves. My mother kisses me on my head.

'I'm so glad you're home, darling. I've missed you.'

'I love you, Mom.'

My parents go into their bedroom and I go into my room and close the door. I don't switch on the light. I walk to the window and look down at our yard. The silver glow of the moon peeks through the trees and illuminates the old tire swing. The metal on the gate gleams and the air is still. Everything is exactly as it was. I look up at the sky dotted with stars and tears gather in my eyes.

I can't do this. I just can't.

I take my phone out of my bag and scroll through my photos until I come to the one of Cash in his disguise. I was so happy that night. I know I said I wouldn't follow Cash's career, but tonight, just this once, because I am feeling extra vulnerable, I will go on the net and see how he is doing.

I won't check his personal life. I won't look to see what new woman he is with. I just want to see how he looks. It will soothe my aching heart.

Sitting in the dark, I navigate to YouTube and type in his name. I scroll down results and see that he has recently, just last week in fact, done an interview on a German TV program. I click into it. An advert for Adidas comes on and I realize I am holding my breath. I make it full screen. The advert finishes and a man in his late forties or fifties with a red/blond scruff on his face appears. He is wearing a grey suit and holding a sheaf of papers. He raps the edges of it on the table ala Jon Stewart, and calls out in a very strong German accent, 'Cash Hunter.'

The in-house band starts playing and the camera cuts to Cash coming into the studio. He is dressed completely in black, suit, shirt with three buttons undone, and shoes. His hair looks lighter and his face more mature. As if it is not months since I saw him, but years. He stops at the top of a white staircase, smiles, and waves to the audience before he walks down it.

I pause the video, my face moving closer to the computer screen.

Wow! He looks like a stranger.

I hit pause again and the video resumes playing. Cash continues walking towards the host. They shake hands and the guy shows him to a plush armchair.

'Cash Hunter, ladies and gentlemen,' the host repeats.

The camera pans to the audience who are all on their feet clapping and cheering. There are a few wolf whistles and Cash smiles and nods towards them.

'Welcome,' the host says.

'Thank you. It's always good to be in Germany. I love the autobahn.'

'Ah, you like having no speed limit while you are driving?'

'Absolutely.'

'So this is a new look for you?' the host comments, his hand waving down Cash's body.

'You gotta look sharp. Take care of those shoes,' Cash drawls, and the audience erupts into cheering and clapping.

'So,' the host says, 'some people are comparing you to Prince, Bob Dylan and Lou Reed. They say the songs you have written for your new album are nothing short of genius.'

'I'll take the comparisons, but there is only one Prince, one Bob Dylan, and one Lou Reed. I grew up listening to their music. They were some of my idols, but maybe one day someone will say there will be only one Cash Hunter.' He smiles.

'Before you started on your solo career you were with one of the most successful bands, Alkaline. Why did you leave? Was it the music? Did you guys fall out?'

Cash shrugs casually. 'I was with the band for close to eight years. That's a long time in this business. It was time to try something new. As someone once told me, "Don't wait any more, reach for the stars, Cash." So I did.'

Oh, my God. I can't believe it. He remembered what I told him on the roof. He actually used me to inspire him to write his own music. I feel a rush of happiness that in some small way I helped his career.

'But this is a departure from the kind of music you were making with the band,' the host prompts.

Cash laughs. 'Yeah it is.'

'That was boyband music.'

'It was pretty bad, wasn't it?

The host waggles his head as if to agree without agreeing. 'What does it feel like to be writing and singing this kind of deep stuff compared to the light pop that you were making before?'

'I was fifteen when I started in the music business. What could I really write about? I didn't understand anything. I hadn't lived yet. I had to figure out who I was. When the band broke up I went into my studio and wrote the songs that I really wanted to write, the kind of music that touched my soul. The way I felt hopefully came out in the album. It's a mixture of the kind of music I grew up listening to and loved.'

The host brings out a CD and opens the jewel case. 'So I have your new single here,' he says showing the cover to the audience. The CD has a picture of a woman's naked chest. Her long blonde hair covers her breasts.

'Of course, not all songs are autobiographical, but judging from the two titles of your songs, She Passed Like A Cloud and I'd Like to Know How You Feel, it would seem these are love songs. Want to tell us who she is?'

Cash's jaw tightens.

The host senses his reaction. 'This is a very sexy cover. Who's the blondie? Do you know her personally?'

'Sure. She's a model.'

'Can I have her number?' he guffaws.

Cash smiles. 'You sure you can handle her?'

The host is still laughing as he reaches under his desk and produces a guitar. 'How about a little song for us?' he asks. The audience erupts into a roar of applause. He lays the guitar on his thigh and plucks experimentally at the strings. 'She Passed Like a Cloud is written around a cord progression that is very similar to the ones the Beatles used, isn't it?'

'Yeah.'

He passes the guitar to Cash and he plays it and sings.

I stop breathing. His voice, the words, the music. It is hauntingly beautiful.

The host shakes his head in awe. 'You are the new star. Yeah, I think, yeah. You will see that in the next few years you will become bigger than ever.'

Cash shrugs modestly. 'Thank you.'

'No, I promise you. You are destined for big things. I saw you perform live once and it was great. You are not just a great composer, but you are also a good singer, a fantastic guitarist and a great dancer as well. The show was exhilarating.'

Cash smiles. 'Welllll, I'm not one to brag, but ...'

The host points at Cash. 'Ladies and gentlemen, Cash Hunter.'

The video ends there and I think about the way his jaw had tightened. Did Cash think of me sometimes? Was I the girl who passed like a cloud? Then I think of the blonde girl on the CD cover. He said he knew her. What if he's slept with her? Oh my God, I can't believe I've let myself go down this path. I switch off my laptop and lie in the darkness. Somehow. Somehow I've got to find a way to heal myself.

Chapter Forty-three

Tori

The sound of my phone buzzing wakes me up. With my eyes still shut, I fumble around and squint at the screen. It's Leah.

'Yeah,' I mumble.

'Are you feeling as bad as I am?' she asks morosely.

'I don't know. I'm not awake yet.'

'Well, wake up and tell me.'

I sit up. 'Why are you up so early?'

'My bed's too comfortable. I couldn't sleep.'

I manage half a laugh. 'So sleep in your sleeping bag then.'

'Might have to do that tonight.'

I yawn.

'Want to meet for lunch or something?'

'I don't know if mom's got something planned. I'll call you later?'

'OK, speak later.'

I close my eyes and fall back to bed. I never got to sleep until late. I had to creep downstairs and cut two cucumber slices to put on my eyelids because I didn't want to wake up with swollen eyes and have everybody know I'd been crying all night. I push my bedclothes away and go to stand in front of the mirror in the bathroom. The cucumber trick worked. My eyes look normal.

As I stare at my own reflection a dream I had last night breaks. Weird. I dreamt Cash and I were sitting in a boat. It must have been a lake because the water was calm. There was no sadness or perpetual pain. In my dream he'd forgiven me. With a sigh I turn away from the mirror.

I use the toilet, wash quickly, and go downstairs in my PJ's. The whole house smells of Italian roast coffee and bacon. My dad has already gone to work, but my mom has got her rubber gloves on and is busy cleaning out one of the shelves.

'Good morning,' she says brightly as she takes her gloves off.

'Morning, Mom,' I reply with fake brightness and a fake cheery smile.

I pour myself a cup of coffee, sit at the kitchen table, and yawn.

'Awww, honey. You're still jetlagged aren't you?'

'I guess so.'

'I knew you'd be missing out on your Southern breakfast so I made the works. How about a nice plate of bacon, ham, sausages, grits and gravy with sunny side up eggs to dip your toast in?'

'Oh no, Mom. I can't today,' I groan. 'I just want cereal.' I get up to take a bowl from the cupboard and my mom steers me back to the chair.

'Bull puckey! You'll do no such thing. I made you a good breakfast this morning and you'll eat it and be grateful for it, young lady. Didn't you say last night how those poor beggar children were starving?'

'You're not going to start using that against me,' I grumble. 'It's not like me eating a big breakfast is going to make a blind bit of difference to them.'

However, mom is already putting a plate on the cooker top to warm it. With a resigned sigh I watch her put the skillet on the stove and lay two thick cut slices of bacon on the black iron.

The bacon has just become limp and mom has just pushed it to one side to make space for the eggs when the doorbell goes. Both mom and me look at each other.

'Who on earth could that be?' mom says.

'I'll go,' I say, and hop off the chair. I peep out of the window and it's a delivery man holding a box. I open the door, sign for the package that is for *me* and come back in.

'Who was it?' mom calls from the kitchen.

'It was a package for me.' I put the package on the kitchen table.

'Who is it from?'

'I don't know. It doesn't say.'

'It's not ticking, is it?' she laughs.

'I don't think so.'

'Well, open it then,' she says giving me a knife.

I slit through the string and brown paper and open the box inside, and stare at the contents.

Mom comes to peer over my shoulder. 'What on earth is all that?'

I look at the measuring tape, the knife, the scissors, clothes pins, and thin and thick rods and I start to laugh.

My mom looks at me strangely.

'These are the items you need for basket weaving, Mom,' I tell her grinning happily.

'Basket weaving? Why in heaven's name would someone send you basket, uh, why're you crying?'

'Mom, your eggs are burning,' I half sob.

She rushes to the skillet and takes it off the stove just as we hear music coming from the back garden. I rush to the back door and wrench it open, and without warning my legs give way. I sink to my knees. My body goes into shock and my little heart feels as if it will burst with happiness.

Cash Hunter is standing in my garden playing the guitar and serenading me! Can this even be real? All those years when I stood in front of the TV and pretended he was singing to me! And now this. Oh my!

You live your life as if it's real.
The girls are young, the music is good,
But your heart is hard.
Hey, look at me, I'm a big star.
There are no limits. You can have anything, man,

But your heart is hard.
I saw her bathing and she didn't even need
moonlight.
She used the sunshine in her hair.
I looked into her eyes, I moved in her
And drank from the pool of her soul.
But my heart was hard.
There are no oceans left for you to swallow, she
said.
They call me diamond
I'll break your hard heart for you, she said.
So she broke it with one kiss.
It lay in a million pieces at her feet
And then she passed on by.
Like a cloud. Like a fuckin' cloud.
Like a cloud. Like a fuckin' cloud.

He stops playing the guitar and walks up the wooden steps on to the back veranda and crouches in front of me. I blink at him. I feel as if I am drowning in a tidal wave of emotion. Cash Hunter is in my backyard and there are a thousand things in his eyes.

I can't think. I can't speak. I can't even breathe.

'I finally stopped being mad and stupid and I read your diary. All of it. Every single word, and I loved you even more after I finished than I did before I started. You're no crazy stalker fan, Tori Diamond. You're the bravest person I know. You travelled half way around the world to chase your dream. I needed a fucking tragedy before I went after mine.'

'I'm so sorry about everything. I honestly didn't mean to hurt anyone.'

He smiles. 'You were always my fate as sure as I am yours. It can't be escaped. Our connection is real. I love you, Tori Diamond.'

With one finger he wipes away the tears that are running down my face.

'I travelled all night to get to you so these better be happy tears,' he says.

I start laughing.

'That's better.'

'Oh, Cash. I love you so much. I thought I would die when I heard Octavia reading my diary. God, I missed you. I can't even describe how much. It's like no matter where I turned I came back to you. It was hell. There was no solace anywhere.'

'Me too, Wildcat. Me too. I couldn't weave a single basket without you.'

'Not a single one?'

He shakes his head slowly. 'Nope.'

With a cry of joy, I throw my arms around his neck and the force of my lunge makes him topple backwards, and we both fall sprawled on the veranda. Me on top of him.

'Oh, Cash. I'm so proud of you. I heard your new stuff last night on a German talk show and your music is just amazing.'

'You made my guitar burn, baby.'

Someone clears their throat. I look up and my mom is standing over us.

'Do you kids want some breakfast?' she asks with a wink.

'Thanks, Mrs. D. I'm starving,' Cash says.

And my heart swells up with joy.

Epilogue

Tori

2 Years Later

https://www.youtube.com/watch?v=-MlR6tFh8Gs
(I'm Your Man)

'**D**on't cry, Mom, or I'm going to start too and it'll ruin my makeup.'

'Oh, honey,' my mom sobs, actually sobs. 'You look so beautiful.'

'That's a good thing, right?' I quip to lighten the mood.

But my mother is already in full flow. 'I still can't believe you're marrying Cash Hunter. Dad and I used to secretly call you Mrs. Hunter.'

'What? When was this?' I ask incredulously.

Mom smiles through her tears. 'When you were young. When you were so crazy about him, we used to joke about it.'

'I never knew.'

'Obviously, we were not going to tell you.'

'I don't know what to do with the information.'

Mom laughs and carefully dabs the corners of her eyes with her handkerchief. 'I'm so happy for you, my darling. Come and see how you look.'

I take a deep breath and walk to the mirror. I look at myself and I have to stare at my own reflection with wide eyes. Wow! Look at me. I decided I didn't want to marry in white, so I went for this astonishingly beautiful strapless multi-colored silk gazar draped ball gown. The bodice is fashioned into a gorgeous rose and the waist is made of pleats that bloom into the gleaming petals of large red and orange roses.

Leah appears next to me in the mirror. She's wearing her bridesmaid's outfit, a pink dress with a darker pink underskirt showing and her shoes are the same deep pink.

'Can you believe it?' she asks with a grin.

'No. Pinch me,' I say softly.

'Neither can I, actually. But I'm so freaking glad you never took my sane advice, and went with the mad option of following your impossible dream instead.'

I laugh.

There is a knock on the door, someone opens it, and my father comes in. I turn towards him and he stops in his tracks.

'Oh my God,' he exclaims unsteadily. He shakes his head in disbelief. 'You look ... did your mother and I really make you?'

'I'm afraid so, Dad.'

His eyes fill with tears as he comes forward to stand in front of me. He takes off his glasses and wipes his eyes. 'You're all grown up now, but you'll always be my baby girl, my little Princess, sitting on my lap telling tales on your brother.'

'I did not,' I mutter.

'I'll be giving you away today, Princess, but not from my heart. Just remember, I'll be here for you, always, until the day I am no more.'

What my mother did not accomplish with her tears my father accomplishes with his words. Tears start rolling down my face and all around me women start tutting and scolding. I am pulled back onto the bed and the woman who did my make-up starts fussing and dabbing at my face.

'No more tears,' she says sternly to no one in particular.

'There's nothing a glass of champagne won't cure,' Britney says putting a glass of bubbling liquid into my hand.

I take it and smile up at her. In my mind I see that day two years ago when Cash came to get me in Georgia and brought me back to his father's house. I was a nervous wreck. I thought she would be angry with me, but she ran up to me, and in her generous wonderful way, hugged me tightly, and said, 'I was never angry with you. You were right. I was a selfish, shallow, self-absorbed creature.' And we both cried our eyes out.

'Bottom's up,' Britney says.

I drink up and thread my hand through my father's.

'I'm ready, Dad.'

https://www.youtube.com/watch?v=9xdyRsGOl6U

Dad squeezes my hand as the car travels in the darkness. Cash and I decided to have a secret midnight wedding.

'I want a marriage not a wedding,' he said, and I couldn't agree more.

Both of us have become publicity shy, and we have learned to guard our privacy fiercely. Neither of us wants paparazzi helicopters swooping overhead, or the frightening packs of paparazzi that seem prepared to do anything just to get that one clear, unique shot they can sell for hundreds of thousands of pounds, gathered outside the gates.

Neither did we want the media circus that ensues when famous guests are jetted in from the four corners of the Earth, or magazine photographers to be present to record the occasion for posterity or a six figure sum.

When Cash asked me where I wanted to have our wedding I didn't even have to think. I couldn't, in fact, I still can't think of a more beautiful place for us to tie the knot than the old Georgian walled garden of the new home that we just bought, renovated and lovingly furnished, but have not moved into yet. It is a magical house and we both fell in love with its beauty, proportions, and tranquility at first glance.

Since we wanted a special occasion in front of only our loved ones we kept our wedding so hush hush that even the caterers were hired under an assumed name from the county of Shropshire, all the wedding guests were sworn to secrecy, and my aunt acted as the wedding planner. Even the minister flew in from Scotland. About five weeks ago we went to see the registrar who granted us a special license so that nobody would find out.

I feel a lump in my throat as the car turns into the tall iron gates. *Our home.* The car goes down the lantern lit driveway and stops outside the garden gate. My father opens the door, and I come out of the car.

'Are you ready?' my father asks.

I nod because I can't speak. I rest my hand on his arm and feel the strength under his sleeve as I lean slightly on it ... and I have a stray thought. One day it will no longer be that strong. I look up at him.

'What is it?'

'Nothing. I love you, Daddy,' I whisper.

'I love you, more,' he whispers, as we round the corner and come to the secret door hidden in the seven feet tall hedges.

At the entrance to the garden, Cora waits with Tabitha and Leah's sister. Cora looks lovely in a cream suit and the girls are wearing their little pink frocks and carrying their baskets of flower petals. Cora dabs her eyes. She always was a soppy romantic.

'Oh, Tori, I'm so happy for you,' she whispers.

She opens the door and my jaw drops. This was Cash's surprise for me. The whole place is like a magical wonderland with fairy lights everywhere you look. On the trees, the hedges, the leaves, the chairs the guests are sitting on, and the rose arbor where my groom is waiting for me.

He has turned to watch me arrive. He is wearing a blue-grey morning suit. His tie is made from the same orange material as my dress. And ... Oh my, it is like the first time. Butterflies go wild in my tummy and I can't stop grinning. Sometimes I still can't believe that I kissed the sexy fucking bastard and he became a prince. I try to suppress a giggle but a muffled sound escapes. It's like a fairytale. I got my prince.

On the loud speakers Bruno Mars starts singing *Marry me.* The girls begin the procession and my father and I sedately walk along the path strewn with rose petals.

Cash smiles slowly at me, his eyes so full of love, my knees become like jelly and I fear I will trip and fall. I tighten my hold on my father. His other hand comes around to pat my hand. I feel grateful to him, but I can't take my eyes off my bridegroom. Finally, we reach him and I inhale deeply.

His scent fills my nostrils. I close my eyes for a moment. So many memories. So many. The first time I wound his hair around my hand. The first time he kissed me. The first time we had sex. The first time we went on holiday. The first time ... I open my eyes. His fingers touch mine. His eyes are wet. I blink.

'You're the most beautiful woman who ever walked this earth,' he purrs.

'And you're the most beautiful man who ever walked this earth.'

His eyes twinkle. 'I know,' he says.

'Oh, Cash. How I love you.'

He bends his head and whispers in my ear. 'I've got a damn woodie for you.'

'And I'm not attracted to you at all,' I whisper. It's our little joke now. We laugh about the days when I used to pretend I didn't find him attractive.

'Not even a bit?' he asks, his eyes gleaming.

'Nope.'

'Then nothing has changed. It's as it has always been and may it always be that way when we are wrinkled and can barely walk.'

Then the minister speaks and I remember we are not alone. Our families and friends are watching.

'Dearly Beloved, we are gathered here today in the presence of these witnesses, to join Cash Hunter and Tori Diamond in holy matrimony commended to be honorable among all; and therefore is not to be entered into lightly but reverently, passionately, lovingly and solemnly. If any person can show just cause why they may not be joined together let them speak now or forever hold their peace.'

He gives it a pause, then smiles, looks to Cash and says, 'Repeat after me: I, Cash Hunter, take you Tori Diamond to be my wife.'

314

Cash repeats.

'To have and to hold from this day forward, for better or for worse,'

Cash says the words looking deeply into my eyes.

'In sickness and in health, to love and to cherish.'

I smile tremulously as Cash says the words.

'From this day forward until death do us part.'

The minister turns to me.

'I, Tori Diamond, take you, Cash Hunter, to be my husband.'

'I, Tori Diamond,' I say, and then laughter starts bubbling up my throat. I see Cash's eyes widen with surprise and that makes me laugh even more. I'm not laughing because it's funny, but I just can't help it. 'Take you, Cash Hunter.' More giggles. I hear the audience start giggling too. Oh, my God. What a disaster. I don't know why I can't stop laughing.

'I'm really sorry,' I apologize to the minister, who is staring at me with a strange expression.

'It's just nerves. Let me start again,' I say, clearing my throat. 'I, Tori Diamond,' I manage, and another fit of laughter overtakes me.

Cash looks at the minister. 'Do you mind?' he asks.

'Of course not,' the startled minister replies immediately.

Catching me around the waist, Cash swoops down and takes my mouth in a deep, passionate kiss. Time rolls back and I am back to our first kiss. It is an instant cure for my laughing fit.

He lifts his head and looks into my dazed eyes.

'Do you, Tori Diamond, take this man to be your lawful wedded husband?' the minister asks quickly.

'I do. Oh, yes, I definitely do.'

That night the sound of laughter, music, and dancing fills the air for hours. Most of the guests are staying in the house and they disappear into one of the twenty-seven rooms. Cash carries me up the stairs, lays me on our bed, and makes love to me for hours, beautiful, passionate love. At first I'm a bit nervous, but the fact that he's really mine is sinking in.

In the early morning hours when I would have dropped off to sleep, he tugs my hand.

'Put some clothes on. I want to show you something.'

'Show me tomorrow,' I say sleepily.

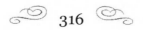

He will have none of it. He pulls me out of bed and wraps me up in a thick dressing gown.

He opens our bedroom door softly. Everyone is fast asleep and the house is very still. He turns to me and places a finger across his lips. Quietly we go down the stairs and hallway and out through the front doors.

'Where are we going?' I whisper.

'To the lake.'

'Now?'

'Yes, now.'

He takes my hand and starts running. By the time we get to the lake I am out of breath and hot. I look around me in wonder. I had no idea when we bought the house that a lake at night would be so peaceful and serene, with a mist hanging over it. A pair of sleeping swans are floating on the water. They glow in the early light of the day.

'Look,' he says, pointing into the trees.

'What?'

'It is the beginning of the rutting season for the red deer. Soon the stag will begin his impressive roaring contest to attract the hinds. In eight months we will see their offspring.'

We sit on the grass and watch that large stag roar and call to his harem. The sound is earthy and truly impressive and reverberates in the still countryside. As the day breaks he begins to mount them. It is so beautiful. Without this precious act there would be no deer, no human, no swans. I rest my head on Cash's shoulder. All girls dream of finding their prince. Mine is no longer a dream.

Last Look Epilogue

Tori

5 Years Later

https://www.youtube.com/watch?v=NGorjBVagoI

In the silence we stand. There is no denying we want each other, an inferno of lust lights our eyes, even the air crackles between us. I smile nervously as Cash begins to walk towards me, all alpha and broodingly sexy. My heart hammers like any of his thousands of adoring screaming female fans. Then his breath is a delicious hot breeze on my neck as he fists my hair and walks me backwards and up against the coldness of the wall.

I always come to him after he has performed. He's always the same. So high with adrenaline that it infects me too, and we tear at each other in a wild frenzy. I watch him, my heart beating with the thunder of desire, as the sweat drips off him. Wetness seeps through my panties, and my nipples pebble as his muscular body presses me tighter to the wall.

He grabs me possessively, rips my dress open, and cups my breasts together. Then his glorious mouth descends and he sucks hard at my nipples, sending crazy sensations coursing through all my nerve ends. I crave him like an addict.

He flicks his tongue from nipple to nipple, teasing and biting until I'm lost in sensual madness I barely feel his hand move my soaked panties to the side. My head rocks back with pure pleasure as he slips his fingers deep inside me.

'Fuck, you're so fucking wet,' he growls.

'I can't wait anymore,' I cry. It's a wild sound.

He hoists me up and holds my throbbing sex over the tip of his erect shaft, and watches me shudder when our flesh touches before he drives his cock into my depths.

I grip his broad shoulders and look into eyes full of fiery passion. I feel his strong hot hands clasp my ass cheeks and bury his cock balls deep inside me. I close my eyes and throw my head back in sheer ecstasy. I can hear his heartbeat and the wet sound of our flesh slapping until my head starts swirling. I dig my fingernails into his skin. My body is in the grip of the most intensely deep orgasm.

'Oh, my God, I'm coming,' I scream.

I feel his whole body stiffen and his rhythm increases dramatically.

'Me too, babe.'

I'm holding him so tight as I feel his cock jolt inside me and then throb uncontrollably inside my sex, I'm surprised that he can still hold me up let alone continue to pile drive into my grasping channel. But he just slams that cock in and out until every drop of cum has been drained from it. When he's finally finished I lean back and look into his satisfied face.

'That was fucking awesome, Mr. Hunter.'

'That's what I fucking love about you, Mrs. Hunter.'

'Yeah, and what's that?'

'You ain't like any of the other girls.'

I roll my eyes. 'Well you've known enough!'

'That's right, baby. I've met tens of thousands and not one of them can hold a candle to you.' His tongue traces my neck slowly and sensually. His cock is still inside me, pulsing and throbbing.

My hand splays on his chest. 'I want to tell you a secret.'

'Oh yeah?'

'Uh huh.'

'Go on then.'

I bite my lip. 'You know that room next to our bedroom that we never use. I think we'll need it in about ... say ... nine months' time.'

He stares at me incredulously. 'What? When? How?'

'When, I just answered, how, you know how, and what? I don't know yet. I hope it's a boy, though.' I grin. 'He can protect his younger sister.'

He takes a breath so shaky I hear it tremble through his chest. He looks at me with wonderment. 'We'll have to buy baby formula,' he says in a hushed voice.

I start to laugh. 'Oh, Cash. I love you so, so, so much.'

The End

Hey Romance Lover,

If you are lusting for a bad boy like Cash Hunter, there's not much we can do, but if you found yourself licking your lips over Cora Bennet's luscious scones, then here's the recipe. :) They will be good the day after baking, but are best straight from the oven.

SCONES

Makes 8 large wedges

INGREDIENTS

- 500g plain flour
- 65g caster sugar
- 2 tbsp baking powder
- 130g cold butter, cut into cubes
- 420ml double cream, plus a little more for brushing on scones
- 1 large egg

METHOD

Preheat the oven to 200C/gas mark 6.

Flour a 23cm cake tin and line a baking sheet with baking parchment.

Sift together the flour, sugar, baking powder and half a teaspoon of salt. Add the butter and rub it

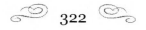

in with your fingertips until the mixture is crumbly with little pea-sized bits of flour-coated butter.

Lightly beat the cream and egg together in a small jug. Make a well in the centre of the flour and gradually add the cream, mixing it in with a butter knife.

Mix just until everything comes together – don't over mix. The dough will be quite sticky.

Put this into the floured cake tin and carefully pat the dough evenly into place. Turn the dough out on to a lightly floured surface and cut the round into eight equal wedges.

Put these on the baking sheet. Brush with the extra double cream.

Transfer to the oven and cook for about 30 minutes. The scones should be golden brown. Leave to cool for five minutes then serve warm.

These are actually still good two days later (well, not quite as good, but they don't deteriorate the way other scones do – just keep them in an airtight container).

http://bit.ly/29e9CjD

Perfect Strawberry Jam

Makes 4 x 200ml jars

INGREDIENTS

2kg small ripe strawberries
1.7kg jam sugar
Juice of 2 lemons

METHOD

1. Hull the strawberries and discard any rotten ones. Set aside about 10 of the smallest berries, and then mash the rest up into a rough pulp. Put into a wide, thick-bottomed pan, add the sugar and the lemon juice, and bring to the boil. Add the remaining strawberries to the pan, and put a saucer in the freezer.

2. Boil the jam for about 15 minutes, stirring regularly checking the setting point every minute or so during the last 5 minutes. To do this, take the cold saucer out of the freezer, put a little jam on it, and put it back in to cool for a minute. If it wrinkles when you push it with your finger, then it's done. Strawberry jam is unlikely to set very solid though, so don't expect the same results as you would with a marmalade.

3. Take off the heat and skim off the pink scum. Pour into sterilised jars and cover with a disc of waxed paper, seal and store.

http://bit.ly/29hFkCg

Coming on the 19th of August ...

Noah's story

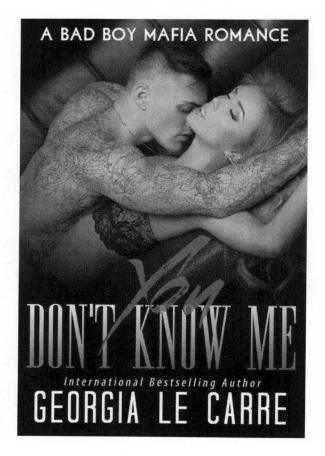

Georgia Le Carre

Please click on this link to receive news of my latest releases and great giveaways.

http://bit.ly/1oe9WdE

and remember

I **LOVE** hearing from readers so by all means come and say hello here:

https://www.facebook.com/georgia.lecarre

Laura Jack

Me, I'll be hanging out here:

http://bit.ly/29n3aZN

Made in the USA
San Bernardino, CA
09 March 2019